Charles Heber Clark

Out of the Hurly-Burly

Life in an odd corner

Charles Heber Clark

Out of the Hurly-Burly
Life in an odd corner

ISBN/EAN: 9783337095499

Printed in Europe, USA, Canada, Australia, Japan

Cover: Foto ©Andreas Hilbeck / pixelio.de

More available books at **www.hansebooks.com**

OUT OF THE HURLY-BURLY;

OR,

LIFE IN AN ODD CORNER.

BY

MAX ADELER.

𝔚𝔦𝔱𝔥 𝔫𝔢𝔞𝔯𝔩𝔶 𝔉𝔬𝔲𝔯 𝔥𝔲𝔫𝔡𝔯𝔢𝔡 𝔍𝔩𝔩𝔲𝔰𝔱𝔯𝔞𝔱𝔦𝔬𝔫𝔰,

BY

ARTHUR B. FROST, FRED. B. SCHELL, WM. L. SHEPPARD AND
ED. B. BENSELL.

PHILADELPHIA:

P. GARRETT & CO.,

706 CHESTNUT STREET.

1879.

DEDICATION.

I HAVE resolved to dedicate this book to a humorist who has had too little fame, to the most delicious, because the most unconscious, humorist, to that widely-scattered and multitudinous comedian who may be expressed in the concrete as

THE INTELLIGENT COMPOSITOR.

To his habit of perpetrating felicitous absurdities I am indebted for "laughter that is worth a hundred groans." It was he who put into type an article of mine which contained the remark, "Filtration is sometimes accomplished with the assistance of albumen," and transformed it into "Flirtation is sometimes accomplished with the resistance of aldermen." It was he who caused me to misquote the poet's inquiry, so that I propounded to the world the appalling conundrum, "Where are the dead, the *varnished* dead?" And it was his glorious tendency to make the sublime convulsively ridiculous that rejected the line in a poem of mine, which declared that a "comet swept o'er the heavens with its trailing skirt," and substituted the idea that a "count slept in the haymow in a traveling shirt." The kind of talent that is here displayed deserves profound reverence. It is wonderful and awful; and thus I offer it a token of my marveling respect.

"Fun is the most conservative element of society, and it ought to be cherished and encouraged by all lawful means. People never plot mischief when they are merry. Laughter is an enemy to malice, a foe to scandal and a friend to every virtue. It promotes good temper, enlivens the heart and brightens the intellect."

PREFACE.

It seems to be necessary to say a few words in reference to the contents of this volume as I offer it to the public. Several of the incidents related in the story have already appeared in print, and have been copied in various newspapers throughout the country. Sometimes they have been attributed to the author; but more frequently they have been given either without any name attached to them, or they have been credited to persons who probably never saw them. The best of the anecdotes have been imitated, but none of them, I believe, are imitations. I make this statement, so that if the reader should happen to encounter anything that has a familiar appearance, he may understand that he has the original and not a copy before him. But a very large portion of the matter contained in the book is entirely new, and is now published for the first time; while all the rest of it has been rewritten and improved, so that it is as good as new.

If this little venture shall achieve popularity, I must attribute the fact largely to the admirable pictures with which it has been adorned by the artists whose names appear upon the title page. All of these gentlemen have my hearty thanks for the efforts they have made to accomplish the best results; but while I express my appreciation of the beautiful landscapes of Mr. Schell, the admirable drawings of Mr. Sheppard and the excellent designs of Mr. Bensell, I wish to direct attention especially to the humorous pictures of Mr. Arthur B.

Frost. This artist makes his first appearance before the public in these pages. These are the only drawings upon wood that he has ever executed, and they are so nicely illustrative of the text, they display so much originality and versatility, and they have such genial humor, with so little extravagance and exaggeration, that they seem to me surely to give promise of a prosperous career for the artist.

It is customary upon these occasions to say something of an apologetic nature for the purpose of inducing the public to believe that the author regards with humility the work of which he is really exceedingly proud—something that will tend to soften the blows which are expected from ferocious and cruel critics. But I believe I have nothing of this kind to offer. If I thought the book required an apology, I would not publish it. Any reviewer who does not like it is at liberty to say so; and I am the more ready to accord him this permission because I am impressed with the conviction that he will hit as hard as he wants to whether I give him leave or withhold it. All I ask is that the volume shall have fair play. If it is successful as an attempt to construct a book of humor which will contribute to innocent popular amusement without violating the laws that govern the construction and orthography of the English language, and as an effort to give pleasure to sensible grown people without offering entertainment to children and idiots, it deserves commendation. If it is a failure in these respects, then it ought to be suppressed, for it certainly has no mighty moral purpose, and it is not designed to reform anything on earth but the personal fortunes of the author.

MAX ADELER.

CONTENTS.

7

CHAPTER V.

CHAPTER VI.

CHAPTER VII.

CHAPTER VIII.

CHAPTER IX.

CHAPTER X.

CHAPTER XI.

CHAPTER XII.

CHAPTER XIII.

CHAPTER XIV.

CHAPTER XV.

CHAPTER XVI.

CHAPTER XVII.

CHAPTER XVIII.

CHAPTER XIX.

CHAPTER XX.

CHAPTER XXI.

CHAPTER XXII.

CHAPTER XXIII.

CHAPTER XXIV.

LIST OF ILLUSTRATIONS.

2*

OUT OF THE HURLY-BURLY.

CHAPTER I.

THE FOUNDER OF NEW CASTLE—A SEARCH FOR QUIETNESS—
LIFE IN THE CITY AND THE VILLAGE—WHY THE LATTER
IS PREFERABLE—PECULIARITIES OF THE VILLAGE—A
SLEEPY OLD TOWN—WE ERECT OUR FAMILY ALTAR.

F Peter Menuit had never been born, it is extremely probable that this book would not have been written. Mr. Menuit, however, had nothing to do with the construction of the volume, and his controlling purpose perhaps was not to prepare the way for it. Peter Menuit was a Swede who in 1631 came sailing up the Delaware River in a queer old craft with bulging sides and with stem and stern high in the air. Moved by some mysterious impulse, he dropped his anchor near a certain verdant shore and landed. Standing there, he surveyed the lovely scene that lay before him in the woodland and the river, and then announced to his companions his determination to remain upon that spot. He began to erect a town upon the bank that went sloping downward to the sandy beach, and his only claim to the immortality that has been allotted to him is that he created what is now New Castle.

It would be pleasant, if it did not seem vain, to hope that New Castle will base its aspirations to enduring fame upon the circumstance that another humble personage came, two hundred years and more after Menuit's arrival, to live in it and to tell, in a homely but amiable fashion, the story of some of its good people, and to say something of a few of their peculiarities, perplexities and adventures.

We were in search of quietness. The city has many charms and many conveniences as a place of residence; and there are those who, having accustomed themselves to the methods of life that prevail among the dense populations of the great towns, can hardly find happiness and comfort elsewhere. But although the gregarious instinct is strong in me, I cannot endure to be crowded. I love my fellow-man with inexpressible affection, but oftentimes he seems more lovable when I behold him at a distance. I yearn occasionally for human society, but I prefer to have it only when I choose, not at all times and seasons without intermission. In the city, how-

ever, it is impossible to secure solitude when it is desired. If I live, as I must, in one of a row of houses, the partition walls upon both sides are likely to be thin. It is possible that I may have upon the one hand a professor of music who gives, throughout the day, madden-
ing lessons to muscular pupils and practices scales himself with energetic persistency during the night. Upon the other

side there may be a family which cherishes two or three infants and sustains a dog. As a faint whisper will penetrate the almost diaphanous wall, the mildest as well as the most violent of the nocturnal demonstrations of the children disturb my sleep; and when these have ceased, the dog will probably become boisterous in the yard.

If there is not a boiler-making establishment in the street at the rear of the house, there will be a saw-mill with a steam whistle, and it is tolerably certain that my neighbor over the way will either have a vociferous daughter who keeps the window open while she sings, or will permit his boy to perform upon a drum. There is incessant noise in street and yard and dwelling. There is perpetual, audible evidence of the active existence of human beings. There is too much crowding and too little opportunity for absolute withdrawal from the confusion and from contact with the restless energy of human life.

It has always seemed to me that village life is the happiest and the most comfortable, and that the busy city man who would establish his home where he can have repose without inconvenience and discomfort should place it amid the trees and flowers and by the grassy highway of some pretty hamlet, where the noise of the world's greater commerce never comes, and where isolation and companionship are both possible without an effort. Such a home, planted judiciously in a half acre, where children can romp and play and where one can cultivate a few flowers and vegetables, mingling the sentimental heliotrope with the practical cabbage, and the ornamental verbena with the useful onion, may be made an earthly Paradise.

There must not be too much ground, for then it becomes a burden and a care. There are few city men who have the agricultural impulse so strong in them that they will find delight, after a day of mental labor and excitement, in rasping a garden with a hoe in the hope of securing a vegetable harvest. A very little exercise of that kind, in most cases, suffices to moderate the horticultural enthusiasm of the inexperienced citizen. It is pleasant enough to weed a few flowers or to toss a spadeful or two of earth about the roots of the grapevine when you feel disposed to such mild indulgence in exercise; but when the garden presents tasks which must be performed no matter what the frame of mind or the condition of the body, you are apt, for the first time, to have a thorough comprehension of the meaning of the curse uttered against the ground when Adam went forth from Eden.   It is far better and cheaper to hire a competent man to cultivate the little field; then in your leisure moments you may set out the cabbage plants upside down and place poles for the strawberry vines to clamber upon, knowing well that if evil is done, it will be corrected on the morrow when the offender is far away, and when the maledic-

tions of the agricultural expert, muttered as he relieves the vegetables from the jeopardy in which ignorance has placed them, cannot reach your ears.

I like a house not too old, but having outward comeliness, with judicious arrangement of the interior, and all of those convenient contrivances of the plumber, the furnace-maker and the bell-hanger which make the merest mite of a modern dwelling incomparably superior in comfort to the most stupendous of marble palaces in the ancient times. I would have no neighbor's house within twenty yards upon either side; I would have noble shade trees about the place, and I would esteem it a most fortunate thing if through the foliage I could obtain constant glimpses of some shining stream upon whose bosom ships come to and fro, and on which I could sometimes find solace and exercise in rowing, fishing and sailing.

Village life is the best. It has all the advantages of residence in the country without the unpleasant things which attend existence in a wholly rural home. There is not the oftentimes oppressive solitude of the country, nor is there the embarrassment that comes from the distance to the station, to the shops and to the post-office. There are the city blessings of the presence of other human beings, and of access to the places where wants may be supplied, without the crowds, without the mixed and villainous perfumes of the streets and without the immoderate taxes. With the conveniences of a civilized community, a village may have pure and healthful air, opportunity for parents and children to amuse themselves out of doors, cheap fare, moderate rent, milk which knows not the wiles of the city dealer, and a moral atmosphere in which a family may grow up away from the temptations and the evil associations which tend to corrupt the young in the great cities.

More than this, I like life in the village because it brings a man into kindlier relations with his fellows than can be obtained elsewhere. In the city I am jostled at every step by those who are strangers to me, who know nothing of me, and who care nothing. In the village I am known by every one, and I know all. If I have any title to respect, it is admitted by the entire society of the place, and perhaps I may even win something of affection if I am worthy of it.

In the country town, too, you may have your morals carefully looked after. There are prying eyes and busy tongues, and you are so conspicuous that unless you walk straightly,

3 *

the little world around you shall know of your slips and
falls. You may quarrel with your wife for ever in the city
and few care to hear the miserable story; but in the village
the details of the conjugal contest are heralded about before
the day is spent.

The interest that is felt in you is amazing. The cost of
your establishment is as well known as if it were blazoned
upon the walls. You cannot impose upon the people with a
pretence of splendor if you have not the reality; one gossiping old woman who has discovered the sham will make you an
object of public scorn in an hour. The village knows how
your children are dressed and trained; how often you have
mutton and the extent of your indulgence in beef. The cost
of your carpets is a matter of common notoriety; your differences with your servants are discussed at the sewing-circle,
and the purchase of new clothing for your family is a concern
of public interest. The arrival of your wife's winter bonnet
actually creates excitement in the village society, and you
are certain, therefore, to get the full worth of your investment
in that article of dress, while the owner obtains unlimited
satisfaction; for winter bonnets are purchased for the benefit
of other people chiefly, not for the convenience and happiness
of the wearers.

Every man is something of a hero-worshiper; and if in
the city I find it difficult to select an idol from among the
many who thrust their greatness upon me, I am not so
embarrassed in the village. Here I will probably find but
one man who is revered as the embodiment of the worshipful
virtues. He has larger wealth than any of his fellow-
villagers; he lives in the most sumptuous house in the
place; he belongs to the oldest family, and his claim to
superiority is admitted almost without question by his
reverent townsmen. It gives me joy to add my voice to the
chorus of admiration, and to feel humble in that *presence*

NEW CASTLE FROM THE RIVER.

wherein my neighbors have humility. Sometimes, of course, I cannot help perceiving that the object of this adoration is, after all, a very pigmy of his kind. I am compelled to admit that his fortune seems large only because mine and Jones's are small; that his house is a palace only for the reason that it dwarfs my little cottage; that if unassisted brains carried the day, and strutting was felonious, he would certainly occupy a much less magnificent position. I know that in a greater community he would be wholly insignificant. And yet I admit his claim to profound respect. It pleases me to see him play his little part, and to observe with what calm, luxurious confidence in his own right and title to homage he passes through life. And I know, after all, that the greater men, out in the busy hurly-burly of the world, are not so very much greater. A good deal of their claim to superiority, too, is a miserable sham; and doubtless, if we could see them as closely as we see our village grandee, we should find that they also depend much upon popular credulity for the stability of their reputations.

My pompous village nabob, too, is honest. I am sure of this. He helps to conduct the government of the community, but he does his duty fairly and he is a gentleman. I could love him for that alone, and for that feel a deeper affection for life in his village. When I go to the city and perceive what creatures wield the power there, when I watch the trickery, the iniquity, the audacious infamy, of the cliques that control the machinery of that great government, and when I look, as I do sometimes, into the faces of those who are thus leagued for plunder and power, only to see there vulgarity, ignorance, vice and general moral filthiness, my soul is made sick. I can turn then with pleasure to the simple methods with which our village is governed, and honestly give my respect to the guileless old gentleman who presides over its destinies.

We wish for quietness, and in New Castle it can be obtained, I think, in a particularly concentrated form. When Swede and Dutchman and Englishman had done contending for possession of the place, there was peace until the Revolution came, and with it ships of war and privateers, and such hurrying of troops and supplies across from New Castle to Frenchtown, from the Delaware to the Chesapeake, as kept the old town in a stir. There was then an interval of repose until the second war with England, when these busy scenes were re-enacted. Later in the century a mighty stir was made by the construction of a railroad, one of the earliest in the country, to Chesapeake Bay; then, as the excitement died away, the old town gradually went to sleep, and for nearly forty years it slumbered so soundly that there seemed to be a chance that it would never wake again. But time achieves wonderful things, and perhaps the day will come when the vicinity of the old town to the bay, the depth of water at its shores and the facilities offered for manufacturing and easy transportation, may make the village a great industrial centre, with hundreds of mills and multitudes of working-people. But as we join ourselves to the community there is no promise of such an awakening. We have still the profound repose and the absence of change that make the place so dear to those who have known it in their childhood. There are the paved streets where the grass grows thickly; the ancient wharves protruding into the stream, deserted but by the anglers and the naked and wicked little boys who go in to swim; the tumbling stone ice-piers, a little way out in the river; the old court-house, whose steeple is the point upon which moves the twelve-mile radial line whose northern end describes the semi-circular boundary of Delaware; the rickety town-hall, the ancient churches and the grim old houses with moss-covered roofs, the Battery, with its drooping willows and its glorious vista of river and shore beyond, and the dense masses of foliage, shutting out the sky here and there as one passes along the streets.

Into such a house as I have described, not far from the river, and with our neighbors at a little more than arm's length, I have come with wife and family, with household gods and domestic paraphernalia generally, to begin the life which will supply the material wherewith to construct the ensuing pages. It may perhaps turn out that the better part of that existence will not be told, but perchance it may be that the events related will be those which will possess for the reader greatest interest and amusement.

CHAPTER II.

A Very Dangerous Invention — The Patent Combination
Step-ladder — Domestic Servants — Advertising for a
Girl — The Peasant-girl of Fact and Fiction — A
Contrast.

A STEP-LADDER is an almost in-
dispensable article to persons who
are moving into a new house.
Not only do the domestics find it
extremely convenient when they
undertake to wash the windows,
to remove the dust from the door
and window-frames, and to perform sundry other household
duties, but the lord of the castle
will require it when he hangs his
pictures, when he fixes the cur-
tains and when he yields to his
wife's entreaty for a hanging shelf
or two in the cellar. I would,
however, warn my fellow-countrymen against the contrivance
which is offered to them under the name of the "Patent
Combination Step-ladder." I purchased one in the city just
before we moved, because the dealer showed me how, by the
simple operation of a set of springs, the ladder could be
transformed into an ironing-table, and from that into a comfortable settee for the kitchen, and finally back again into a
step-ladder, just as the owner desired. It seemed like get-

36

ting the full worth of the money expended to obtain a trio
of such useful articles for a single price, and the temptation
to purchase was simply irresistible. But the knowledge
gained by a practical experience of the operation of the
machine enables me to affirm that there is no genuine eco-
nomical advantage in the use of this ingenious article.

Upon the day of its arrival, the servant-girl mounted the
ladder for the purpose of removing the globes from the
chandelier in the parlor, and while she was engaged in the
work the weight of her body unexpectedly put the springs
in motion, and the machine was suddenly converted into an

ironing-table, while the maid-servant was prostrated upon
the floor with a sprained ankle and amid the fragments of
two shattered globes.

Then we decided that the apparatus should be used
exclusively as an ironing-table, and to this purpose it would
probably have been devoted permanently if it had suited.
On the following Tuesday, however, while half a dozen

shirts were lying upon it ready to be ironed, some one knocked against it accidentally. It gave two or three ominous preliminary jerks, ground two shirts into rags, hurled the flat-iron out into the yard, and after a few convulsive movements of the springs, settled into repose in the shape of a step-ladder.

It became evident then that it could be used with greatest safety as a settee, and it was placed in the kitchen in that shape. For a few days it gave much satisfaction. But one night when the servant had company the bench was perhaps overloaded, for it had another and most alarming paroxysm; there was a trembling of the legs, a violent agitation of the back, then a tremendous jump, and one of the visitors was hurled against the range, while the machine turned several somersaults, jammed itself halfway through the window-sash, and appeared once more in the similitude of an ironing-table.

It has now attained to such a degree of sensitiveness that it goes through the entire drill promptly and with celerity if any one comes near it or coughs or sneezes close at hand. We have it stored away in the garret, and sometimes in the middle of the night a rat will jar it, or a current of air will pass through the room, and we can hear it dancing over the floor and getting into service as a ladder, a bench and a table fifteen or twenty times in quick succession.

The machine will be disposed of for a small fraction of the original cost. It might be a valuable addition to the collection of some good museum. I am convinced that it will shine with greater lustre as a curiosity than as a household utensil.

Perhaps we may attribute to the fantastic capers of this step-ladder the dissatisfaction expressed by the servant who came with us from the city; at any rate, she gave us notice at the end of the first week that she would not remain. She is the ninth that we have had within four months. Mrs.

Adeler said she was not sorry the woman intended to go, for she was absolutely good for nothing; but I think a poor servant is better than none at all. Life is gloomy enough

without the misery which comes from rising before daylight to fumble among the fires, and without living upon short rations because one's wife has no time to attend to the cooking.

I am not sure, at any rate, that it would be a very great advantage to have thoroughly good servants, for then women would be deprived of the very evident pleasure they now take in discussing the shortcomings of their domestics. The practice is so common that there must be supreme consolation in the sympathy and in the relief to the overcharged feelings that are permitted by such communion.

Place two women together under any circumstances, and it makes no difference where the conversation starts from, for it will be perfectly certain to work around to the hired-girl question before many minutes have elapsed. I have seen an elderly housekeeper, with experience in conducting the talk in the desired direction, break in upon a discussion of Pythagoras and the doctrine of the transmigration of souls, and switch off the entire debate with such expedition that a careless listener would for some moments have an indistinct impression that the conversation referred to the inefficiency of Pythagoras as a washer and ironer, and to the tendency of that heathen philosopher to take two Thursdays out every week.

And when a woman has an unusually villainous servant, is it not interesting to observe how she glories in the superior intensity of her sufferings as compared with those of

4

her neighbors, and to perceive how she rejoices in her misery? A housewife who possesses a really good girl is always in a condition of wretchedness upon such occasions, and is apt to listen in envious silence while her companions unburden their souls to each other.

Mrs. Adeler intimated that these accusations were slanderous, but she ventured to observe that the practical question which required immediate consideration was, How shall we get another girl?

"There is but one method, Mrs. A.: it is to advertise. Do not patronize the establishments which, in bitter irony, are styled 'intelligence offices.' An intelligence office is always remarkable for the dense stupidity of everybody connected with it. But a single manifestation of intelligence gleams through the intellectual darkness that enshrines the souls of the beings who maintain such places. I refer to the singular ability displayed in extracting two-dollar bills from persons who know that they will get nothing for their money."

Mrs. Adeler admitted that it would perhaps be better to advertise.

"How would it answer to insert in the daily paper an advertisement in which sarcasm is mingled with exaggeration in such a way that it shall secure an unlimited number of applications, while we shall give expression to the feeling of bitterness that is supposed to exist in the bosom of every housekeeper?"

She said she thought she hardly caught the idea precisely.

"Suppose, for instance, we should publish something like this: 'Wanted: a competent girl for general housework. The most strenuous effort will be made to give such a person complete satisfaction. If she is not pleased with the furniture already in the kitchen, we are willing to have the range silver plated, the floor laid in mosaic and the dresser covered with pink plush. No objection will be made to breakage. The domestic will be permitted at any time to disport in the china closet with the axe. We consider hair in the breakfast-rolls an improvement; and the more silver forks that are dropped into the drain, the more serene is the happiness which reigns in the household. Our girl cannot have Sunday out. She can go out every day but Sunday, and remain out until midnight if she wishes to. If her relations suffer for want of sugar, she can supply them with ours. We rather prefer a girl who habitually blows out the gas, and who is impudent when complaint is made because she soaks the mackerel in the tea-kettle. If she can sprinkle hot coals over the floor now and then, and set the house afire, we will rejoice the more, because it will give the fire-department healthful and necessary exercise. Nobody will interfere if she woos the milkman, and she will confer a favor if she will discuss family matters across the fence with the girl who lives next door. Such a servant as this can have a good home, the second-story front room and the whole of our income with the exception of three dollars a week, which we must insist, reluctantly, upon reserving for our own use.'

"How does that strike you, Mrs. Adeler?"

She said that it struck her as being particularly non-sensical. She hoped I wouldn't put such stuff as that in the paper.

"Certainly not, Mrs. A. If I did, we should cause a general immigration of the domestics of the country to New Castle. We will not precipitate such a disaster."

The insertion of a less extended advertisement, couched in the usual terms, secured a reply from a young woman named Catherine. And when Catherine's objections to the size of the family, to the style of the cooking-range, to the dimensions of the weekly wash and to sundry other things had been overcome, she consented to accept the position.

"I hope she will suit," exclaimed Mrs. Adeler, with a sigh and an intonation which implied doubt. "I do hope she will answer, but I am afraid she won't, for according to her own confession she doesn't know how to make bread or to iron shirts or to do anything."

"That is the reason why she demanded such exorbitant wages. Those servants who are entirely ignorant always want the largest pay. If we ever obtain a girl who understands her business in all its departments, I cherish the conviction that she will work for us for nothing. The wages of domestics are usually in inverse ratio to the merit of the recipients. Did you ever reflect upon the difference between the real and the ideal Irish maiden?"

Mrs. A. admitted that she had not considered the subject with any degree of attention.

"The ideal peasant-girl lives only in fiction and upon the stage. We are largely indebted to Mr. Boucicault for her

existence, just as we are under obligations to Mr. Fennimore Cooper for a purely sentimental conception of the North American Indian. Have you ever seen the *Colleen Bawn?*"

"What is that?" inquired Mrs. Adeler, as she bit off a piece of thread from a spool.

"It is a play, a drama, my dear, by Mr. Dion Boucicault."

"You know I never go to theatres."

"Well, in that and in many other of his dramas Mr. Boucicault has drawn a particularly affecting portrait of the imaginary peasant-girl of Ireland. She is, as depicted by him, a lovely young creature, filled with tenderest sensibility, animated by loftiest impulses and inspired perpetually by poetic enthusiasm. The conversation of this fascinating being sparkles with wit; she overflows with generosity; she has unutterable longings for a higher and nobler life; she loves with intense and overpowering passion; she is capable of supreme self-sacrifice; and she always wears clean clothing. If such charming girls really existed in Ireland in large numbers, it would be the most attractive spot in the world. It would be a particularly profitable place for young bachelors to emigrate to. I think I should even go there myself."

Mrs. Adeler said she would certainly accompany me if I did.

"But these persons have no actual existence. We know, from a painful experience, what the peasant-girl of real life is, do we not? We know that her appearance is not prepossessing; we are aware that her lofty impulses do not lift her high enough to enable her to avoid impertinence and to conquer her unnatural fondness for cooking wine. She will withhold starch from the shirt collars and put it in the underclothing; she will hold the baby by the leg, so that it is in perpetual peril of apoplexy, and she will drink the milk. All of her visitors are her cousins; and when they have spent a festive evening with her in the kitchen, is it not curious to remark with what certainty we find low tide in the sugar-box and an absence of symmetry about the cold beef? The only evidence that I can 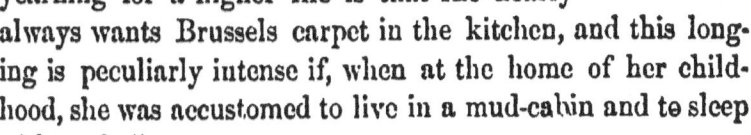 discover of the existence in her soul of a yearning for a higher life is that she nearly always wants Brussels carpet in the kitchen, and this longing is peculiarly intense if, when at the home of her childhood, she was accustomed to live in a mud-cabin and to sleep with a pig."

4 *

But I do not regret that Mr. Boucicault has not placed this person upon the stage. It is, indeed, a matter for rejoicing that she is not there. She plays such a part in the drama of domestic life that in contemplation of the virtues of the fabulous being we find intense relief.

THE VIEW DOWN THE RIVER.

CHAPTER III.

E have a full view of the
river from our chamber
window, and it is a mag-
nificent spectacle that
greets us as we rise in
the morning and fling
the shutters wide open.
The sun, in this early
summer-time, has al-
ready crept high above
the horizon of the pine-
covered shore opposite, and has flooded the unruffled waters
with its golden light until they are transformed for us into
a sea of flame. There comes a fleet of grimy coal schooners
moving upward with the tide, their dingy sails hanging
almost listless in the air; now they float, one by one, into
the yellow glory of the sunshine which bars the river from
shore to shore. Yonder is a tiny tug puffing valorously as it
tows the great merchantman—home from what distant land
of wonders?—up to the wharves of the great city. And
look! there is another tug-boat going down stream, with a
score of canal-boats moving in huge mass slowly behind it.
They come from far up among the mountains of the Lehigh

47

and the Schuylkill with their burdens of coal, and they are bound for the Chesapeake. Those men lounging lazily about upon the decks while the women are getting breakfast ready spend their lives amid some of the wildest and noblest scenery in the world. I would rather be a canal-boat captain, Mrs. Adeler, and through all my existence float calmly and serenely amid those regions of beauty and delight, without ever knowing what hurry is, than to be the greatest and busiest of statesmen—that is, if one calling were as respectable and lucrative as the other.

That fellow upon the boat at the rear is playing upon his bugle. The canal-boat bugler is not an artist, but he makes

 wonderful music sometimes when he blows a blast up yonder in the heart of Pennsylvania, and sets the wild echoes flying among the cañons of those mighty hills. And even now it is not indifferent. Listen! The tones come to us mellowed by the distance, and so indistinct that they have lost all but the sweetness which makes them seem so like the sound of

"Horns of Elfland, faintly blowing."

That prosaic tooter floating there upon the river doubtless would be surprised to learn that he is capable of such a suggestion; but he is.

Off there in the distance, emerging from the shadowy mantle of mist that rests still upon the bosom of the stream to the south, comes the steamboat from Salem, with its decks loaded down with rosy and fragrant peaches, and with baskets of tomatoes and apples and potatoes and berries, ready for the hungry thousands of the Quaker City. The schooner

lying there at the wharf is getting ready to move away, so
that the steamer may come in. You can hear the screech
made by the block as the tackle of the sail is drawn swiftly
through it. Now she swings out into the stream, and there,
right athwart her bows, see that fisherman rowing homeward
with his net piled high in tangled meshes in the bow of his
boat. He has a hundred or two silver-scaled shiners at his
feet, I'll warrant you, and he is thinking rather of the price
they will bring than of the fact that his appearance in his
rough batteau gives an especially picturesque air to the
beauty of that matchless scene. I wish I was a painter. I
would pay any price if I could fling upon canvas that background of hazy gray, and place against it the fiery splendor
of the sunlit river, with steamer and ship and weather-
beaten sloop and fishing-boat drifting to and fro upon the
golden tide. .

There, too, is old Cooley, our next-door neighbor on the
east. He is out early this morning, walking about his garden, pulling up a weed here and there, prowling among his
strawberry vines and investigating the condition of his early
raspberries. That dog which trots behind him,
my dear, is the one that barked all night. I
shall have to ask Cooley to take him in the
house after this. We had enough of that
kind of disturbance in the city; we do not
want it here.

"I don't like the Cooleys," remarked Mrs. A.

"Why not?"

"Because they quarrel with each other. Their girl told
our girl that 'him and her don't hit it,' and that Mr. Cooley
is continually having angry disputes with his wife. She
says that sometimes they even come to blows. It is
dreadful."

"It is indeed dreadful. Somebody ought to speak to

Cooley about it. He needs overhauling. Perhaps he is too ignorant a man to have perceived the true road to happiness. Of course, Mrs. A., *you* know the secret of real happiness in married life?"

She said she had never thought much about it. She was happy, and it seemed natural to be so. She thought it very strange that there should ever be any other condition of things between man and wife.

"Mrs. Adeler, the secret of conjugal felicity is contained in this formula: demonstrative affection and self-sacrifice. A man should not only love his wife dearly, but he should tell her he loves her, and tell her very often. And each should be willing to yield, not once or twice, but constantly and as a practice, to the other. The man who never takes the baby from his wife, who never offers to help her in her domestic duties, who will sit idly by, indulging himself with repose while she is overwhelmed with care and work among the children, or with other matters, is a mean wretch who does not deserve to have a happy home. And a wife who never holds up her husband's hands in his struggle with the world, who displays no interest in his perplexities and trials, who has never a word of cheer for him when he staggers under his heavy burden, is not worthy the name of a wife. Selfishness, my dear, crushes out love, and most of the couples who are living without affection for each other, with cold and dead hearts, with ashes where there should be a bright and holy flame, have destroyed themselves by caring too much for themselves and too little for each other."

"To me," said Mrs. Adeler, "the saddest thing about such coldness and indifference is that both the man and the woman must sometimes think of the years when they loved each other."

"Yes, and can you imagine anything that would be more likely to give a woman the heartache than such a recollection? When her husband comes home and enters the house without a smile or a word of welcome; when he growls at his meals, and finds fault with this and that domestic arrangement; when he buries his nose in his newspaper after supper, and never resurrects it excepting when he has a savage word of reproof for one of his children, or when he goes out again to spend the evening and leaves his wife alone, the picture which she brings up from the past cannot be a very pleasant one.

"Indeed, my dear, the man's present conduct must fill the woman's soul with bitter pain when she contrasts it with that which won her affection. For there must have been a time when she looked forward with joy to his coming, when he caressed her and covered her with endearments, when he looked deep into her eyes and said that he loved her, and when he said that he could have no happiness in this world unless she loved him wholly and truly. When a man makes such a declaration as that to a woman, he is a villain if he ever treats her with anything but loving-kindness. And I take the liberty of doubting whether he who leads a young girl into wedlock with such pledges, and then acts in direct violation of them, ought not to be prosecuted for obtaining valuable consideration upon false pretences. It is infinitely worse, in my opinion, than stealing ordinary property."

Mrs. Adeler expressed the opinion that death at the stake might be regarded as an appropriate punishment for criminals of this class.

"But there is a humorous side even to this melancholy business. Do you remember the Sawyers, who used to live near us in the city? Well, before Sawyer's marriage I was his most intimate friend; and when they returned from their wedding-trip, of course I called upon them. Mrs. Sawyer alone was at home, and after a brief discussion of the weather, the conversation turned upon Sawyer. I had

known him for many years, and I took pleasure in making
Mrs. Sawyer believe that he had as much virtue as an omni-
bus load of patriarchs. Mrs. Sawyer assented joyously to
it all, but I thought I detected a shade of sadness on her
face while she spoke. I asked her if anything was the
matter—if Sawyer's health was not good.

"'Oh yes,' she said, 'very good indeed, and I love him
dearly. He is the best man in the world; but—but—'

"Then I assured Mrs. Sawyer that she might speak frankly
to me, as I was Sawyer's friend, and could probably smooth
away any little unpleasantness that might mar their happiness. She then said it was nothing. It might seem foolish
to speak of it; she knew it was not her dear husband's fault,
and she ought not to complain; but it was hard, hard to
submit when she reflected that there was but one thing to
prevent her being perfectly happy; yes, but one thing, 'for
oh, Mr. Adeler, I would ask for nothing more in this world

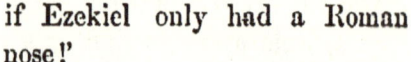

if Ezekiel only had a Roman
nose!'

"It is an awful thing, Mrs.
Adeler, to think of two young
lives being made miserable for
want of one Roman nose, isn't
it?"

Mrs. A. gently intimated that
she entertained a suspicion that
I had made up the story; and
if I had not, why, then Mrs. Sawyer certainly was a very
foolish woman.

My wife's cousin, Bob Parker, came down a fortnight ago
to stay a day or two on his way to Cape May, with the
intent to tarry at that watering-place for a week or ten days,
and then to return here to remain with us for some time.
Bob is a bright youth, witty in his own small way, fond of

using his tongue, and always overflowing with animal spirits. He came partly to see us, but chiefly, I think, because he cherishes a secret passion for a certain fair maid who abides here.

He brought me a splendid present in the shape of an American agave, or century plant. It was offered to him in Philadelphia by a man who brought it to the store and wanted to sell it. The man said it had belonged to his

grandfather, and he consented to part with it only because he was in extreme poverty. The man informed Bob that the plant grew but half an inch in twenty years, and blossomed but once in a century. The last time it bloomed, according to the information obtained from the gray-haired grandsire of the man, was in 1776, and it would therefore certainly burst out again in 1876. Patriotism and a desire to have such a curiosity in the family combined to induce Mr. Parker to purchase it at the price of fifty dollars.

I planted the phenomenon on the south side of the house.

5

against the wall. Two days afterward I called Bob's attention to the circumstance that the agave had grown nearly three feet since it was placed in the ground. This seemed somewhat strange after what the man said about the growth of half an inch in two decades. But we concluded that the surprising development must be due to the extraordinary 'fertility of the soil, and Bob exulted as he thought how he had beaten the man by getting a century plant so much larger and so much more valuable than he had supposed. Bob said that the man would be wofully mad if he should call and see that century plant of his grandfather's getting up out of the ground so splendidly.

That afternoon we all went down to Cape May, and for two weeks we remained there. Upon our return, Bob remarked, as we stepped from the boat, that he wanted to go around the first thing and see how the plant was coming on. He suggested gloomily that he should be bitterly disappointed if it had perished from neglect during our absence.

But it was not dead. We saw it as soon as we came near the house. It had grown since our departure. It had a trunk as thick as my leg, and the branches ran completely over three sides of the house; over the window shutters, which were closed so tightly that we had to chop the century plant away with a hatchet; over the roof, down the chimneys, which were so filled with foliage that they wouldn't draw; and over the grapevine arbor, in such a fashion that we had to cut away vines and all to get rid of the intruder.

The roots, also, had thrown out shoots over every available square foot of the yard, so that I had eight or ten thousand century plants in an exceedingly thriving condition, while a branch had grown through the open cellar window, and was getting along so finely that we could only reach the coal-bin by tramping through a kind of an East Indian jungle.

Mr. Parker, after examining the vegetable carefully, observed:

"I'm kind of sorry I bought that century plant, Max. I have half an idea that the man who sold it to me was a humorist, and that his Revolutionary grandfather was an octogenarian fraud."

If anybody wants a good, strong, healthy century plant that will stand any climate, and that is warranted to bloom in 1876, mine can be had for a very reasonable price. This may be regarded as an unparalleled opportunity for any young agriculturist who does not want to wait long for his vegetables to grow.

CHAPTER IV

JUDGE PITMAN—HIS EXPERIMENT IN THE BARN—A LESSON IN
NATURAL HISTORY—CATCHING THE EARLY TRAIN—ONE OF
THE MISERIES OF LIVING IN A VILLAGE — BALL'S LUNG
EXERCISE—MR. COOLEY'S IMPERTINENCE.

Y next-door neighbor upon the west is Judge Pitman. I heard his name mentioned before I became acquainted with him, and I fancied that he was either a present occupant of the bench, or else that he had gone into retirement after spending his active life in dispensing justice and unraveling the tangles of the law. But it appears that he has never occupied a judicial position, and that his title is purely complimentary, having no relation whatever to the nature of his pursuits either in the past or in the present. The judge, indeed, is merely the owner of a couple of steam-tugs and one or two wood sloops which ply upon the river and upon Chesapeake Bay. He spends most of his time at home, living comfortably upon the receipts of a business which is conducted by his hired men, and perhaps also upon the interest of a few good investments in this and other places.

A very brief acquaintance with the judge suffices to convince any one that he has never presided in court. He is a rough, uneducated man, with small respect for grammar, an irrepressible tendency to distort the language, and very little information concerning subjects which are not made familiar by the occurrences of every-day life. But he is hearty, genial, sincere and honest, and I very soon learned to like him and to find amusement in his quaint simplicity.

My first interview with the judge was somewhat remarkable. I came home early one afternoon for the purpose of training some roses and clematis against my fence. While I was busily engaged with the work, the judge, who had been

digging potatoes in his garden, stuck his spade in the earth and came to the fence. After looking at me in silence for a few moments, he observed,

"Fine day, cap!"

The judge has the habit of conferring titles promiscuously and without provocation, particularly upon strangers. To call me "cap." was his method of expressing a desire for sociability.

"It *is* a beautiful day," I observed, "but the country needs rain."

5 *

"It never makes no difference to me," replied the judge, "what kinder weather there is; I'm allers satisfied. 'Twon't rain no sooner for wishin' for it."

As there was no possibility of our having a controversy upon this point, I merely replied, "That is true."

"How's yer pertaters comin' on?" inquired the judge.

"Very well, I believe. They're a little late, but they appear to be thriving."

"Mine's doin' first rate," returned the judge. "I guannered them in the spring, and I've bin a-hoein' at 'em and keepin' the weeds down putty stiddy ever since. Mons'ous sight o' labor growin' good pertaters, cap."

"I should think so," I rejoined, "although I haven't had much practical experience in that direction thus far."

"Cap.," observed the judge, after a brief interval of silence, "you're one of them fellers that writes for the papers and magazines, a'n't you?"

"Yes, I sometimes do work of that kind."

"Well, see here: I've got somethin' on my mind that's bin a-botherin' me the wust kind for a week and more. You've read the 'Atlantic Monthly,' haven't you?"

"Yes."

"Well, my daughter bought one of 'em, and I was a-readin' it the other night, when I saw it stated that guanner could be influenced by music, and that Professor Brown had made some git up and come to him when he played a tune on the pianner."

I remembered, as the judge spoke, that the magazine in question did contain a paragraph to the effect that the *iguana* was susceptible of such influence, and that Mrs. Brown had succeeded in taming one of these animals, so that it would run to her at the sound of music. But I permitted Mr. Pitman to continue without interruption.

"Of course," said he, "I never really believed no such

nonsense as that, but it struck me as kinder sing'lar, and I thought I'd give the old thing a trial, anyhow. So I got down my fiddle and went to the barn, and put a bag of guanner in the middle of the floor and begun to rake out a tune. First I played ' A Life on the Ocean Wave and a Home on the Rollin' Deep' three or four times; and there that guanner sot, just as I expected 'twould. Then I begun agin and sawed out a lot o' variations, but still she didn't budge. Then I put on a fresh spurt and jammed in a passel o' extra sharps and flats and exercises; and I played that tune backward and sideways and cat-a-cornered. And

I stirred in some scales, and mixed the tune up with Old Hundred and Mary Blaine and some Sunday-school songs, until I nearly fiddled my shirt off, and nary time did that guanner bag git up off o' that floor. I knowed it wouldn't. I knowed that feller wa'n't tellin' the truth. But, cap., don't it strike you that a man who'd lie like that ought to have

somethin' done to him?   It 'pears to me 's if a month or two
in jail 'd do that feller good."

The lesson in natural history which I proceeded to give to
the judge need not be repeated here.   He acknowledged
that the laugh was fairly against him, and ended his affir-
mation of his new-born faith in the integrity of the Atlantic
Monthly. by inviting me to climb over the fence and taste
some of his Bartlett pears.   The judge and I have been
steady friends ever since.

I find that one of the most serious objections to living out
of town lies in the difficulty experienced in catching the
early morning train by which I must reach the city and my
business.   It is by no means a pleasant matter, under any
circumstances, to have one's movements regulated by a time-
table and to be obliged to rise to breakfast and to leave
home at a certain hour, no matter how strong the temptation to delay may be.   But sometimes the horrible punctu-
ality of the train is productive of absolute suffering.   For
instance: I look at my watch when I get out of bed and find
that I have apparently plenty of time, so I dress leisurely,
and sit down to the morning meal in a frame of mind which
is calm and serene.   Just as I crack my first egg I hear the
down train from Wilmington.   I start in alarm; and taking
out my watch, I compare it with the clock and find that it is
eleven minutes slow, and that I have only five minutes left
in which to get to the dépôt.

 I endeavor to scoop the egg from the shell,
but it burns my fingers, the skin is tough, and
after struggling with it for a moment, it mashes
into a hopeless mess.   I drop it in disgust and
seize a roll, while I scald my tongue with a.
quick mouthful of coffee.   Then I place the roll in my
mouth while my wife hands me my satchel and tells me
she thinks she hears the whistle.   I plunge madly around

looking for my umbrella, then I kiss the family good-bye as well as I can with a mouth full of roll, and dash toward the door.

Just as I get to the gate, I find that I have forgotten my duster and the bundle my wife wanted me to take up to the city to her aunt. Charging back, I snatch them up and tear down the gravel-walk in a frenzy. I do not like to run through the village: it is undignified and it attracts attention; but I walk furiously. I go faster and faster as I get away from the main street. When half the distance is accomplished, I actually do hear the whistle;  there can be no doubt about it this time. I long to run, but I know that if I do I will excite that abominable speckled dog sitting by the sidewalk a little distance ahead of me. Then I really see the train coming around the curve close

by the dépôt, and I feel that I *must* make better time; and I do. The dog immediately manifests an interest in my

movements. He tears after me, and is speedily joined by
five or six other dogs, which frolic about my legs and bark
furiously. Sundry small boys, as I go plunging past, contribute to the excitement by whistling with their fingers, and
the men who are at work upon the new meeting-house stop
to look at me and exchange jocular remarks with each other.
I do feel ridiculous; but I must catch that train at all
hazards.

I become desperate when I have to slacken my pace until
two or three women who are standing upon the sidewalk,
discussing the infamous price of butter, scatter to let me
pass. I arrive within a few yards of the station with my
duster flying in the wind, with my coat tails in a horizontal
position, and with the speckled dog nipping my heels, just as
the train begins to move. I put on extra pressure, resolving

to get the train or perish, and I reach it just as the last
car is going by. I seize the hand-rail; I am jerked violently
around, but finally, after a desperate effort, I get upon the

step with my knees, and am hauled in by the brakeman, hot, dusty and mad, with my trousers torn across the knees, my legs bruised and three ribs of my umbrella broken.

Just as I reach a comfortable seat in the car, the train stops, and then backs up on the siding, where it remains for half an hour while the engineer repairs a dislocated valve. The anger which burns in my bosom as I reflect upon what now is proved to have been the folly of that race is increased as I look out of the window and observe the speckled dog engaged with his companions in an altercation over a bone. A man who permits his dog to roam about the streets nipping the legs of every one who happens to go at a more rapid gait than a walk, is unfit for association with civilized beings. He ought to be placed on a desert island in mid-ocean, and be compelled to stay there.

This will do as a picture of the experience of one morning—one melancholy morning. Of course it is exceptional. Rather than endure such agony of mind and discomfort of body frequently, I would move back to the city, and abandon for ever my little paradise by the Delaware.

I hardly think I shall get along so well with my neighbor on the other side, Cooley, as I do with Pitman. He is not only exceedingly ill-natured, but he inclines to be impertinent. Several times he has volunteered advice respecting the management of my garden and grounds, and has displayed a disposition to be somewhat sarcastic when his plans did not meet with my approval. I contrived, however, to avoid a breach of our amicable relations until the other day, when his conduct became absolutely unendurable.

I observed in the last number of Ball's *Journal of Health* some suggestions concerning a good method of exercising the lungs and expanding the chest. They were to this effect:

"Step out into the purest air you can find; stand perfectly erect,

with the head up and the shoulders back, and then, fixing the lips as
though you were going to whistle, draw the air, not through the
nostrils, but through the lips, into the lungs. When the chest is
about half full, gradually raise the arms, keeping them extended with
the palms of the hands down, as you suck in the air, so as to bring
them over the head just as the lungs are quite full. Then drop
the thumbs inward, and after gently forcing the arms backward and
the chest open, reverse the process by which you draw your breath
till the lungs are empty. This process should be repeated three or
four times immediately after bathing, and also several times through
the day."

This seemed reasonable, and I determined to give it a
trial. For that purpose I went out into the yard; and
pinning the directions to a tree, I stood in front of them

where I could see them.
Just as I began, Cooley
came out; and perceiving
me, he placed his elbows
upon the fence, rested his
chin upon his arms and
watched me with a very
peculiar smile upon his face.
I was exceedingly annoyed
and somewhat embarrassed,
but I was determined that
he should not have the
gratification of driving me
away from my own ground.
I made up my mind that I
would continue the exercise

without appearing to notice him. In a few moments, however, he remarked:

"Training for a prize-fight, Adeler?"

I made no reply, but continued the exercise. When I
had gone through the programme once, I began again. As

I arrived at that portion of it where the instructions direct the arrangement of the lips, Mr. Cooley, by this time somewhat incensed at my silence, observed,

"Whistle us a tune, Adeler. Give us something lively!"

As I paid no attention to this invitation, Cooley embraced the opportunity afforded by the upward motion of my arms, in accordance with the directions, to ask me if I was going to dive, and to offer to bring me out a tub in case I cherished such a design.

Then I completed the exercise and went into the house without giving Cooley any reason to suppose that I was aware of his presence. The next day I performed the ceremony at the same place, at the same hour. On the third day Cooley evidently expected me, for as soon as I appeared he came up to the fence and assumed his old position. He had with him a couple of friends, whom he must have summoned for the express purpose of tormenting me. When I had gone through the movements once, Cooley said:

"See here, Adeler, I don't want to do you any harm, but let me advise you as a friend to go to an asylum. I have known much worse cases than yours to be cured. It isn't kind to your family for you to remain at large. You're afflicted with only a mild form now; but if you don't do something, you'll have a violent paroxysm some day, and smash things. Now, take my advice, and put yourself under treatment."

Silence upon my part.

"How would you take it now," inquired Cooley, in a tone indicative of yearning tenderness, "if I should get over the fence and chain you to the pump while I go for the doctor? I really think you are getting dangerous."

"Mr. Cooley," I said, "I wish you would attend to your own business. I do not wish to quarrel with you, sir, but I will not have any interference on your part with my affairs

6

If it will make you any happier to learn what I am doing, I will tell you, seeing that you are so much interested in the matter, that I am exercising, under medical direction, for the benefit of my lungs."

"Exercising for the benefit of his lungs!" moaned Cooley. "His mind is entirely gone."

"Yes, sir," I said, angrily, "I am exercising for the benefit of my lungs, according to the directions of Dr. Ball, and I will thank you to keep your tongue quiet about it."

"He has them awfully bad," exclaimed Cooley, with a

pathetic look. "There is no such man as Dr. Ball, you know," he remarked, in a confidential tone, to one of his companions.

"I wish you distinctly to understand that I will not tolerate this impertinence much longer, sir," I exclaimed, indignantly. "What right have you to interfere with me upon my own ground, you ruffian?"

"His intellect's completely shattered," said Cooley, with a mournful shake of his head, to his companions. "Poor Mrs.

Adeler! It will be a terrible blow for her and for the children. My heart bleeds for them."

"Mr. Cooley," I said, "I want no more of this. I shall discontinue Dr. Ball's exercise at this place for the present, but I will tell you before I go that I consider you an insolent, unendurable idiot, and I will repay you some day or other for your outrageous behavior to me."

"Sad, sad, indeed!" said Cooley to his friends. "Strange how he clings to that fancy about a man named Ball, isn't it?"

One of Cooley's companions observed that the deranged were apt to get such notions in their heads, and he supplemented this statement with the remark, "This is a very interesting case—very."

Then I went into the house, and from the window saw Cooley and his companions walk away laughing. Not even the unpardonable insolence of Cooley can disguise the fact that the affair has a certain comic aspect; and when I became calmer, I confess that I appreciated this phase of the occurrence with some keenness, even though I happened to occupy an exceedingly unpleasant position as the victim of the joke. But I shall be even with Cooley for this. I will devise a scheme for tormenting him which will cause him to rue the day that he interfered with my pulmonary gymnastics. Dr. Ball's recipe, however, I think I will toss into the fire. I will expand my lungs by learning to sing or to play upon the flute. My family can then participate in my enjoyment. A married man has no right to be selfish in his pleasures.

CHAPTER V.

ISS BESSIE MAGRU-
DER is the object upon
which the affections of Mr.
Bob Parker are fixed at the
present moment. He met
her, I believe, while she was
attending school in the city
last winter, and what with
accompanying her to mati-
nees, taking her to church
and lingering by her side in
the parlor oftentimes in the
evening with the gas turned
low, the heart of Mr. Parker
gradually was induced to
throb only for the pretty
maid from New Castle. She has been very
gracious to him during all the time that he
has devoted himself to her, and has seemed to
like him so well that there is really no reason
for doubting that when the climax of the little

drama is reached and the question asked, she will droop her
eyelids, crimson her cheeks with blushes and whisper "Yes."

But Mr. Parker's courage has not yet been quite equal to the presentation of the proposition in a definite form. When I asked him the other day, good-humoredly, if he had explained himself to Miss Magruder, he told me confidentially that he had not.  At least a dozen times he had prepared the question in a graceful and effective form, and after committing it to memory he had started out with a valiant determination to declare his passion in that precise language the very moment he should encounter Miss Magruder.

"The words seem all right enough when I'm not with her," sighed Bob. "The very way I wrote 'em out appears to express exactly what I want to say, and as I go along the street I repeat 'em over and think to myself: 'By George, I'll do it now or die!' But as soon as I see her it seems ridiculous to blurt out a speech like that the first thing. So we begin to talk about something else, and then it seems 's if I couldn't break right in abruptly on the conversation. Then I  get to wondering how she'd feel if she knew what I was thinking about. Then very likely somebody comes in, and the chance is gone and I have to put it off. It worries me nearly to death. I'll go down there some day soon and plump it right out without saying another word first; I will, by George!"

It is an odd circumstance that every man who finds him-

6 *

self in the position occupied by Mr. Parker should entertain
the conviction that he is the first human being who ever suffered such embarrassment. Bob, my dear boy, you are traveling an old, a very old road, and all those rough and stony
places whereupon you endure distress, and where your timid
feet stumble, have been passed for hundreds of centuries by
love-sick wayfarers who were as eager, as unwise and as
cowardly as you!

It is very curious to observe how quickly the partiality
of a young man for a maid is perceived by their acquaintances, and with what zest the gossiping tongues tell the tale.
Women, of course, display deepest interest and acutest perception in such matters. A movement made in the direction
of courtship by a young fellow sends a strong ripple of excitement circling over the surface of the little world in which
they live; and there is something wonderful in the rapidity
with which the involved questions of suitability, social standing and financial condition are considered and settled. It is
soon perceived whether the business is a serious one upon
both sides; and as the two chief actors proceed slowly toward the moment when their hearts shall be unfolded to
each other, sharp eyes are watching them, and though they
think they are keeping their secret very fast from their
friends, every step of their progress is perceived, and the
gentle excitement of suspense increases and intensifies day
by day among the watchers until it culminates in the formal
announcement that they are engaged.

So they remain objects of general and tender consideration
until that other grand climax—the wedding—is at last attained; and the bride, with her orange blossoms and her veil,
with her satin, her silver-ware and her sweetness, becomes
the central figure of a happy festival whose gayety is tem-
pered by the solemn thoughts which will come concerning
that great unknown future whose threshold is being passed.

And then, when all this is over, when the lights are out, the wedding garments folded away, the practical domestic life begun and the period of romance passed, the interest which followed the pair from the first blossom of their love expires, and, as far as sentiment is concerned, their day—a time full of pleasant things, of grateful happiness in the present and joyful expectation for the future—is done for ever. Thenceforward their lives will be but prosy and dull to the world, however full to them the years may be of serenity and peace.

I have been making some inquiries concerning the Magruder family, in order to satisfy my wife that Bob's prospective relations are "the right kind of people." The expression, I know, is vague; and now that we have learned something of the Magruders, my inability to determine precisely what qualifications are necessary in order to make people of the right kind forbids the formation of a definite opinion upon my part concerning them. But Mrs. Adeler will decide; women are always mistresses of such subjects.

Mr. Magruder is apparently a man of leisure and of comparative wealth; his social position is very good, and he has enough intelligence and cultivation to enable him to get along comfortably in the society of very respectable persons. Mrs. Magruder, it seems, is rather inclined to emphasize herself. She is a physician, an enthusiast in the study and practice of medical science, and a woman of such force that she succeeds in keeping Mr. Magruder, if not precisely in a state of repression, at least slightly in the background. He married her, according to report, shortly after her graduation; and as he was at that time an earnest advocate of the theory that women should practice medicine, a belief prevails that he became attached to her while under her treatment. She touched his heart, we may presume, by exciting activity in his liver. He loved her, let us say, for the blisters she had spread, and demanded her hand because he had observed the singular dexterity with which it cut away tumors and tied up veins.

But if what Dr. Tobias Jones, our family physician, tells me is true, the sentiments of Magruder upon the subject of medical women have undergone a radical change in consequence of an exuberance of enthusiasm on the part of Mrs. Magruder. Dr. Jones entertains the regular professional hatred for Mrs. Dr. Magruder, and so I have my private doubts respecting the strict accuracy of his narrative.

He said that a few years ago the Magruders lived in

Philadelphia, and Mrs. Magruder was a professor in the Woman's Medical College. At that time Magruder was in business; and as he generally came home tired, he had a habit of lying on the sitting-room sofa in the evening, for the purpose of taking a nap. Several times when he did so, and Mrs. Magruder had some friends with her down stairs, he noticed upon awaking that there was a peculiar feeling of heaviness in his head and a queer smell of drugs in the room. When he questioned Mrs. Magruder about it, she invariably colored and looked confused, and said he must have eaten something which disagreed with him.

Ultimately the suspicions of Magruder were aroused. He suspected something wrong. A horrible thought crossed his • mind that Mrs. Magruder intended to poison him for his

skeleton—to sacrifice him so that she could dangle his bones on a string before her class, and explain to the seekers after medical truth the peculiarities of construction which enabled the framework of her husband to move around in society.

So Magruder revealed his suspicions to his brother, and engaged him to secrete himself in a closet in the room while he took his usual nap on a certain evening upon the sofa.

When that night arrived, Mrs. Magruder pretended to have the "sewing circle" from the church in the parlor, while her husband went to sleep in the sitting-room with that vigilant relative of his on guard. About nine o'clock Mr. Magruder's brother was surprised to observe Mrs. Magruder softly stealing up stairs, with the members of the "sewing  circle" following her noiselessly in single file. In her hand Mrs. Magruder carried a volume. If her brother-in-law had conceived the idea that the book might contain the tender strains of some sweet singer amid whose glowing imagery this woman reveled with the ecstasy of a sensitive nature, he would have been mistaken, for the work was entitled "Thompson on the Nervous System;" while those lines traced in a delicate female hand, upon the perfumed note-paper, and carried by Mrs. Magruder, so far from embodying an expression of the gentlest and most sacred emotions of her bosom, were merely a diagnosis of an aggravated case of fatty degeneration of the heart.

I give the story literally as I received it from that eminent practitioner Jones.

When the whole party had entered the room, Mrs. Magruder closed the door and applied chloroform to her husband's nose. As soon as he became completely insensible, the sewing in the hands of the ladies was quickly laid aside, and to Magruder's secreted brother was disclosed the alarming fact that this was a class of students from the college.

If Dr. Jones is to be believed, Professor Magruder began her lecture with some very able remarks upon the nervous system; and in order to demonstrate her meaning more plainly, she attached a galvanic battery to her husband's toes, so that she might make him wriggle before the class. And he did wriggle. Mrs. Magruder gave him a dozen or two shocks and poked him with a ruler to make him jump around, while the students stood in a semi-circle, with note-books in their hands, and exclaimed, "How very interesting!"

Magruder's brother thought it awful, but he was afraid to come out when he reflected that they might want *two* skeletons at the college.

Mrs. Magruder then said that she would pursue this branch of the investigation no further at that moment, because Mr. Magruder's system was somewhat debilitated in consequence of an overdose of chlorate of potash which she had administered in his coffee upon the previous day for the purpose of testing the strength of the drug.

Mrs. Magruder then proceeded to "quiz" the class concerning the general construction of her husband. She said, for instance, that she had won what was called the heart of Mr. Magruder, and she asked the students what it was that she had really won.

"Why, the cardia, of course," said the class; "it is an azygous muscle of an irregular pyramid shape, situated obliquely and a little to the left side of the chest, and it rests on the diaphragm."

One fair young thing said that it didn't rest on the diaphragm.

Another one said she would bet a quart of paregoric it did, and until the dispute was settled by the professor, Magruder's brother's hair stood on end with fear lest they should go to probing around inside of Magruder with a butcher-knife and a lantern, for the purpose of determining the actual condition of affairs respecting his diaphragm.

Mrs. Magruder continued. She explained that when she accepted Mr. Magruder he seized her hand, and she required the class to explain what it was that Mr. Magruder actually had hold of.

The students replied that he held in his grip twenty-seven distinct bones, among which might be mentioned the phalanges, the carpus and the metacarpus.

The beautiful creature who was incredulous concerning the diaphragm suggested that he also had hold of the deltoid. But the others scornfully suggested that the deltoid was a muscle; they knew, because they had dissected one that very morning. The discussion became so exciting that thumb-lancets were drawn, and there seemed to be a prospect of bloodshed, when the professor interfered and demanded of the girl who had begun to cry about the deltoid what was the result when Mr. Magruder kissed her.

"Why merely a contraction of the orbicularis oris muscle; thus," said the student as she leaned over and kissed Mr. Magruder.

Magruder's brother, in the closet, thought maybe it wasn't so very solemn for Magruder after all. He considered this portion of the exercises in a certain sense soothing.

But all the students said it was perfectly scandalous. And the professor herself, after informing the offender that hereafter when illustration of any point in the lesson was needed it would be supplied by the professor, ordered her to go to the foot of the class, and to learn eighty new bones as a punishment.

"Do you hear me, miss?" demanded the professor, when she perceived that that blooming contractor of the orbicularis oris did not budge.

"Yes," she said, "I am conscious of a vibration striking against the membrana tympanum, and being transmitted through the labyrinth until it agitates the auditory nerve, which conveys the impression to the brain."

"Correct," said the professor. "Then obey me, or I will call my biceps and flexors and scapularis into action and put you in your place by force."

"A GENERAL ATTACK ON THE SUBJECT."

"Yes, and we will help her with our spinatus and infra-spiralis," exclaimed the rest of the class.

Magruder's brother in the gloom of his closet did not comprehend the character of these threats, but he had a vague idea that the life of that lovely young saw-bones was menaced by firearms and other engines of war of a peculiarly deadly description. He felt that the punishment was too severe for the crime. Magruder himself, he was convinced, would have regarded that  orbicularis operation with courageous fortitude and heroic composure.

Mrs. Magruder then proceeded to give the class practice in certain operations in medical treatment. She vaccinated Magruder on the left arm, while one of the students bled his right arm and showed her companions how to tie up the vein. They applied leeches to his nose, under the professor's instructions; they cupped him on the shoulder blades; they exercised themselves in spreading mustard plasters on his back; they timed his pulse; they held out his tongue with pincers and examined it with a microscope, and two or three enthusiastic students kept hovering around Magruder's leg with a saw and a carving-knife, until Magruder's brother in retirement in the closet shuddered with apprehension.

But the professor restrained these devotees of science; and when the other exercises were ended, she informed the students that they would devote a few moments in conclusion to study of the use of the stomach-pump.

Dr. Jones continued : " I shall not enter into particulars concerning the scene that then ensued. There is a certain want of poetry about the operation of the weapon just named, a certain absence of dignity and sentiment, which, I may say, render it impossible to describe it in a manner which will elevate the soul and touch the moral sensibilities. It will

7

suffice to observe that as each member of the class attacked Magruder with that murderous engine, Magruder's brother, timid as he was, solemnly declared to himself that if the class would put away those saws and things he would rush out and rescue his brother at the risk of his life.

"He was saved the necessity of thus imperiling his safety. Magruder began to revive. He turned over; he sat up; he stared wildly at the company; he looked at his wife; then he sank back upon the sofa and said to her, in a feeble voice:

"'Henrietta, somehow or other I feel awfully hungry!'

"Hungry! Magruder's brother considered that, after that

last performance of the class, Magruder ought to have a relish for a couple of raw buffaloes, at least. He emerged from the closet, and seizing a chair, determined to tell the whole story. Mrs. Magruder and the class screamed, but he proceeded. Then up rose Magruder and discussed the subject with vehemence, while his brother brandished his chair and joined in the chorus. Mrs. Magruder and the class cried, and said Mr. Magruder was a brute, and he had no love for science. But Mr. Magruder said that as for himself, 'hang science!' when a woman became so infatuated with it as to chop up her husband to help it along. And his brother said he ought to put in even stronger terms than that. What followed upon the adjournment of the class is not known. But Magruder seems somehow to have lost much of his interest in medicine, and since then there has been a kind of coolness between him and the professor."

I shall repeat this extraordinary narrative to Mr. Parker. He ought to be aware of the propensities of his prospective mother-in-law beforehand, so that he may not encounter the dangers which attend her devotion to her profession without realizing the fact of their existence. Admitting that Jones adheres closely to truth in his statement, we may very reasonably fear that Mrs. Magruder would not hesitate to vivisect a mere son-in-law, or in an extreme case to remove one of his legs. A mother-in-law with such dangerous proclivities ought not to be accepted rashly or in haste. Prudence requires that she should be meditated upon.

"I want to ask you a question," observed Mr. Parker, as we sat out upon the porch after tea with Mrs. Adeler. "I notice that you always say 'is being done,' and not 'is doing.' Now, which is correct? I think you're wrong. Some of those big guns who write upon such subjects think so too. Grind us out an opinion."

"The subject has been much discussed, Bob, and a good many smart things have been said in support of both theories. But I stick to 'is being done,' first, because it is more common, and therefore handier, and second, because it is the only form that is really available in all cases. Suppose, for instance, you wished to express the idea that our boy Agamemnon is enduring chastisement; you would say, 'Agamemnon is being spanked,' not 'Agamemnon is spanking.' The difference may seem to you very slight, but it would be a matter of considerable importance to Agamemnon; and if a choice should be given him, it is probable that he would suddenly select the latter form."

"Just so," exclaimed Mr. Parker.

"You say again, 'Captain Cook is being eaten.' Certainly this expresses a very different fact from that which is conveyed by the form, 'Captain Cook is eating.' I venture to say that Captain Cook would have insisted upon the latter as by far the more agreeable of the two things."

"Precisely," said Mr. Parker.

"And equally diverse are the two ideas expressed by the phrases 'The mule is being kicked' and 'The mule is kicking.' But it is to be admitted that there are occasions when the two forms indicate a precisely similar act. You assert, I will say, that 'Hannah is hugging.'"

"Which would be a very improper thing for Hannah to do," suggested Mr. P.

"Of course it would; but there is an extreme probability that you would indicate Hannah's action under the circumstances if you should say, 'Hannah is being hugged.' It is in most cases a reciprocal act. Or suppose I say, 'Jane is kissing'?"

"And her mother ought to know about it if she is," remarked Bob.

"It is nearly the same as if I should say, 'Jane is being kissed,' for one performance in most cases presupposes the other. It will not, however, be necessary for you to attempt to prove this fact by practice anywhere in the neighborhood of the Magruder mansion. If you find it necessary to explain to Miss Magruder my views of this grammatical question, it will be better to confine your illustrations to the case of Captain Cook. But you can safely continue to say, 'is being built.' Nobody will object to that but a few superfine people who are so far ahead of you in such matters that they will be tolerably sure to regard you as an idiot whichever form you happen to use, while if you adopt the other form in conversation with your unfastidious acquaintances, you will be likely to confuse your meaning very often in such a manner as to impress them with the conviction that your reason is dethroned."

7 *

CHAPTER VI.

 THE editor of our daily paper, *The Morning Argus*, is Col. Bangs — Colonel Mortimer J. Bangs. The colonel is an exceedingly important personage in the village, and he bears about him the air of a man who is acutely conscious of the fact. The gait of the colonel, the peculiar way in which he carries his head, the manner in which he swings his cane, and the art he has of impressing any one he happens to address with a feeling that he is performing an act of sublime condescension in permitting himself to hold communication with an inferior being, combine to excite in the vulgar mind a sentiment of awe. The eminent journalist manifests in his entire bearing his confidence in the theory that upon him devolves the responsibility of forming the public opinion

of the place; and there is a certain grandeur in the manner in which he conveys to the public mind, through the public eye, the fact that while he appreciates the difficulties of what seemed to be an almost superhuman task, which would surely overwhelm men of smaller intellectual calibre, the work presents itself to his mind as something not much more formidable than pastime.

The appearance of Colonel Bangs is not only imposing, but sometimes it inclines to be almost ferocious. The form in which he wears his whiskers, added to the military nature of his title, would be likely to give to timid strangers an idea not only that the colonel has a raging and insatiable thirst for blood and an almost irresistible appetite for the horrors of war, but that upon very slight provocation he would suddenly grasp his sword, fling away the scabbard, and then proceed to wade through slaughter to a throne and shut the gates of mercy on mankind. But I rejoice to say that the colonel has not really such murderous and revolutionary inclinations. His title was obtained in those early years of peace when he led the inoffensive forces of the militia upon parade, and marshaled them as they braved the perils of the target-shooting excursion.

I think I am warranted in saying that Colonel Bangs would never voluntarily stand in the imminent deadly breach if there happened to be a man there with a gun who wanted him to leave, and that he will never seek the bubble reputation at the cannon's mouth unless the cannon happens to be unloaded. Place Colonel Bangs in front of  an empty cannon, and for a proper consideration he would remain there for years without the quiver of a muscle.

Charge that piece of ordnance with powder and ball, and not all the wealth of the world would induce him to stand anywhere but in the rear of the artillery.

The *Argus* has never appeared to me to be an especially brilliant journal. To the intelligent and critical reader, indeed, the controlling purpose of the colonel seems to be to endeavor to ascertain how near he can bring the paper to imbecility without actually reaching that condition; and it is surprising how close a shave he makes of it. When we first came to the village, a gleam of intelligence now and then appeared in the editorial columns of the *Argus*, and this phenomenon was generally attributed to the circumstance that Colonel Bangs had permitted his assistant editor to spread his views before the public. On such occasions it was entertaining to observe in what manner the colonel would assume the honors of the authorship of his assistant's articles. Cooley, for instance, meeting him upon the street would observe:

"That was an uncommonly good thing, colonel, which appeared in the *Argus* this morning on The Impending Struggle; whose was it?"

COLONEL BANGS (with an air of mingled surprise and indignation). Whose was it? Whose was that article? I suppose you are aware, sir, that *I* am the editor of *The Morning Argus!*"

COOLEY. "Yes; but I thought perhaps—"

COLONEL (with grandeur). "No matter, sir, what you thought. When an article appears in my own paper, Mr. Cooley, there is but a single inference to be drawn. When I find myself unable to edit the *Argus*, I will sell out, sir—I will sell out!"

COOLEY (calmly). "Well, but Murphy, your assistant, told me distinctly that he wrote that editorial himself."

COLONEL (coming down). "Ah! yes, yes! that is partly true, now I remember. I believe Murphy did scratch off the body of the article, but I overhauled it; it was necessary for me to revise it, to touch it up, to throw it into shape, as it were, before it went into type. Murphy means well, and with a little guidance—just a l-e-e-t-l-e careful training —he will do."

But Murphy did not remain long. One of the colonel's

little nephews died, and a man who kept a marble-yard in Wilmington thought he might obtain a gratuitous advertisement by giving to the afflicted uncle a substantial expression of his sympathy. So he got up a gravestone for the departed child. The design, cut upon the stone in basrelief, represented an angel carrying the little one in his arms and flying away with it, while a woman sat weeping upon the ground. It was executed in a most dreadful manner. The tombstone was sent to the colonel, with a simple request that he would accept it. As he was absent, Mr. Murphy determined to acknowledge the gift, although he had not the slightest idea what it meant. So the next morning he burst out in the *Argus* with the following remarks:

"ART NEWS.

"We have received from the eminent sculptor, Mr. Felix Mullins of Wilmington, a comic *bas-relief* designed for an ornamental fireboard. It represents an Irishman in his night-shirt running away with the little god Cupid, while the Irishman's sweetheart demurely hangs her head in the

corner. Every true work of art tells its own story; and we understand, as soon as we glance at this, that our Irish friend has been coqueted with by the fair one, and is pretending to transfer his love to other quarters. There is a lurking smile on the Irishman's lips which expresses his mischievous intentions perfectly. We think it would have been better, however, to have clothed him in something else than a night-shirt, and to have smoothed down his hair. We have placed this *chef d'œuvre* upon a shelf in our office, where it will undoubtedly be admired by our friends when they call. We are glad to encourage such progress in Delaware art."

This was painful. When the colonel returned next day, Mr. Mullins called on him and explained the tombstone to him, and that very night Mr. Murphy retired from the *Morning Argus*, and began to seek fresh fields for the exercise of his talents.

Colonel Bangs affords me most entertainment in the *Argus* when an election is approaching.

Your city editor often displays a certain amount of vehemence at such times, but his wildest frenzy is calmness, is absolute slumberous repose itself, when compared with the frantic enthusiasm manifested by Colonel Bangs. The latter succeeds in getting up as much fury over a candidate for constable as a city editor does over an aspirant for the Presidency. He will turn out column after column of double-leaded type, in which he will demonstrate with a marvelous profusion of adjectives that if you should roll all the prophets, saints and martyrs into one, you would have a much smaller amount of virtue than can be found in that one humble man who wants to be constable. He will prove to you that unless that particular person is elected, the entire fabric of American institutions will totter to its base and become a bewildering and hopeless ruin, while the merciless despots who grind enslaved millions beneath their iron heels will greet the hideous and irreclaimable chaos with fiendish laughter, and amid the remnants of a once proud republic they will erect bastiles in which they will forge chains to fetter the wrists of dismayed and heart-broken patriots. He will ask you to take your choice between electing that man constable and witnessing the annihilation of the proud work for which the Revolutionary patriots bled and died.

The man who runs against the candidate of the *Argus* will be proved to be a moral and intellectual wreck, and it will be shown that all the vices which have corrupted the race since the fall of man are concentrated in that one individual. The day after election, if his man wins, Colonel Bangs will decorate his paper with a whole array of roosters and a menagerie of 'coons, and inform a breathless world that the nation is once more saved. If he loses, he will omit any reference to the frightful prophecies uttered during the campaign, keep his roosters in the closet, and mildly assert that the opposition man is not so bad, after all, and that the right party must triumph next time for certain. Then Colonel Bangs will keep his enthusiasm cool for a year, and during that period will rest his overwrought brain, while he edits his paper with a pair of predatory shears and a dishonest paste-pot.

It is extremely probable that we shall lose our servant-girl. She was the victim of a very singular catastrophe a night or two since, in consequence of which she has acquired a prejudice against the house of Adeler. We were troubled with dampness in our cellar, and in order to remove the difficulty we got a couple of men to come and dig the earth out to the depth of twelve or fifteen inches and fill it in with a cement-and-mortar floor. The material was, of course, very soft, and the workmen laid boards upon the surface, so that access to the furnace and the coal-bin was possible. That night, just after retiring, we heard a woman screaming for help, but after listening at the open window, we concluded that Cooley and his wife were engaged in an altercation, and so we paid no more attention to the noise.

Half an hour afterward there was a violent ring at the front-door bell, and upon going to the window again, I found Pitman standing upon the door-step below. When I spoke to him, he said:

"Max" (the judge is inclined sometimes, especially during periods of excitement, to be unnecessarily familiar), "there's somethin' wrong in your cellar. There's a woman down there screechin' and carryin' on like mad. Sounds 's if somebody's a-murderin' her."

I dressed and descended; and securing the assistance of Pitman, so that I would be better prepared in the event of burglars being dis-covered, I lighted a lamp and we went into the cellar.

There we found the maid-ser-vant standing by the refrigera-tor, knee-deep in the cement, and supporting herself with the handle of a broom, which was also half submerged. In seve-ral places about her were air-holes marking the spot where the milk-jug, the cold veal, the lima beans and the silver-plated butter-dish had gone down. We procured some additional boards, and while Pitman seized the suf-

ferer by one arm I grasped the other. It was for some time doubtful if she would come to the surface without the use of more violent means, and I confess that I was half inclined to regard with satisfaction the prospect that we would have to blast her loose with gunpowder. After a desperate struggle, during which the girl declared that she would be torn in pieces, Pitman and I succeeded in

8

getting her safely out, and she went up stairs with half
a barrel of cement on each leg, declaring
that she would leave the house in the morning.

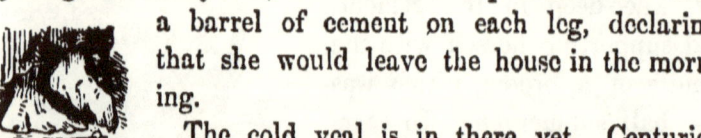

The cold veal is in there yet. Centuries
hence some antiquarian will perhaps grub
about the spot whereon my cottage once stood, and will blow
that cold veal out in a petrified
condition, and then present it to
a museum as the fossil remains
of some unknown animal. Perhaps, too, he will excavate the
milk-jug and the butter-dish, and
go about lecturing upon them as
utensils employed in bygone ages by **a race** of savages
called "the Adelers." I should like to be alive at the time
to hear that lecture. And I cannot avoid the thought that

if our servant had been completely buried in the cement, and thus carefully preserved until the coming of that antiquarian, the lecture would be more interesting, and the girl more useful than she is now. A fossilized domestic servant of the present era would probably astonish the people of the twenty-eighth century.

"I see," said Mrs. Adeler, who was looking over the evening paper upon the day following the accident, "that Mlle. Willson, the opera-singer, has been robbed of ten thousand dollars' worth of diamonds in St. Louis. What a dreadful loss!"

"Dreadful, indeed, Mrs. A. These singing women are very unfortunate. They are constantly being robbed, or rolled over embankments in railway cars, or subjected to deadly perils in some other form; and the astonishing thing about it all is that these frightful things invariably occur precisely at the times when public interest in the victims begins to flag a little, and the accounts always appear in the papers of a certain city just before the singers begin an engagement in that place. It is very remarkable."

"You don't think this story is false, do you, and that all such statements are untrue?"

"Certainly not. I only refer to the fact because it shows how very wonderful coincidences often are. I have observed precisely the same thing in connection with other contributors to popular entertainment. But in these cases sometimes we may trace the effects directly to the cause. Take menageries, for example. The peculiar manifestations which frequently attend the movements of these collections of wild animals through the land can be attributed only to the wonderful instinct of the beasts. If I am to judge from the reports that appear occasionally in the provincial newspapers, it invariably happens that the animals come to the rescue of the menagerie people when the latter begin their campaigns and are badly in want of advertisements for which they are disinclined to pay.

"Regularly every season these ferocious beasts proceed to do something to secure sensational allusions to themselves in the papers. If the rhinoceros does not plunge through the

side of the tent and prowl about until he comes home with an entire Sunday-school class of small boys impaled on his horn, the Nubian lion is perfectly certain to bite its keeper in half and lunch upon his legs. If the elephant should neglect to seize his attendant and fling him into the parquet circle, while at the same time it crushes the hyena into jelly, the Bengal tiger is very sure not to forget to tear half a dozen ribs out of the ticket agent, and then to assimilate ten or twelve village children who are trying to peep under the tent. Either the brass

band, riding upon the den of lions, finds the roof caving in, and at last is rescued with the loss of the cymbal player and the operator upon the key bugle, and of a lot of legs and arms snatched from the bass drummer and the man with the triangle, or else there is a railroad accident which empties the cars and permits kangaroos, panthers, blue-nose baboons and boa-constrictors to roam about the country reducing the majorities of the afflicted sections previous to the election.

"You may find hundreds of accounts of such accidents in the rural press during the summer season; and whenever I read them, I am at a loss to determine which is more wonderful, the remarkable sagacity and the self-sacrificing devotion of these beasts, which perceive that something must be done and straightway do it, or the childlike confidence, the bland simplicity, of the editors who give gratuitous circulation to these narratives."

"Talking about menageries," observed Mr. Bob Parker, "did I ever tell you about Wylie and his love affair?"

"No."

"Wylie, you know, was the brother of the porter in our store; and when he had nothing to do, he used to come around and sit in the cellar among the boxes and bales, and we fellows would go down when we were at leisure and hear him relate his adventures.

"One time, several years ago, he was awfully hard up, and he accepted a situation in a traveling show. They dressed him up in a fur shirt and put grizzly bears' claws on his feet and daubed some stuff over his face, and advertised him as 'The Wild Man of Afghanistan.' Then, when the show was open, he would stand in a cage and scrouge up against the bars and growl until he would scare the children nearly to death. The fat woman used to sit near him during the exhibitions just outside the cage, and by degrees he learned to love her. The keeper of the concern himself, it appears, also cherished a tender feeling for the corpulent young creature, and he became jealous of the Wild Man of Afghanistan."

"And the professor of avoirdupois—whom did she affect?"

"Well, when the visitors came, the keeper would procure a pole with a nail in the end, and he would stir up the Wild

8 *

Man and poke him. Then he would ridicule the Wild Man's legs and deliver lectures upon the manner in which he turned in his toes; and he sometimes read to the audience

chapters out of books of natural history to show that a being with a skull of such a shape must necessarily be an idiot. Then he would poke the Wild Man of Afghanistan a few more times with the pole and pass on to the next cage with some remarks tending to prove that the monkeys therein and the Wild Man were of the same general type.

"And all the time the fat woman would sit there and smile a cold and disdainful smile, as if she believed it all,  and hated such legs and despised toes that turned in. At last the Wild Man of Afghanistan had his revenge. One day when all hands were off duty, the keeper fell asleep on the settee in the ticket-office adjoining the show-room. Then Mr. Wylie threw a blanket over him and went for the fat woman. He led her by the hand and asked her to be seated while he told her about his love. Then she suddenly sat down on the keeper."

" And killed him, I suppose, of course?"

"Wylie informed me that you could have passed the remains under a closed door without scraping the buttons of
the waistcoat. They merely slid him into a crack in the

ground when they buried him, and
the fat woman pined away until she
became thin and valueless. Then
the Wild Man married her, and began life again on a new basis."

"Was Mr. Wylie what you might
consider a man of veracity?"

"Certainly he was; and his story
is undoubtedly true, because his
toes did turn in."

"That settles the matter. With
such incontrovertible evidence as
that at hand, it would be folly to
doubt the story. We will go quietly
and confidently to tea instead of discussing it."

CHAPTER VII.

The Battery and its Peculiarities—A Lovely Scene—
Swede and Dutchman Two Hundred Years Ago—Old
Names of the River—Indian Names Generally—Cooley's
Boy—His Adventure in Church—The Long and the
Short of It—Mr. Cooley's Dog and Our Troubles
with It.

HE closing hours of the long summer afternoon can be spent in
no pleasanter place than by the
water's side. And after tea I
like to take my little group of
Adelers out from the hot streets
over the grassy way which leads
to the river shore, and to find a
comfortable loitering-place upon
the Battery. That spot is adorned
with a long row of rugged old
trees whose trunks are gashed
and scarred by the penknives of
idlers. Their branches inter-
lock overhead and form one
great mass of tender green foliage, here sweeping down
almost to the earth, and there hanging far out over the
water, trembling and rustling in the breeze. Beneath, there
is a succession of hewn logs, suggesting the existence of some
sort of a wharf in the remote past, but now serving nicely
for seats for those who come here to spend a quiet hour.

Around there is a sod which grows lush and verdant, excepting where the tread of many feet has worn a pathway backward to the village

In front is as lovely a scene as any the eye can rest upon in this portion of the world. Below us the rising and the ebbing tides hurl the tiny ripples upon the pebbly beach, and the perpetual wash of the waves makes that gentle and constant music which is among the most grateful of the sounds of nature.

Away to the southward sweeps the Delaware shore line in a mighty curve which gives the river here the breadth and magnificence of a great lake, and at the end of the chord of the arc the steeples and the masts at Delaware City rise in indistinct outline from the waves. To the left, farther in the distance, old Fort Delaware lifts its battlements above the surface of the stream. And see! A puff of white smoke rises close by the flag-staff. And now a dull thud comes with softened cadence across the wide interval. It is the sunset gun. Far, far beyond, a sail glimmers with rosy light caught from the brilliant hues of the clouds which make the western heavens glorious with their crimson drapery; and while here as we gaze straight out through the bay there is naught in the perspective but water and sky, to the right the low-lying land below the island fortress seems, somehow, to be queerly suspended between river and heaven, until as it recedes it grows more and more shadowy, and at last melts away into the mist that creeps in from the ocean. It is pure happiness to sit here beneath the trees and to look upon the scene while the cool air pours in from the water and lifts into the upper atmosphere the oppressive heat that has mantled the earth during the day.

I do not know why the place is called "the Battery." Perhaps a couple of centuries ago the Swedes may have built here a breastwork with which to menace their hated

THE BATTERY.

Dutch rivals who held the fort just below us there upon the river bank. (We will walk over to the spot some day, Mrs. Adeler.) And who can tell what strange old Northmen in jerkin and helmet have marched up and down this very stretch of level sward, carrying huge fire-lock muskets and swearing mighty oaths as they watched the intruding Dutchman in his stronghold, caring little for the placid loveliness of the view which the rolling tide of the majestic river ever offered to their eyes!

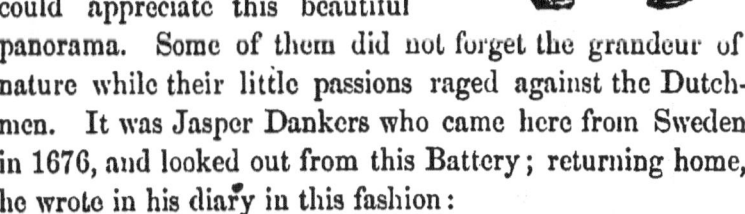

But some of those people could appreciate this beautiful panorama. Some of them did not forget the grandeur of nature while their little passions raged against the Dutchmen. It was Jasper Dankers who came here from Sweden in 1676, and looked out from this Battery; returning home, he wrote in his diary in this fashion:

, "The town is situated upon a point which extends out with a sandy beach, affording a good landing-place. It lies a little above the bay where the river bends and runs south from there, so that you can see down the river southwardly. The greater portion of it presents a beautiful view in perspective, and enables you to see from a distance the ships come out from the great bay and sail up the river."

The sandy beach is gone, and the ships which float upward from the bay are not such craft as Dankers saw; but the stream has its ancient majesty, and the wooded banks, I like to think, present to our eyes nearly the same sweet picture that touched the soul of that old Swede two long centuries ago.

Another thing has changed—yes, it has changed many times. The Indians, Mrs. A., called the bay Poutaxat and the river Lenape Wihittuck. The stream, too, was named the Arasapha, and also Mackerish Kitton—a title pretty enough in its way, but oddly suggestive of mackerel and kittens. But the Swedes came, and with that passion which burned in the bosoms of all the early European immigrants for prefixing the word "new" to the names of natural objects, they entitled the river New Swedeland Stream. Then the Dutch obtained the mastery here, and it became the South River, the Hudson being the North River, and finally the English obtained possession, and called it Delaware.

What a pity it is that they didn't suffer one of the original titles to remain! The Lenape would have been a beautiful name for the river—far better than the Gallic compound that it bears now. The men who settled this country seem to have had for Indian names the same intense dislike that they entertained for the savages themselves, and as a rule they rejected with scorn the soft, sweet syllables with which mountain and forest and stream were crowned, substituting too often most barbarous words therefor. Even Penn and his Quakers disdained the Indian names. How much better Pennsylvania would have been treated if that grand old State had been called Susquehanna or Juniata or Allegheny! And would it not have been wiser if the city, instead of bringing its name from Asia, had sought it among its own surroundings, and had grown to greatness as Wissahickon or Wingohocking? The Indian names that still remain here and there to designate a stream, a district or a town are the few distinctly American words in existence. We have thrown away the others, although they were a very precious part of the legacy which we received from the race we have supplanted. One such word as Wyoming is worth an entire volume of such names as New York, Philadelphia,

Baltimore, Maryland and the like; and I have always wondered at the blundering folly of the man who, with such musical syllables at hand ready to be used, dubbed the town of Wilkes Barre with that particularly poor name.

While we were sitting by the river discussing these and other matters, Cooley's boy, a thoroughly disagreeable urchin, who had been playing with some other boys upon the wharf near by, tumbled into the water. There was a terrible screaming among his companions, and a crowd quickly gathered upon the pier. For a few moments it seemed as if the boy would drown, for no one was disposed to leap in after him, and there was not a boat within saving distance. But fortunately the current swept him around to the front of the Battery, where the water is shallow, and before he was seriously hurt he was safely landed in the mud that stretches below the low-water mark. Then the excitement, which had been so great as to attract about half the population of the village, died away, and people who had just been filled with horror at the prospect of a tragedy began to feel a sense of disappointment because their fears had not been realized. I cannot of course say that I was sorry to see the youngster once more upon dry land; but if fate had robbed us of him, we should have accepted the dispensation without grievous complaint.

We did not leave all the nuisances behind us in the city. Cooley's dog and his boy are two very sore afflictions which make life even here very much sadder than it ought to be in a place that pretends to be something in the nature of an

9

earthly paradise. The boy not only preys upon my melon-patch and fruit trees and upon those of my neighbors, but he has an extraordinary aptitude for creating a disturbance in whatever spot he happens to be. Only last Sunday he caused such a terrible commotion in church that the services had to be suspended for several minutes until he could be removed. The interior of the edifice was painted and varnished recently, and I suppose one of the workmen must have left a clot of varnish upon the back of Cooley's pew, which is directly across the aisle from mine. Cooley's boy was the only representative of the family at church upon that day, and he amused himself during the earlier portions of the

service by kneeling upon the seat and communing with Dr. Jones's boy, who occupied the pew immediately in the rear. Sometimes, when young Cooley would resume a proper position, Jones's boy would stir him up afresh by slyly pulling his hair, whereupon Cooley would wheel about and menace Jones with his fist in a manner which betrayed utter indifference to the proprieties of the place and the occasion, as well as to the presence of the congregation. When Cooley finally sank into a condition of repose, he placed his head, most unfortunately, directly against the lump of undried varnish, while he amused himself by reading the commandments and the other scriptural texts upon the wall behind the pulpit.

In a few moments he attempted to move, but the varnish had mingled with his hair, and it held him securely. After making one or two desperate but ineffectual efforts to release himself, he became very angry; and supposing that Jones's boy was holding him, he shouted:

"Leg go o' my hair! Leg go o' my hair, I tell you!"

The clergyman paused just as he was entering upon consideration of "secondly," and the congregation looked around in amazement, in time to perceive young Cooley, with his head against the back of the pew, aiming dreadful blows

over his shoulder with his fist at some unseen person behind him. And with every thrust he exclaimed:

"I'll smash yer nose after church! I'll go for you, Bill Jones, when I ketch you alone! Leg go o' my hair, I tell you, or I'll knock the stuffin' out o' yer," etc., etc.

Meanwhile, Jones's boy sat up at the very end of his pew, far away from Cooley, and looked as solemn as if the sermon had made a deep impression upon him.

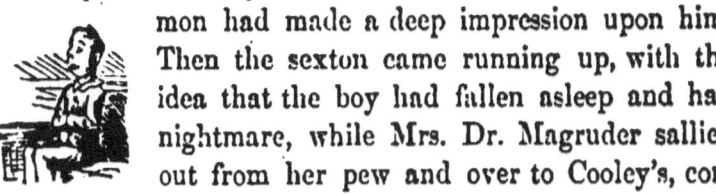

Then the sexton came running up, with the idea that the boy had fallen asleep and had nightmare, while Mrs. Dr. Magruder sallied out from her pew and over to Cooley's, convinced that he had a fit. When the cause of the disturb-

ance was ascertained, the sexton took out his knife, and after
sawing off enough of Cooley's hair to release him, dragged
him out of church.   The victim retreated unwillingly,

glancing around at Jones's boy and shaking his fist at that
urchin as if to indicate that he cherished a deadly purpose
against Jones.

Then the sermon proceeded.   I suppose a contest between
the two boys has been averted, for only yesterday I saw
Jones and Cooley, the younger, playing hop-scotch together
in the street in apparent forgetfulness of the sorrows of the
sanctuary.

Judge Pitman tells me that one of the reasons why Cooley

and his wife disagree is that there is such a difference in their height. Cooley is tall, and Mrs. Cooley is small. Mrs. Cooley told Mrs. Pitman, if the judge is to be believed, that Cooley continually growled because she could not keep step with him. They always start wrong, somehow, when they go out together, and then, while he tries to catch step with her, she endeavors to get in with him. After both have been shuffling about over the pavement for several minutes in a perfectly absurd manner, they go ahead out of step just as before.

When Cooley tried to take short steps like hers, his gait was so ridiculous as to excite remark; while if she tried to make such long strides as his, people stopped and looked at her as if they thought she was insane. Then she would strive to take two steps to his one, but she found that two and a half of hers were equal to one of his; and when she undertook to make that fractional number in order to keep up with him, he would frown at her and say,  "Mrs. Cooley, if you are going to dance the polka mazourka upon the public highway, I'm going home."

I do not receive this statement with implicit confidence in its truthfulness. Pitman's imagination sometimes glows with unnatural heat, and he may have embellished the original narrative of Mrs. Cooley.

I shall probably never receive from any member of the Cooley family a correct account of the causes of the unpleasant differences existing therein, for we are on worse terms than ever with Cooley.

His dog became such an intolerable nuisance because of his nocturnal vociferation that some practical humanitarian in the neighborhood poisoned him. Cooley apparently cherished the conviction that I had killed the animal, and he flung the carcass over the fence into my yard. I threw it back. Cooley returned it. Both of us remained at home that day, and spent the morning handing the inanimate brute to each other across the fence. At noon

I called my man to take my place, and Cooley hired a colored person to relieve him. They kept it up until nightfall, by which time I suppose the corpse must have worn away to a great extent, for at sundown my man buried the

tail by my rose-bush and came in the house, while Cooley's representative resigned and went home.

The departed brute left behind him but one pleasant recollection; and when I recall it, I feel that he fully avenged my wrongs upon his master. Cooley went out a week or two ago to swim in the creek, and he took the dog with him to watch his clothing. While Cooley
bathed the dog slept; but when Cooley emerged from the water, the dog did not recognize him in his nude condition, and it refused to let him come near his garments. Whenever Cooley would attempt to seize a boot or a stocking or a shirt,

the dog flew at him with such ferocity that he dared not attempt to dress himself. So he stood in the sun until he was almost broiled; then he went into the water and remained there, dodging up and down for the purpose of avoiding the people who passed occasionally along the road. At last the dog went to sleep again, and Cooley, creeping softly behind the brute, caught it suddenly by the tail and flung it across the stream.   Before the dog could recover its senses and swim back, Cooley succeeded in getting some of his clothing on him, and then the dog came sidling up to him looking as if it expected to be rewarded for its extraordinary vigilance.   The

manner in which Cooley kicked the faithful animal is said to have been simply dreadful.

I should have entertained a positive affection for that dog if it had not barked at night. But I am glad it is gone.   We came here to have quietness, and that was unattainable while Cooley's dog remained within view of the moon.

CHAPTER VIII.

A RATHER unusual sensation has been excited in the village by the *Morning Argus* within a day or two; and while most of the readers of that wonderful sheet have thus been supplied with amusement, the soul of the editor has been filled with gloom and wrath and despair. Colonel Bangs recently determined to engage an assistant to take the place made vacant by the retirement of the eminent art-critic, Mr. Murphy, and he found in one of the lower counties of the State a person who appeared to him to be suitable. The name of the new man is Slimmer. He has often contributed to the *Argus* verses of a distressing character, and I suppose Bangs must have become acquainted with him through the medium of the correspondence thus begun. No one in the world but Bangs would ever have selected such a poet for an editorial position. But Bangs is singular—he is excep-

tional. He never operates in accordance with any known laws, and he is more than likely to do any given thing in such a fashion as no other person could possibly have adopted for the purpose. As the *Argus* is also *sui generis*, perhaps Bangs does right to conduct it in a peculiar manner. But he made a mistake when he employed Mr. Slimmer.

The colonel, in his own small way, is tolerably shrewd. He had observed the disposition of persons who have been bereaved of their relatives to give expression to their feelings in verse, and it occurred to him that it might be profitable to use Slimmer's poetical talent in such a way as to make the *Argus* a very popular vehicle for the conveyance to the public of notices of deaths. That kind of intelligence, he well knew, is especially interesting to a very large class of readers, and he believed that if he could offer to each advertiser a gratuitous verse to accompany the obituary paragraph, the *Argus* would not only attract advertisements of that description from the country round about the village, but it would secure a much larger circulation.

When Mr. Slimmer arrived, therefore, and entered upon the performance of his duties, Colonel Bangs explained his theory to the poet, and suggested that whenever a death-notice reached the office, he should immediately write a rhyme or two which should express the sentiments most suitable to the occasion.

"You understand, Mr. Slimmer," said the colonel, "that when the death of an individual is announced I want you, as it were, to cheer the members of the afflicted family with the resources of your noble art. I wish you to throw your-self, you may say, into their situation, and to give them, f'r instance, a few lines about the deceased which will seem to be the expression of the emotion which agitates the breasts of the bereaved."

"To lighten the gloom in a certain sense," said Mr. Slim-mer, "and to—"

"Precisely," exclaimed Colonel Bangs. "Lighten the

gloom. Do not mourn over the departed, but rather take a joyous view of death, which, after all, Mr. Slimmer, is, as it were, but the entrance to a better life. Therefore, I wish you to touch the heart-strings of the afflicted with a tender hand, and to endeavor, f'r instance, to divert their minds from contemplation of the horrors of the tomb."

"Refrain from despondency, I suppose, and lift their thoughts to—"

"Just so! And at the same time combine elevating sen-timent with such practical information as you can obtain from the advertisement. Throw a glamour of poesy, f'r instance, over the commonplace details of the every-day life of the deceased. People are fond of minute descriptions. Some facts useful for this purpose may be obtained from the man who brings the notice to the office; others you may perhaps be able to supply from your imagination."

"I think I can do it first rate," said Mr. Slimmer.

"But, above all," continued the colonel, "try always to take a bright view of the matter. Cause the sunshine of smiles, as it were, to burst through the tempest of tears; and if we don't make the *Morning Argus* hum around this town, it will be queer."

Mr. Slimmer had charge of the editorial department the next day during the absence of Colonel Bangs in Wilming-

ton. Throughout the afternoon and evening death-notices arrived; and when one would reach Mr. Slimmer's desk, he would lock the door, place the fingers of his left hand among his hair and agonize until he succeeded in completing a verse that seemed to him to accord with his instructions.

The next morning Mr. Slimmer proceeded calmly to the office for the purpose of embalming in sympathetic verse the memories of other departed ones. As he came near to the establishment he observed a crowd of people in front of it, struggling to get into the door. Ascending some steps upon the other side of the street, he overlooked the crowd, and could see within the office the clerks selling papers as fast as they could handle them, while the mob pushed and yelled in frantic efforts to obtain copies, the presses in the cellar meanwhile clanging furiously. Standing upon the curbstone in front of the office there was a long row of men, each of whom was engaged in reading *The Morning Argus* with an

earnestness that Mr. Slimmer had never before seen displayed by the patrons of that sheet. The bard concluded that either his poetry had touched a sympathetic chord in the popular heart, or that an appalling disaster had occurred in some quarter of the globe.

He went around to the back of the office and ascended to the editorial rooms. As he approached the sanctum, loud voices were heard within. Mr. Slimmer determined to ascertain the cause before entering. He obtained a chair, and placing it by the side door, he mounted and peeped over the door through the transom. There sat Colonel Bangs, holding *The Morning Argus* in both hands, while the fringe which grew in a semicircle around the edge of his bald head stood straight out, until he seemed to resemble a gigantic gun-swab. Two or three persons stood in front of him in threatening attitudes. Slimmer heard one of them say:

"My name is McGlue, sir!—William McGlue! I am a brother of the late Alexander McGlue. I picked up your paper this morning, and perceived in it an outrageous insult to my deceased relative, and I have come

around to demand, sir, WHAT YOU MEAN by the following
infamous language:

    "'The death-angel smote Alexander McGlue,
       And gave him protracted repose;
    He wore a checked shirt and a Number Nine shoe,
       And he had a pink wart on his nose.
    No doubt he is happier dwelling in space
       Over there on the evergreen shore.
    His friends are informed that his funeral takes place
       Precisely at quarter-past four.'

"This is simply diabolical! My late brother had no wart
on his nose, sir. He had upon his nose neither a pink wart
nor a green wart, nor a cream-colored wart, nor a wart of
any other color. It is a slander! It is a gratuitous insult
to my family, and I distinctly want you to say *what do you
mean* by such conduct?"

"Really, sir," said Bangs, "it is a mistake. This is the
horrible work of a miscreant in whom I reposed perfect con-

fidence. He shall be punished by my own hand for this outrage. A pink wart! Awful! sir—awful! The miserable scoundrel shall suffer for this—he shall, indeed!"

"How could I know," murmured Mr. Slimmer to the foreman, who with him was listening, "that the corpse hadn't a pink wart? I used to know a man named McGlue, and *he* had one, and I thought *all* the McGlues had. This comes of irregularities in families."

"And who," said another man, addressing the editor, "authorized you to print this hideous stuff about my deceased son? Do you mean to say, Bangs, that it was not with your authority that your low comedian inserted with my advertisement the following scandalous burlesque? Listen to this:

> "'Willie had a purple monkey climbing on a yellow stick,
> And when he sucked the paint all off it made him
>   deathly sick;
> And in his latest hours he clasped that monkey in
>   his hand,
> And bade good-bye to earth and went into a better
>   land.

> "'Oh! no more he'll shoot his sister with his little wooden gun;
> And no more he'll twist the pussy's tail and make her yowl, for fun.
> The pussy's tail now stands out straight; the gun is laid aside;
> The monkey doesn't jump around since little Willie died.'

"The atrocious character of this libel will appear when I say that my son was twenty years old, and that he died of liver complaint."

"Infamous!—utterly infamous!" groaned the editor as he cast his eyes over the lines. "And the wretch who did this still remains unpunished! It is too much!"

"And yet," whispered Slimmer to the foreman, "he told me to lighten the gloom and to cheer the afflicted family with the resources of my art; and I certainly thought that idea about the monkey would have that effect, somehow. Bangs is ungrateful!"

Just then there was a knock at the door, and a woman entered, crying.

"Are you the editor?" she inquired of Colonel Bangs.

Bangs said he was.

"W-w-well!" she said, in a voice broken by sobs, "wh. what d'you mean by publishing this kind of poetry about m-my child? M-my name is Sm-Smith; and wh-when I looked this m-morning for the notice of Johnny's d-death in your paper, I saw this scandalous verse:

> "'Four doctors tackled Johnny Smith—
>   They blistered and they bled him;
> With squills and anti-bilious pills
>   And ipecac. they fed him.
> They stirred him up with calomel,
>   And tried to move his liver;
> But all in vain—his little soul
>   Was wafted o'er The River.'

"It's false! false! and mean! Johnny only had *one* doctor. And they d-didn't bl-bleed him and b-blister him.

It's a wicked falsehood, and you're a hard-hearted brute f-f-for printing it!"

"Madam, I shall go crazy!" exclaimed Bangs. "This is not my work. It is the work of a villain whom I will slay with my own hand as soon as he comes in. Madam, the miserable outcast shall die!"

"Strange! strange!" said Slimmer. "And this man told me to combine elevating sentiment with practical information. If the information concerning the squills and ipecac. is not practical, I have misunderstood the use of that word. And if young Smith didn't have four doctors, it was an outrage. He ought to have had them, and they ought to have excited his liver. Thus it is that human life is sacrificed to carelessness."

At this juncture the sheriff entered, his brow clothed with thunder. He had a copy of *The Morning Argus* in his hand. He approached the editor, and pointing to a death-notice, said,

"Read that outrageous burlesque, and tell me the name of the writer, so that I can chastise him."

The editor read as follows:

"We have lost our little Hanner in a very painful manner,
    And we often asked, How can her harsh sufferings be borne?
When her death was first reported, her aunt got up and snorted
    With the grief that she supported, for it made her feel forlorn.

"She was such a little seraph that her father, who is sheriff,
    Really doesn't seem to care if he ne'er smiles in life again.
She has gone, we hope, to heaven, at the early age of seven
    (Funeral starts off at eleven), where she'll nevermore have pain."

"As a consequence of this, I withdraw all the county advertising from your paper. A man who could trifle in this manner with the feelings of a parent is a savage and a scoundrel!"

10 *

As the sheriff went out, Colonel Bangs placed his head upon the table and groaned.

"Really," Mr. Slimmer said, "that person must be deranged. I tried, in his case, to put myself in his place, and to write as if I was one of the family, according to instructions. The verses are beautiful. That allusion to the grief of the aunt, particularly, seemed to me to be very happy. It expresses violent emotion with a felicitous combination of sweetness and force. These people have no soul—no appreciation of the beautiful in art."

While the poet mused, hurried steps were heard upon the stairs, and in a moment a middle-aged man dashed in

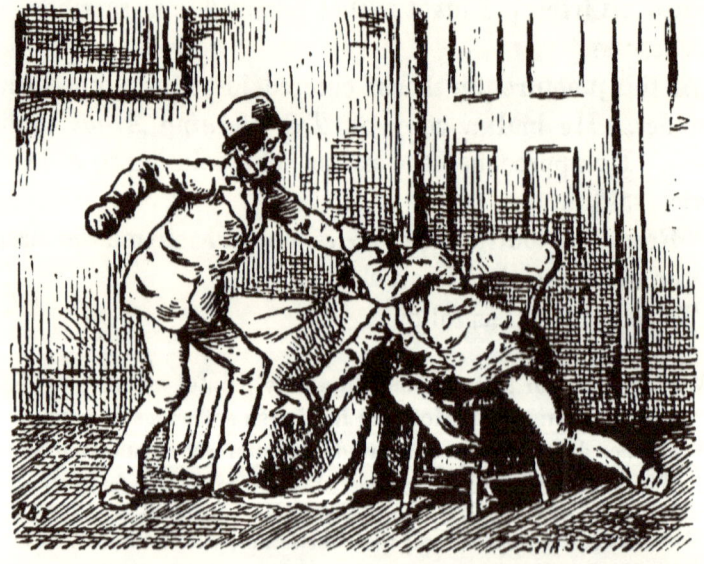

abruptly, and seizing the colonel's scattered hair, bumped his prostrate head against the table three or four times with considerable force. Having expended the violence of his emotion in this manner, he held the editor's head down with one hand, shaking it occasionally by way of emphasis, and with the other hand seized the paper and said,

"You disgraceful old reprobate! You disgusting vampire! You hoary-headed old ghoul! What d'you mean by putting such stuff as this in your paper about my deceased son? What d'you mean by printing such awful doggerel as this, you depraved and dissolute ink-slinger—you imbecile .quill-driver, you!

> "'Oh! bury Bartholomew out in the woods,
> In a beautiful hole in the ground,
> Where the bumble-bees buzz and the woodpeckers sing,
> And the straddle-bugs tumble around ;
> So that, in winter, when the snow and the slush
> Have covered his last little bed,
> His brother Artemas can go out with Jane
> And visit the place with his sled.'

"I'll teach you to talk about straddle-bugs! I'll instruct you about slush! I'll enlighten your insane old intellect on the subject of singing woodpeckers! What do *you* know about Jane and Artemas, you wretched buccaneer, you despicable butcher of the English language? Go out with a sled! I'll carry you out in a hearse before I'm done with you, you deplorable lunatic!"

At the end of every phrase the visitor gave the editor's head a fresh knock against the table. When the exercise was ended, Colonel Bangs explained and apologized in the humblest manner, promising at the same time to give his assailant a chance to flog Mr. Slimmer, who was expected to arrive in a few moments.

"The treachery of this man," murmured the poet to the foreman, "is dreadful. Didn't he desire me to throw a glamour of poesy over commonplace details? But for that I should never have thought of alluding to woodpeckers and bugs, and other children of Nature. The man objects to the remarks about the sled. Can the idiot know that it was necessary to have a rhyme for 'bed'? Can he suppose that

I could write poetry without rhymes? The man is a lunatic! He ought not to be at large!"

Hardly had the indignant and energetic parent of Bartholomew departed when a man with red hair and a ferocious glare in his eyes entered, carrying a club and accompanied by a savage-looking dog.

"I want to see the editor," he shouted.

A ghastly pallor overspread the colonel's face, and he said,

"The editor is not in."

"Well, when *will* he be in, then?"

"Not for a week—for a month—for a year—for ever! He will never come in any more!" screamed Bangs. "He has gone to South America, with the intention to remain there during the rest of his life. He has departed. He has fled. If you want to see him, you had better follow him to the equator. He will be glad to see you. I would advise you, as a friend, to take the next boat—to start at once."

"That is unfortunate," said the man; "I came all the way from Delaware City for the purpose of battering him up a lot with this club."

"He will be sorry," said Bangs, sarcastically. "He will regret missing you. I will write to him, and mention that you dropped in.

"My name is McFadden," said the man. "I came to break the head of the man who wrote that obituary poetry about my wife. If you don't tell me who perpetrated the following, I'll break *yours* for you. Where's the man who wrote this? Pay attention:

> " ' Mrs. McFadden has gone from this life;
>   She has left all its sorrows and cares;
>   She caught the rheumatics in both of her legs
>   While scrubbing the cellar and stairs.
>   They put mustard-plasters upon her in vain;
>   They bathed her with whisky and rum;
>   But Thursday her spirit departed, and left
>   Her body entirely numb.' "

"The man who held the late Mrs. McFadden up to the scorn of an unsympathetic world in that shocking manner," said the editor, "is named James B. Slimmer. He boards in Blank street, fourth door from the corner. I would advise you to call on him and avenge Mrs. McFadden's wrongs with an intermixture of club and dog-bites."

"And this," sighed the poet, outside the door, "is the man who told me to divert McFadden's mind from contemplation of the horrors of the tomb. It was this monster who counseled me to make the sunshine of McFadden's smiles burst through the tempest of McFadden's tears. If that red-headed monster couldn't smile over that allusion to whisky and rum, if those remarks about the rheumatism in her legs could not divert his mind from the horrors of the tomb, was it *my* fault? McFadden grovels! He knows no more about poetry than a mule knows about the Shorter Catechism."

The poet determined to leave before any more criticisms were made upon his performances. He jumped down from his chair and crept softly toward the back staircase.

The story told by the foreman relates that Colonel Bangs at the same instant resolved to escape any further persecution, and he moved off in the direction taken by the poet. The two met upon the landing, and the colonel was about to begin his quarrel with Slimmer, when an enraged old woman who had been groping her way up stairs suddenly  plunged her umbrella at Bangs, and held him in the corner while she handed a copy of the *Argus* to Slimmer, and pointing to a certain stanza, asked him to read it aloud. He did so in a somewhat tremulous voice and with frightened glances at the enraged colonel. The verse was as follows:

" Little Alexander's dead ;
    Jam him in a coffin ;
Don't have as good a chance
    For a fun'ral often.
Rush his body right around
    To the cemetery ;
Drop him in the sepulchre
    With his Uncle Jerry."

The colonel's assailant accompanied the recitation with such energetic remarks as these ;

"Oh, you willin! D'you hear that, you wretch? What d'you mean by writin' of my grandson in that way? Take that, you serpint! Oh, you wiper, you! tryin' to break a lone widder's heart with such scand'lus lies as them! There, you willin! I kemmere to hammer you well with this here umbreller, you owdacious wiper, you! Take that, and that, you wile, indecent, disgustin' wagabone! When you know well enough that Aleck never had no Uncle Jerry, and never had no uncle in no sepulchre anyhow, you wile wretch, you!"

When Mr. Slimmer had concluded his portion of the entertainment, he left the colonel in the hands of the enemy anà fled. He has not been seen in New Castle since that day, and it is supposed that he has returned to Sussex county for the purpose of continuing in private his dalliance with the Muses. Colonel Bangs appears to have abandoned the idea of establishing a department of obituary poetry, and the *Argus* has resumed its accustomed aspect of dreariness.

It may fairly boast, however, that once during its career it has produced a profound impression upon the community.

Mr. Bob Parker came home at a very late hour last night; and when I opened the front door to let him in, he muttered something to the effect that he was "sorry for being out so late." Then he pushed by me suddenly and went up stairs in a very odd fashion, keeping his face as much as possible toward the door, where I remained standing, astonished at

his very strange behavior. When I closed the door and went to my room, it occurred to me that something of a serious nature might have happened; and impelled partly by curiosity and partly by a desire to be of service, I knocked at Bob's door.

"Anything the matter?" I inquired.

"Oh no. I was detained down town," replied Bob.

"I can't do anything for you, then?"

"No; I'll be in bed in a couple of minutes."

"You acted so peculiarly when you came in that I thought you might be ill."

"I was never better in my life. I went up stairs that way because I was tired."

"A very extraordinary effect of fatigue," I said.

"I say!" cried Bob, "don't say anything to your wife about it. There's no use of getting up an excitement about nothing."

I went to bed convinced that something was wrong, and determined to compel Bob to confess on the morrow what it was. After breakfast we sat smoking together on the porch, and then I remarked:

"Bob, I wish you to tell me plainly what you meant by that extraordinary caper on the stairs last night. I think I ought to know. I don't want to meddle with your private affairs, but it seems to me only the proper thing for you to give me a chance to advise you if you are in trouble of any kind. And then you know I am occupying just now a sort of a parental relation to you, and I want to overhaul you if you have been doing anything wrong."

"I don't mind explaining the matter to you," replied Bob. "It don't amount to much, anyhow, but it's a little rough on a fellow, and I'd rather not have the whole town discussing it."

"Well?"

"You know old Magruder's? Well, I went around there last night to see Bessie; and as it was a pleasant evening, we thought we would remain out on the porch. She sat in a chair near the edge, and I placed myself at her feet on one of the low wooden steps in front. We stayed there talking about various things and having a pretty fair time, as a matter of course, until about nine o'clock, when I said I thought I'd have to go."

"You came home later, I think."

"Well, you know, some mutton-headed carpenter had been there during the day mending the rustic chairs on the porch, and he must have put his glue-pot down on the spot where I sat, for when I tried to rise I found I couldn't budge."

"You and Cooley's boy seem to have a fondness for that particular kind of adventure."

"Just so. And when I made an effort to get upon my feet, Bessie said, 'Don't be in a hurry; it's early yet,' and I told her I believed I would stay a little while longer. So I sat there for about two hours, and during the frightful gaps in the conversation I busied myself thinking how I could get away without appearing ridiculous. It hurts a man's chances if he makes himself ridiculous before a woman he is fond of. So you see I didn't know whether to ask Bessie to go in the house while I partially disrobed and went home in

11

Highland costume, or whether to give one terrific wrench and then proceed down the yard backward. I couldn't make up my mind; and as midnight approached, Bessie, who was dreadfully sleepy, said, at last, in utter despair, she would have to excuse herself for the rest of the evening.

"Then, you understand, I was nearly frantic, and I asked her suddenly if she thought her father would lend me

his front steps for a few days. She looked sort of scared.

and went in after old Magruder. When he came out, I
made him stoop down while I explained the situation to
him. He laughed and
hunted up a hatchet and
saw, and cut away the sur-
rounding timber, so that I
came home with only about
a square foot of wood on
my trousers. Very good of
the old man, wasn't it, to
smash up his steps in that
manner? And the reason
why I kind of sidled up
stairs was that I feared
you'd see that wooden
patch and want to know
about it. That's all. Queer
sort of an affair, wasn't it?"

Then Mr. Parker darted off for the purpose of overtaking
Miss Magruder, who at that moment happened to pass upon
the other side of the street.

As Mr. Parker disappeared, Mrs. Adeler came out upon
the porch from the hall, and placing her hand upon my
shoulder, said,

"You are not going to publish that story of the attempt
of the *Argus* to establish a department of obituary poetry,
are you?"

"Of course I am. Why shouldn't I?"

"Don't you fear it might perhaps give offence? There
are some people, you know, who think it right to accompany
a notice of death with verses. Besides, does it seem precisely proper to treat such a solemn subject as death with
so much levity?"

"My dear, the persons who use those ridiculous rhymes which sometimes appear in the papers for the purpose of

parading their grief before the public cannot have very nice sensibilities."

"Are you sure of that? At any rate, is it not possible that a verse which appears to you and me very silly may be the attempt of some bereaved mother to give in that forlorn fashion expression to her great agony? I shouldn't like to ridicule even so wretched a cry from a suffering heart."

"The suggestion is creditable to your goodness. But I would like to retain the story of Slimmer's folly, and I'll tell you what I will do: I will publish your opinions upon the subject, so that those who read the narrative may understand that the family of Adeler is not wholly careless of propriety." So here are the story and the protest; and those to whom the former is offensive may find what consolation can be obtained from the fact that the latter has been offered in advance of any expression of opinion by indignant readers whose grief for the departed tends to run into rhyme.

11 *

CHAPTER IX.

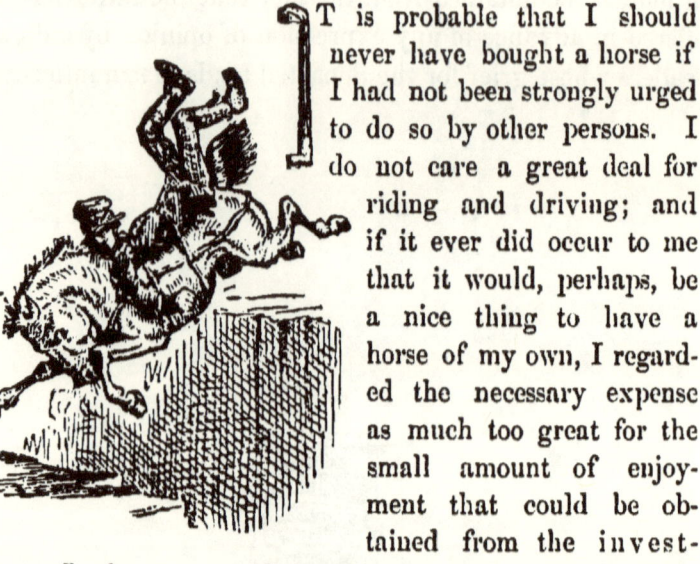

T is probable that I should never have bought a horse if I had not been strongly urged to do so by other persons. I do not care a great deal for riding and driving; and if it ever did occur to me that it would, perhaps, be a nice thing to have a horse of my own, I regard- ed the necessary expense as much too great for the small amount of enjoy- ment that could be ob- tained from the invest- ment. It always seemed to me to be much cheaper to hire a horse at a livery-stable if only an occasional drive was desired; and I cling to that theory yet. But everybody else seemed to think I ought to own a horse. Mrs. Adeler was especially anxious about it. She insisted that we were doing very well in the world, and she could not see the use of hav- ing means if we were to live always as we did when we were poor. She said she often wanted to take a little drive along the river-road in the evening with the children, and she frequently wished to visit her friends in the country, but she couldn't bear to go with a strange horse of which she knew nothing.

My friends used to say, "Adeler, I wonder you don't keep a horse and take your family out sometimes;" and they hammered away at the theme until I actually began to feel as if the public suspected me of being a niggardly and cruel tyrant, who hugged my gold to my bosom and gloated over the misery of my wife and children—gloated because they couldn't have a horse. People used to come down from the city to see us, and after examining the house and garden, they would remark, "Very charming!—very charming, indeed! A little paradise, in fact; but, Adeler, why don't you buy a horse?"

I gradually grew nervous upon the subject, and was tolerably well convinced that there would never be perfect happiness in my family until I purchased a steed of some kind. At last, one day Cooley had a yellow horse knocked down to him at one of those auction-sales which are known in the rural districts as "Vandues." And when I saw Cooley drive past the house, every afternoon, with that saffron brute, and his family in a dearborn wagon, and observed how he looked in at us and smiled superciliously, as if he was thinking, "There lives a miserable outcast who has no horse and can't get one," I determined to purchase at once.

I have not had much experience with horses, but I found one whose appearance and gait were fairly good, and I was particularly drawn toward him because the man recommended him as being "urbane." I had heard many descriptions of the points of a good horse, but this was the first time I had ever met a horse whose most prominent characteristic was urbanity. It seemed to me that the quality was an excellent one, and I made a bargain on the spot and drove home.

"Mrs. Adeler," I said, as I exhibited the purchase to her, "I do not think this horse is very fast; I do not regard him as in the highest sense beautiful; he may even be deficient in wind; his tail certainly is short; and I think I can detect

in his forelegs a tendency to spring too far forward at the knees; but, Mrs. Adeler, the horse is urbane. The man said that his urbanity amounted to a positive weakness, and that is why I bought him. If a horse is not urbane, my dear, it is useless, no matter what its merit in other respects."

She said that had been her opinion from early childhood.

"I do not care greatly, Mrs. Adeler, for excessive speed. Give me a horse that can proceed with merely a tolerable degree of celerity and I am content. I never could comprehend why a man whose horse can trot a mile in two minutes and forty seconds should be made unhappy because another man's horse trots the same distance one second sooner—that is, of course, supposing that they are not running for money. One second of time never makes any especial difference to me, even when I am in a hurry. What I want in a horse is not swiftness, but urbanity. I would rather have a kind-hearted horse, like ours, than the most rapid trotter with a wicked disposition."

For a while I enjoyed having a horse, and I felt glad I had bought him. It seemed very good to drive down by the river-bank upon a pleasant evening, with the cool breeze blowing in from the water, and the country around beautiful with the bright foliage of early autumn. There was a sufficient compensation for the heat and wretchedness of the busy day in that quiet journey over the level road and past the fragrant fields in the early twilight; and as we came home amid the deepening shadows, we could find pleasure in watching the schooners far off in the channel flinging out their lights, and we could see the rays streaming across the wide interval of rippling surface, and moving weirdly and strangely with the motion of the water.

Sometimes, upon going out, we would overtake Cooley in his dearborn; and then it was felicitous to observe how, when I touched my horse with the whip, the animal put his head down, elevated his abbreviated tail to a horizontal position and left Cooley far, far behind, flogging his tawny horse with such fury as would surely have subjected him to the reproaches of the Society for the Prevention of Cruelty to Animals if that excellent organization had been present. My horse could achieve a tolerably rapid gait when he de-

sired to do so. That fact made existence in this world of
anguish and tears seem even more sad to Cooley than it had
done previously. I feel sure that he would have given fabulous sums if his horse could have trotted a mile in a minute

—just once—when we were upon the road together. I began to think that it was just as well, after all, to have a pro-
gressive horse as a slow one.

But when the novelty of the thing had passed, my old
indisposition to amusement of that kind gradually returned.
I drove less frequently. One day my man said to me:

"Mr. Adeler, that hoss is a-eatin' his head off, sir. If you
don't take him out, he'll be so wild that he'll bu'st the machine to flinders, sir."

The threatened catastrophe seemed so alarming that I
took him out, although I had important work to do at home.
The next day I wanted to stay up in the city to go to a lecture; but that morning, early, the horse again displayed an
alarming amount of friskiness, and I felt as if I must go
down and exercise him. I drove him for three hours at a
rapid gait, and succeeded in working off at least the exuberance of his spirits.

On the following Wednesday I came home in the afternoon, exhausted with work, and intending to retire at an early hour. At half-past six o'clock, Judge Pitman came in. He remarked:

"Adeler, that horse of yourn 'll certainly go crazy if you don't move him around. Mind me. He kicks like a flintlock musket now if you come within forty foot of the stable."

I went out and hitched up, and that night I drove twenty-four miles at a frightful speed. Horses have, perhaps, gone farther and faster, but few have been pushed forward with a smaller regard for consequences. Nothing but a recollection of the cost of the horse restrained me from driving him into the river and leaving him there.

By degrees the despicable brute became the curse of my existence. If I desired to go on a journey, the restlessness of the horse had first to be overcome. If I received an invitation to a party, the horse must be exercised beforehand. If I had an important article to write, I must roam around the country behind that horse for two or three hours, holding him in with such force that my hands were made too unsteady for penmanship. If I wanted to take a row on the river—an exercise of which I am passionately fond— that detestable animal had to be danced up and down the turnpike in order to keep him from kicking the stable to pieces. And he was recommended to me as "urbane"!

He made my life unhappy. I became depressed and morose. Sometimes when, amid a circle of friends, there was a provocation to laughter, and I participated in the general hilarity, I would suddenly become conscious of the fact that the horse was in active existence, and the mirth would be extinguished in gloom. He mingled with my dreams. Visions of a bob-tailed horse consuming spectral oats, and kicking with millions of legs, disturbed my rest at night. I rushed with him over countless leagues of shadowy road, and plunged with him over incomprehensible precipices. He organized himself into hideous nightmare shapes, and

charged wildly over me as I slept, and filled all the air of that mysterious slumber-land with the noise of his demoniac neighing.

The reality was bad enough without the unreal nocturnal horrors. I might have sold the brute, but my wife really wanted to have a horse, and I wished to oblige her. But it was very wearing to bear about constantly the feeling of responsibility which the animal engendered. I had to choose between driving him continually and having the lives of the members of my family imperiled when they took him out; and the consciousness that whether there was sickness or business, storm or earthquake, calamity or death, the horse must be driven, gradually placed me in the position of a man who is haunted by some dreadful spectre that clings to him and overshadows him for ever and for ever.

The perpetual nervous worry told upon me. I became thin. My clothing hung loose upon me. I took up two inches in my waistcoat strap. The appetite which enabled me to find enjoyment at the table deserted me. The food seemed tasteless; and if in the midst of a meal the neigh of the horse came eddying up through the air from the stable, I turned away with a feeling of disgust, and felt as if I wanted to prod somebody with the carving-knife.

One day my wife said to me:

"Mr. Adeler, you know that I urged you strongly to buy that horse, and I thought he would do, but—"

"But now you want to sell him! ha! ha!" I exclaimed, with delight. "Very well, I'll send him to the auctioneer this very day."

"I wasn't going to say that," she remarked. "What I wanted to mention was that nearly everybody in good cir-cumstances about here drives a pair, and I think we ought to get another horse; don't you, my dear? It's so much nicer than having only one."

"Mrs. Adeler," I said, solemnly, "that one horse down there in the stable has reduced me to a skeleton and made me utterly miserable. I will do as you say if you insist upon it, but I tell you plainly that if another horse is brought upon these premises I shall go mad."

"Don't speak in that manner, my dear."

"I tell you, Mrs. Adeler, that I shall go stark, staring mad! Take your choice: go without the other horse or have a maniac husband."

She said, of course, she would do without the horse.

But the affliction was suddenly and unexpectedly removed

My horse had a singularly brief tail, and I thought it might be that some of his violent demonstrations in the stable were induced by his inability to switch off the flies which alighted upon sensitive portions of the body. It occurred to me to

get him up an artificial tail for home use, and I procured a piece of thick rope for the purpose. There was, too, a certain humorousness about the idea that pleased me; and as the amount of jocularity which that horse had occasioned had, thus far, been particularly small, the notion had peculiar attractiveness.

I unraveled about eighteen inches of the rope and fastened the other end to the horse's tail. This, I estimated, would enable him to switch a fly off the very end of his nose when he had acquired a little practice. Unfortunately, I neglected to speak to my man upon the subject; and when he came to the stable that evening, he examined the rope and concluded that I was trying experiments with

some new kind of hitching-strap; so he tied the horse to the stall by the artificial continuation. By morning the feed-box was kicked into kindling-wood, and the horse was stand ing on three legs, with the other leg caught in the hay-rack, while he had chewed up two of the best boards in the side of the stable in front of him.

Subsequently I explained the theory to the man and re-adjusted the rope. But the patent tail annoyed the hostler so much while currying the horse that he tied a stone to it to hold it still. The consequence was that in a moment of unusual excitement the horse flung the stone around and inflicted· a severe wound upon the man's head. The man resigned next morning.

I then concluded to introduce an improvement. I pur-chased some horse-hair and spliced it upon the tail so neatly that it had the appearance of a natural growth. When the new man came, he attempted to comb out the horse's tail, and the add-ed portion came off in his hand. He had profound confidence in his veterinary skill, and he im-agined that the occurrence indi-cated a diseased condition of the horse. So he purchased some powders and gave the animal an enormous dose in a bucket of warm "mash." In half an hour that pestilential horse was seized with convulsions, during which  he kicked out the stable-door, shattered the stall to pieces, hammered four more boards out of the partition, dislocated his off hind leg and expired in frightful agony.

He was more urbane after death than he had been during his life, and I contemplated his remains without shedding a tear. He was sold to a glue-man for eight dollars; and when he had departed, I felt that he would fulfill a wiser and better purpose as a contributor to the national stock of glue than as the unconscious persecutor of his former owner.

"Mrs. Adeler, do you feel any interest in the subject of pirates?"

She said the question was somewhat abrupt, but she thought she might safely say she did not.

"I make the inquiry for the reason that I have just written a ballad which has for its hero a certain bold corsair. This is the first consequence of the death of our horse. In the exuberance of joy caused by that catastrophe, I felt as if I would like to perpetrate something which should be purely ridiculous, and accordingly I organized upon paper this piratical narrative. You think the subject is an odd one? Not so. I do not pretend to explain the fact, but it

is true that by this generation a pirate is regarded as a comic personage. Perhaps the reason is that he has been so often presented to us in such a perfectly absurd form in melodrama and in the cheap and trashy novels of the day. At any rate, he is susceptible of humorous treatment, as you will perceive.

"I have had a stronger impulse to write of buccaneers, too, because I am in New Castle; for, somehow, I always associate those freebooting individuals with this village. A certain ancestor of mine sailed away from this town in 1813, in a brig commissioned as a privateer, and played havoc with the ships of the enemy upon the Atlantic. In my childhood I used to hear of his brave deeds, and, somehow, I conceived the idea

that he was a genuine pirate with a black flag, skull and
cross-bones, and a disagreeable habit of compelling his cap-
tives to walk the plank. I was much more proud of him
then, Mrs. Adeler, than I should be now had he really been
such a ruffian. But he was not. He was a gallant sailor
and a brave and honest gentleman, who served his country
faithfully on the ocean, and then held a post of honor as
warden of the port of Philadelphia until his death. But I
never go to the river's side in New Castle without involun-
tarily recalling that fine old man in the character of an out-
lawed rover upon the high seas.

"Here, my dear, is the ballad. When I have read it to
you, I will send it to the *Argus*. Since Mr. Slimmer's retirement there has been a dearth of poetry in the columns of that
great organ."

MRS. JONES'S PIRATE.

A sanguinary pirate sailed upon the Spanish main
In a rakish-looking schooner which
   was called the "Mary Jane."
She carried lots of howitzers and
   deadly rifled guns,
With shot and shell and powder and
   percussion caps in tons.

The pirate was a homely man, and
   short and grum and fat;
He wore a wild and awful scowl beneath his slouching hat.
Swords, pistols and stilettos were arranged around his thighs,
And demoniacal glaring was quite
   common with his eyes.

His heavy black moustaches curled away beneath his nose,
And drooped in elegant festoons about his very toes.

12 *

He hardly ever spoke at all; but when such was the case,
His voice 'twas easy to perceive was quite a heavy bass.

He was not a serious pirate; and despite his anxious cares,
He rarely went to Sunday-school and seldom said his prayers.
He worshiped lovely women, and his hope in life was this:
To calm his wild, tumultuous soul with pure domestic bliss.

When conversing with his shipmates, he very often swore
That he longed to give up piracy and settle down on shore.
He tired of blood and plunder; of the joys that they could bring;
He sighed to win the love of some affectionate young thing.

One morning as the "Mary Jane" went bounding o'er the sea

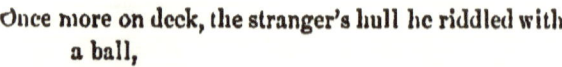

The pirate saw a merchant bark far
off upon his lee.
He ordered a pursuit, and spread all
sail that he could spare,
And then went down, in hopeful mood,
to shave and curl his hair.

He blacked his boots and pared his
nails and tied a fresh cravat;
He cleansed his teeth, pulled down his
cuffs and polished up his hat;
He dimmed with flour the radiance of
his fiery red nose,
For, hanging with that vessel's wash,
he saw some ladies' hose.

Once more on deck, the stranger's hull he riddled with
a ball,
And yelled, "I say! what bark is that?" In answer to his call
The skipper on the other boat replied in thunder
tones:
"This here's the bark Matilda, and her captain's name is Jones."

The pirate told his bold corsairs to man the jolly-boats,
To board the bark and seize the crew, and slit their tarry throats,
And then to give his compliments to Captain Jones, and say
He wished that he and Mrs. Jones would come and spend the day.

They reached the bark, they killed the crew, they threw them in the
    sea,
And then they sought the cap-
    tain, who was mad as he
    could be,
Because his wife—who saw the
    whole sad tragedy, it
    seems—
Made all the ship vociferous with
    her outrageous screams,

But when the pirate's message
    came, she dried her stream-
    ing tears,
And said, although she'd like to
    come, she had unpleasant
    fears
That, his social status being very
    evidently low,
She might meet some common
    people whom she wouldn't care to know.

Her husband's aged father, she admitted, dealt in bones,
But the family descended from the famous Duke de Jones;

> And such blue-blooded people, that the rabble
> might be checked,
> Had to make their social circle excessively
> select.
>
> Before she visited his ship she wanted him to
> say
> If the Smythes had recognized him in a social,
> friendly way;
> Did the Jonsons ever ask him 'round to their
> ·   ancestral halls?

Was he noticed by the Thomsons? Was he asked to Simms's balls?

The pirate wrote that Thomson was his best and oldest friend,
That he often stopped at Jonson's when he had a week to spend;
As for the Smythes, they worried him with their incessant calls;
His very legs were weary with the dance at Simms's balls.

> (The scoundrel fibbed most
> shamelessly. In truth he
> only knew
> A lot of Smiths without a y—a
> most plebeian crew.
> His Johnsons used a vulgar h,
> his Thompsons spelled
> with p,
> His Simses had one m, and they
> were common as could be.)
>
> Then Mrs. Jones mussed up her
> hair and donned her best
> delaine,
> And went with Captain Jones
> aboard the schooner Mary
> Jane.

The pirate won her heart at
> once by saying, with a smile,
He never saw a woman dressed in such exquisite style.

The pirate's claim to status she was very sure was just
When she noticed how familiarly the Johnsons he discussed.
Her aristocratic scruples then were quickly laid aside,
And when the pirate sighed at her, reciproc'ly she sighed.

No sooner was the newer love within her bosom born
Than Jones was looked upon by her with hatred and with scorn.
She said 'twas true his ancestor was famous Duke de Jones,
But she shuddered to remember that his father dealt in bones.

So then they got at Captain Jones and hacked him with a sword,
And chopped him into little bits and tossed him overboard.

The chaplain read the
   service, and the cap-
   tain of the bark
Before his widow's weep-
   ing eyes was gobbled
   by a shark.

The chaplain turned the
   prayer-book o'er ;
   the bride took off
   her glove ;

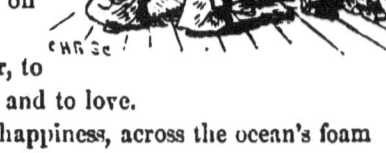

They swore to honor, to
   obey, to cherish and to love.
And, freighted full of happiness, across the ocean's foam
The schooner glided rapidly toward the pirate's home.

And when of ecstasy and joy their hearts could hold no more,
That pirate dropped his anchor down and rowed his love ashore.
And as they sauntered up the street he gave his bride a poke,
And said, "In them there mansions live the friends of whom I
   spoke."

She glanced her eye along the plates of brass upon each door,
And then her anger rose as it had never done before.
She said, "That Johnson has an h ! that Thompson has a p !
The Smith that spells without a y is not the Smith for me !"

And darkly scowled she then upon that rover of the wave;

"False! False!" she shrieked, and spoke of him as "Monster, ·traitor, slave!"
And then she wept and tore her hair, and filled the air with groans,
And cursed with bitterness the day she let them chop up Jones.

And when she'd spent on him at last the venom of her tongue,
She seized her pongee parasol and stabbed him in the lung.
A few more energetic jabs were at his heart required,

And then this scand-'lous buccaneer rolled over and expired.

Still brandishing her parasol she sought the pirate boat;

She loaded up a gun and jammed her head into its throat;
And fixing fast the trigger, with string tied to her toe,
She breathed "Mother!" through the touch-hole, and kicked and let her go.

A snap, a fizz, a rumble; some stupendous roaring tones—
And where upon earth's surface was the recent Mrs. Jones?
Go ask the moaning winds, the sky, the mists, the murmuring sea;
Go ask the fish, the coroner, the clams—but don't ask me.

CHAPTER X

A PICTURESQUE CHURCH—SOME REFLECTIONS UPON CHURCH
MUSIC—BOB PARKER IN THE CHOIR—OUR UNDERTAKER—
A GLOOMY MAN—OUR EXPERIENCE WITH THE HOT-AIR
FURNACES—A SERIES OF ACCIDENTS—MR. COLLAMER'S
VOCALISM—AN EXTRAORDINARY MISTAKE.

HERE are but few old vil-
lages in the United States
that contain ancient churches so picturesque in situation
and in appearance as that
which stands in the centre
of our town, the most conspicuous of its buildings.
The churchyard is filled with
graves, for the people still
cling to that kindly usage
which places the sacred
dust of the departed in holy
ground. And so here, be-
neath the trees, and close to
the shadow of the sanctuary walls, villagers of all ages and
generations lie reposing in their final slumber, while from
among them the snow-white spire rises heavenward to point
the way their souls have gone. There are many of us who
were not born here, and who are, as it were, almost strangers
in the town, who can wander down the narrow paths of the
yard, to out-of-the-way corners, where the headstones are
gray with age and sometimes covered with a film of moss,

and read in the quaint characters with which the marble is
inscribed our own family names. Here lies the mortal part
of men and women who were dear to our
grandsires; of little children too, sometimes,
whose departure brought sorrow to the
hearts of those who joined them in Paradise
long, long before we began to play our parts
in the drama of existence. The lives that
ended in this quiet resting-place are full of
deepest interest to us; they have a controlling influence upon our destiny, and yet
they are very unreal to us. The figures
which move by us as we try to summon up
the panorama of that past are indistinct
and obscure. They are shadows walking in
the dusk, and we strive in vain to vest them
with a semblance of the personality which
once was theirs. They should seem very
near to us their kindred, and yet, as we
attempt to come closer to them, they appear
so remote, so far away in the dead years,
that we hardly dare to claim fellowship with them, or to
speak of them as of our flesh and blood.

It makes no difference where the empty shell is cast when
the spiritual man is gone, but I reverence that human
instinct which induces a man to wish to be laid at the last
by the side of his ancestors and near to those whom he has
loved in life. It is at least a beautiful sentiment which
demands that those who are with each other in immortality
should not be separated here on earth, but together should
await the morning of the resurrection.

I like this old church for its simplicity; not only for the
absence of splendor in its adornment, but for the methods
of worship of which it approves. The choir, from its station

in the organ-loft, never hurls down upon the heads of the saints and sinners beneath any of those surprising sounds which rural choirs so often emit, with a conviction that they are achieving wonderful feats of vocalism, and no profane fingers compel the pipes of the microscopic organ to recall to the mind of the listener the music of the stage and the concert-room. From the instrument come only harmonies round, sweet and full, melting in solemn cadences from key to key and rolling down through the church, bringing the souls of the worshipers into full accord with the spirit of the place and the occasion, or else pouring forth some stately melody on which the voices of the singers are upborne. The choir fulfills its highest purpose by leading the people through the measures of those grand old tunes, simple in construction but sublime in spirit, which give to the language of the spiritual songs of the sanctuary a more eloquent beauty than their own. I would rather hear such music as may be found in "Federal Street," in "Old Hundred," in "Hursley" and in the "Adeste Fideles," sung by an entire assembly of people

who are in earnest in their religion, than to listen to the most intricate fugue worked out by a city choir of hired singers, or the most brilliant anthem sung by a congregation of surpliced boys who quarrel with each other and play wicked games during the prayers. Such tunes as these are filled with solemn meaning which is revealed to him whose singing is really an act of worship. There is more genuine religious fervor in "Hursley" than in a library of ordinary oratorios. A

THE OLD CHURCH.

church which permits its choir to do all the singing might as well adopt the Chinese fashion of employing a machine to do its praying. A congregation which sits still while a quartette of vocalists overhead utters all the praises, need not hesitate to offer its supplications by turning a brass wheel with a crank. Our people do their singing and their praying for themselves, and the choir merely takes care that the music is of a fitting kind.

Miss Magruder sits in the organ-loft now that she is at home, and I doubt not she contributes much to the sweetness of the strains which float from out that somewhat narrow enclosure. Her presence, I observe, ensures the regular attendance of young Mr. Parker at the church, and last Sunday he even ventured to sit with the choir and to help with the singing. I have never considered him a really good performer, although he cherishes a conviction that he has an admirable voice, and such acquaintance with the art of using it as would have given him eminence if he had chosen the career of a public singer. After service I had occasion to speak to the clergyman for a moment, and as soon as he saw me he said:

"Mr. Adeler, did you notice anything about the organ or the choir to-day that was peculiar?"

"No; I do not think I did."

"It is very odd; but it seemed to me when they were singing the two last hymns that something must be the matter with one of the pipes. There was a sort of a rough, buzzing, rasping sound which I have never observed before. The instrument must need repairing."

"I think I know what it was," remarked Mr. Campbell, the basso, who stepped up at that moment.

"The valves a little worn, I suppose?" said the minister.

"Well, no," replied Campbell; "the fact is that extraordinary noise was produced by Mr. Parker, who was making a strenuous effort to sing bass. He seemed to be laboring under a strong conviction that the composers had made some mistakes in the tunes, which he proposed to correct as he went along. Parker's singing is like homœopathic medicine—a very little of it is enough."

Bob attributes the criticism of Campbell to professional jealousy, but he will probably sit down stairs after this. He prefers not to waste his talents upon provincial people who cannot appreciate genuine art. He will content himself with walking home with the fair Magruder after service.

There is one thing about the church with which I must

find fault. I have never been able to comprehend why it is customary throughout this country, even in the large cities, to permit undertakers to decorate the exteriors of churches with their advertisements, as ours is decorated by our undertaker. In old times, when the sexton was the grave-digger and general public functionary, it was well enough to give publicity to his residence by posting its whereabouts in a public place. There were oftentimes little offices which he had to perform for the congregation and for the neighborhood, and it was necessary that he should be found quickly. But the present fashion, which allows an undertaker—who has no other connection with the church than that he sits in a pew occasionally and goes to sleep during the sermon—to nail a tin sign, bearing a picture of a gilt coffin, right by the church door, so that no man, woman or child can enter that sanctuary without thinking of the grave, is monstrous.

It is very proper that the minds of the people should be turned to contemplation of the certainty of death whenever they go to church. But it is hardly necessary to disturb a man's reflections upon the necessity of preparing for the grave by confronting him with an advertisement which compels him to remember how much it is going to cost his relations to put him ·there. Besides this, it makes the undertakers covetous, and fills their gloomy souls with murderous wishes.

I have seen ours standing against the wall in the church-yard on a Sunday morning with his hands in his pockets, glowering at the congregation as they go in, eyeing and criticising the members, and muttering to himself, "Splendid fit *he'd* make in that mahogany coffin I've got at home!" "There goes a man who ought to have died five years ago if *I'd* been treated right!" "I'll souse that Thompson un-

derground some of these fine days!" "Those Mulligan girls
certainly can't give the old man anything less than a four-
hundred-dollar funeral when *he* dies!" " Healthiest looking
congregation of its size *I ever* saw !" etc., etc.

If I were in authority in the church, I would suppress
that gilded advertisement and try to convert the owner of it.

No man should be permitted to waste his Sabbaths in vain
longings for the interment of his fellow-men.

They are very busy now at the church putting in new
furnaces in order to be prepared for the cold weather. New
ones were introduced last winter, I am told, but they were
not entirely successful in operation. The first time the fire
was put in them was on Saturday morning, and on Sunday

the smoke was so dense in the church that nobody could see the clergyman. The workman had put the stove-pipe into the hot-air flue. Next Saturday night the fires were lighted, out on Sunday morning only the air immediately under the roof was warm, and the congregation nearly froze to death.

The sexton was then instructed to make the fire on Thursday, in order to give the church a chance to become thoroughly heated. He did so, and early Sunday morning the furnaces were so choked up with ashes that the fires went out, and again the thermometer in the front pew marked zero.

Then the sexton received orders to make that fire on Thursday, and to watch it carefully until church-time on the following Sabbath. He did so, and both furnaces were in full blast at the appointed hour. That was the only warm Sunday we had last winter. The mercury was up to eighty degrees out of doors, while in the church everybody was in a profuse perspiration, and the bellows-blower at the organ fainted twice. The next Sunday the sexton tried to keep the fires low by pushing in the dampers, and consequently the church was filled with coal-gas, and the choir couldn't

sing, nor could the minister preach without coughing between his sentences.

Subsequently the sexton removed one of the cast-iron registers in the floor for the purpose of examining the hot-air flue. He left the hole open while he went into the cellar for a moment, and just then old Mr. Collamer came in to hunt for his gloves, which he thought he had left in  his pew. Of course he walked directly into the opening, and was dragged out in a condition of asphyxia. That very day one of the furnaces burst and nearly fired the church. The demand for heaters of another kind seemed to be imperative.

Old Collamer, by the way, is singularly unfortunate in his experiences in the sanctuary. He is extremely deaf, and a few Sundays ago he made a fearful blunder during the sermon. The clergyman had occasion to introduce a quotation, and as it was quite long, he brought the volume with him; and when the time came, he picked up the book and began to read from it. We  always sing the Old Hundred doxology after sermon at our church, and Mr. Collamer, seeing the pastor with the book, thought the time had come, so while the minister was reading he opened his hymn-book at the place. Just as the clergyman laid the volume down the man sitting next to Mr. Collamer began to yawn, and Mr. Collamer, thinking he was about to sing, immediately broke out into Old Hundred, and roared it at the top of his voice. As the clergyman was just beginning "secondly," and as there was of course perfect silence in the church, the effect of Mr. Collamer's vociferation was very startling. But the good old man failed to notice that anything was the matter, so he kept right on and sang the verse through.

When he had finished, he observed that everybody else seemed to be quiet, excepting a few who were laughing, so he leaned over and said out loud to the man who yawned,

"What's the matter with this congregation, anyhow? Why don't they go home?"

The man turned scarlet, and the perspiration broke out all over him, for he felt that the eyes of the congregation were upon him, and he knew that he would have to yell to make Mr. Collamer hear. So he touched his lips with his fingers as a sign for the old man to keep quiet. But Mr. Collamer misunderstood the motion:

"Goin' to sing another hymn, hey? All right."

And he began to fumble his hymn-book again. Then the sexton hurried up the aisle, and explained matters out loud to Mr. Collamer, and that gentleman subsided, while the minister proceeded with his discourse. The clergyman has written Mr. Collamer a note requesting him in the future not to join in the sacred harmony. The effect is too appalling upon the ribald boys in the back pews.

CHAPTER XI.

T is said that there is good fishing in this vicinity. Several of my neighbors who have been out lately have brought home large quantities of fish of various kinds, together with glowing reports of the delightful character of the sport. A craving to indulge in this form of amusement was gradually excited in the mind of Mr. Bob Parker by the stories of the anglers and by the display of their trophies, and he succeeded in persuading me to assist in the organization of an expedition down the river to the fishing-grounds. Yesterday was selected for the undertaking. I hired a boat from a man at the wharf; and after packing a generous luncheon in the fish-basket and securing a box full of bait, we tossed our lines into the boat, together with a heavy stone which was to serve as an anchor, and then we pushed out into the stream.

It was early morning when we started, and to my dismay I found that the tide was running up with remarkable

velocity. As we had to pull four miles down the river, this was a consideration of very great importance. Mr. Parker is not an especially skillful oarsman, and before he had fairly seated himself and dipped his blade in the water we had drifted two hundred yards in the wrong direction. After very severe labor for half an hour, we succeeded in getting three-quarters of a mile below the town, and then Bob informed me that he thought he could row better with my oar. Accordingly, I changed places with him, and during the time thus expended the boat went back a third of the distance we

had gained. Another prolonged and terrible effort enabled us to proceed two miles toward our destination, and then Parker observed that he must stop and rest; he said he would die if he rowed another stroke. So we lay upon our oars for a while, and embraced the opportunity to wipe away the perspiration and to cool our blistered hands in the river. Parker then asked me if I would mind changing places with him again. He said he was now convinced that he had made a mistake in leaving his first position. We fell back half a mile during this period; and when we finally reached the grounds, the morning was far advanced. Bob

was nearly worn out, and he proposed that we give up the idea of catching fish and row ashore, where we could lie down under the trees and begin operations upon the luncheon.

But as we had come to fish, I was determined to do so. I informed Bob that I should be ashamed to go home without bringing any game. I should be afraid to look in the face of the man who owned the boat when he asked me what luck I had. So we tied a rope around the stone, and tossing the stone overboard, we came to anchor. Our hooks were baited and the lines were thrown out, and then Bob and I waited patiently for bites.

It required a great deal of patience, for the fish did not take the bait with a remarkable degree of freedom. In fact, we only had a nibble or two at first, and then even this mani-

festation of the presence of the fish ceased. We were sitting with our backs to the shore, watching the corks in front of us, when Bob suddenly uttered an exclamation. Upon look-ing around, I found that we had drifted half a mile up stream and out into the middle of the river, which is here nearly four miles wide. The stone had dropped from the knot in the rope and released the boat.

Then we rowed back to shore and landed for the purpose of obtaining another stone. We could not find one, so we pulled out again; and sticking one of the oars in the mud, we fastened the boat to that. Then Bob had a bite. He pulled up, and dragged to the surface of the water a crab, which instantly let go and  sidled under the boat. Then we each  caught a small sunfish, and with this our enthusiasm began to revive. Just then the oar came out of the mud, slipped through the loop in the cable and floated off. The prospect of having to take the boat home with one oar seemed so appalling that I hastily threw off my coat and shoes and swam after the fugitive oar. Meantime, the boat floated off, and I reached it and was hauled in by Bob just as I had made up my mind to give up and go to the bottom.

We then fastened the oar down again, and I held it with one hand and my fishing-line with the other. Suddenly each of us had a splendid bite, and we both pulled in vigorously. The fish seemed to struggle violently all the way to the surface; but when the hooks came into view, we found that our lines were entangled, and that neither of us had a

14

fish. The next time Bob attempted to take in his line his hook caught upon the bottom; and when, in a fit of exas-

peration, he tried to jerk it loose, the cord snapped and the hopes of the fisherman were blasted for that day. Then, as Bob tipped the boat while he wash-ed his hands, the bait-box fell overboard, and so matters came to a definite conclusion, and we determined to quit.

When we started for home, the tide had turned, and we did not reach town until dark. The man who owned the craft had just telegraphed to Delaware City for the purpose

of ascertaining if two sus-picious men had landed there and attempted to sell a boat. He compelled me to pay half a day's hire ex-tra for staying out so late, together with the cost of the telegram.

I consider it beneath me to notice the unnecessary violence of his language or the insolence of his criti-cisms upon our skill as fish-ermen.

This I could have borne with patience, but it was hard, very, very hard, upon arriv-ing home, to have Mrs. Adeler come to the door with a smile upon her face and ask, "Where are the fish?" while she informed us that she had asked the Magruders over to tea, and had depended upon us to supply the principal dish, so that now she had not a thing in the house that she could cook.

"Mrs. Adeler, we return with two diminutive sunfish, one demoralized ham-sandwich, two crimson noses and a thorough, sincere, whole-souled and earnest disgust for the wretched business which some men choose to regard in the light of amusement. No, Mrs. Adeler, we have no fish that are worthy of the name, and hereafter when we wish to have some, we will purchase them from the unhappy beings who catch them. A fisherman deserves all the money he can get, my dear. I wouldn't be a professional piscator for the mines of Golconda and the wealth of a nabob to boot."

Our unfortunate experiences upon the river tempt me to refer in detail to the ills to which amateur fishermen, as a class, are exposed. The pleasures of angling have been said and sung by a vast multitude of sentimental people reaching all the way from old Izaak Walton to Mr. Prime; but the story of the suffering that too often accompanies the sport has not yet been narrated with a sufficient amount of vigor. The martyr fishermen have been too long kept in the background. The time has come for them to have a hearing. I have chosen to present their complaint in the somewhat singular form of a letter to Mr. Benjamin F. Butler, because at the time of the negotiation of the Washington treaty he manifested much indignation at the wrongs heaped upon American fishermen by that instrument, and because he is a very suitable person to figure in a remonstrance which has about it perhaps a slight flavor of burlesque, even though it is a narrative of real misery.

The Sorrows of the Fisherman.

Dear General: I have given a great deal of reflection, lately, to the fishery question, and I am convinced that your opposition to the fishery clauses of the Washington treaty had a basis of sound common sense. The treaty, in my opinion, wholly fails to consider in a spirit of wise statesmanship the causes which move the fisherman to complaint, and supplies no adequate means for securing their removal. Permit me to suggest to you the propriety of urging upon the government the reassembling of the joint high commission for the purpose of obtaining a reconsideration of the fishery question with the new light which I propose to shed upon it.

My experience in fishing has convinced me that one of the most serious of the primary obstacles to be overcome is the difficulty of procuring worms. Perhaps you may have observed an enthusiastic fisherman in pursuit of worms? The day is always warm, and his performance upon the shovel conduces to profuse perspiration. He seems never to strike precisely the spot where the worms frolic. He labors with tremendous energy until he has excavated a couple of cellars and a rifle-pit, from which he rescues but two or three worms, while all around him the earth is perforated with holes, into

which other vermicular creatures are perceived to disappear before he can lay his hands on them. The alacrity with which a worm draws himself into a hole in the ground, and dives down apparently to the centre of the globe, when you want him, is a constant source of aggravation to the fisherman. The fishery interests suffer on account of it.

If a joint high commission would address itself in a con-
ciliatory spirit to the work of obtaining concerted action

from the civilized nations of the world upon the
subject of the reformation of worms, blessed
results would undoubtedly accrue. I know a
fisherman who could make a speech in Congress
on the subject of worms which would make that
body weep the rotunda full of tears.

And even when bait has been secured, you are aware,
perhaps, that the fisherman will sit for hours upon the bank
of the stream watching his cork
until he is nearly blinded, and
until his head swims. At last,
when his patience is exhausted
and he is convinced that there
are no fish about, he pulls up
for the purpose of trying another
spot, and finds that some disreputable fish has sucked the bait
off the hook an hour before
without making a perceptible
nibble.

Perhaps a clause in the treaty
upon the general subject of nibbles might be of service. I
think a paragraph could be constructed on nibbles which

would create more amazement and produce a
greater sensational effect in diplomatic circles
than anything that ever appeared in a treaty.
The introduction of the subject of nibbles to in-
ternational law would give that science refresh-
ing variety and probably prevent devastating wars.

It is another cause of suffering to the fisherman that when
he has thrown in again, and has waited an hour for a bite,
and waited in vain, he considers it safe to drop his rod for a

14 *

moment, so that he can light his pipe.   It is a peculiar circumstance, I say, that just as he

has struck his last match he al-
ways gets the most vigorous bite
of the whole day. The cork pulls
under in the most exciting manner several times, and only floats
up again permanently at the moment when the angler seizes his
rod in eager haste and finds that
the fish is gone. ·

It is this kind of thing that
makes the fisherman feel as if he
would be relieved by the use of
violent language.   The British
premier, I am sure, will consent to the negotiation of another
treaty if you will press this matter on him.   He must see at
once that unless bites are arranged with a greater regard for
the feelings of the fisherman and for the sanctity of the law
against profane swearing, the fishery interests will languish
and the crop prove a humiliating failure.

I have often remarked, too, that when the fisherman has
nearly landed a fish, which drops off the hook just as it appears to be safe, he collects all his energies for the next bite.
He grasps the rod tightly with both hands, he rises and
plants his legs firmly upon the ground, he watches the cork
carefully, with his lips compressed and with fiery determination gleaming from his eyes.   The cork moves slightly.   It
goes under; he has a good bite; he pulls up with frightful
energy, determined not to lose this one, and the next instant his line hits the limb of the tree overhead, and winds
around it as closely as if it was put there on purpose to
splice that limb, so as to make it perfectly secure throughout
the unending ages of eternity.

I always excuse the man for taking a gloomy view of life, and for saying over with ardor and vehemence his en-tire reserve stock of objurga-tions as he shins up the tree. But has the government no duty in the matter? What is the use of joint high com-missions if these things are to be allowed? We have made the republic successful, we have fought mighty bat-tles, we have paid millions of indebtedness and we have given the civilization of the world a tremendous impulse forward; now let us do some-thing for the disgusted fish-erman who has to fumble

around out on that limb. Let us have a special treaty on that particular branch of the subject.

If something could be done in relation to eels, I think the government of our beloved country would rest upon a foun-dation of greater stability and have a more permanent hold upon popular affection. Perhaps you have fished for eels? The eel gently pulls the cork under and lets go. You pull up suddenly, and throw in again. The eel tenderly draws the cork beneath the surface, and, wild with fury, you jerk out your line a second time. This exhilarating exercise con-tinues for some moments, and you make up your mind that existence will be a burden, the world a hollow sham, and groceries and marketing useless baubles, unless you catch that eel. Finally you do hook him and draw him out. He is active, playful and vivacious. He wriggles; he forms himself in quick succession into S's, C's and Q's. He points

to all the four quarters of the compass at once. He swal-
lows himself and spits himself out. He wraps himself
around your boot and shoots up
your leg and covers your trow-
sers with slime, and tangles your
line into a mess by the side of
which the Gordian knot was the
perfection of simpli-
city. When you get
your foot firmly on
him, you find that he
has swallowed the
hook, and you have to cut him
completely open, from head to
tail, to get the hook out, and
then, as likely as not, the eel will
flip back into the water and escape. I think eels rarely die.

A joint high commission which would devote itself with
philanthropic ardor and untiring energy to a dispassionate
consideration of the subject of the immortality of eels might,
perhaps, achieve important results. Any settlement of the
fishery question which overlooked the hideous wickedness of
eels would be a cruel mockery of human woe.

But for pure pathos, I can conceive of nothing that will
equal the anguish of the fisherman when he imagines he has
a catfish upon his hook. His cork is drawn slowly under
the surface, and it goes down, down, down, until it sinks completely out of sight. He is certain it is a catfish—they always pull in this manner, he says; and he draws in his line
gently, while the fish tugs and pulls at the other end.
Gradually, v-e-r-y gradually, the fisherman pulls it in, in
order to be sure to keep the prey upon the hook. It is
evidently a very large fish, and he is determined to land
it through the shallow water, so that it cannot drop back

and escape. Slowly it comes up, and just as the hook nears the surface the angler gives a sudden jerk, and out comes a terrific snag with a dozen branches and covered with mud. And meanwhile, during all the fisherman's troubles, there is that infamous small boy sitting on the opposite bank of the creek pulling up fish by the dozen with a pinhook and some wrapping twine.

It would gratify me if the new treaty would devote one clause to a definite settlement of the question of the bearing of snags upon the miseries of mankind, and about eight stupendous clauses to a determination of the fate that is deserved by that boy. My own humanitarian tendencies incline me to urge that he

should be summarily shot. If a boy with a pin-hook is to be allowed thus to destroy the peace of older American citizens, the sooner we ask some efficient and reliable despot to come over here and break up the government and trample on us, the happier we shall be.

I commend the subject to your enlightened consideration, and ask for an earnest appeal to the next Congress in behalf of suffering fishermen. If we cannot obtain redress by peaceful means, let us have it by force. I am ready to overturn the government, massacre the people, burn the cities and carry desolation, devastation and death into every home in the land, rather than to per-

mit these outrages against justice longer to continue and these
unhappy men to endure further persecution.

There are indications that the course of Bob Parker's
true love will not run entirely smooth. The officers stationed at Fort Delaware, below here, come up to the village
constantly upon social errands, and they are exceedingly
popular with the young ladies. Lieutenant Smiley is, I
think, the favorite; and as he has become a somewhat frequent visitor at Magruder's, Bob's jealousy has been aroused.
He hates Smiley with a certain deadly hatred. Mr. Parker
is not naturally warlike in his tendencies, but I believe he
would willingly engage in hostilities with the lieutenant with
an utterly reckless disregard of the consequences.

Smiley comes to see us sometimes; and Bob, I fear, regards even this family with gloom and suspicion because we
receive the lieutenant courteously. But he says very little
upon the subject; for when he begins to abuse Smiley, I
always ask him why he does not propose to Miss Magruder
at once and thus relieve himself from his agony of apprehension. Then he beats a retreat. He would rather face a
regiment of Smileys armed with Dahlgren guns than to discuss the subject of his cowardice respecting the beautiful
Magruder.

We like the lieutenant well enough, and we should like
him better but for his propensity for telling incredible stories.
He was in the naval service for eight or ten years; and when
he undertakes to give accounts of his adventures, he is very
apt to introduce anecdotes of which Munchausen would have
been ashamed. It is one of Smiley's favorite theories that
he sojourned for a considerable period among the Fiji
Islands, and many of his narratives relate his experiences
in that region. There was a missionary meeting at the
church a night or two ago, and the lieutenant, having been

defeated by Bob in his attempt to escort Miss Magruder to her home, came to our house; and very naturally he began the conversation with a story of missionary enterprise with which he assumed to have become familiar during his visit to the South Seas.

"Mr. Adeler," he said, "I was very much interested in the proceedings at that meeting to-night, but it seems to me that there is one defect in the system of preparing men for the work of propagating the gospel among the heathen."

"What is that?"

"Why they ought to teach the science of mesmerism in the divinity schools."

"I don't exactly understand the purpose of the—"

"Perhaps you never heard of the Rev. Mr. Blodgett, missionary to the Fiji Islands? Well, he saved his life once merely by practicing mesmerism. He has told me the story often."

"I should like to hear it."

"It seems that Blodgett in his sinful youth had been a traveling professor of mesmerism; but he had abandoned the business to go into the ministry and to preach

to the heathen in Fiji. Well, his church out there got up a Sunday-school picnic, it appears; and when the people all arrived upon the ground, they learned that the provisions had been forgotten. A meeting of the vestry was called, and after a brief consultation it was decided that the only thing which could be done to meet the emergency was to barbecue the minister. The inducement to this course was all the stronger because his salary was six months in arrears, and the church was entirely out of funds. So they built a huge fire; and seizing Blodgett, they began to strip him and to stick him with forks.

" In order to save himself, he immediately mesmerized each member of the vestry; and when they were all fixed, he called up the Sunday-school scholars, class by class, and put them comfortably to sleep. Having them all completely under his influence, he gave an entire class to each one of the vestrymen, and assured them that the innocent children were the most luscious kind of missionary. Thereupon the hypnotized vestry immediately ate up the somnambulistic Sunday-school and picked the bones clean. Blodgett was a very conscientious man in the performance of his sacerdotal functions, so he read the funeral service over each class as it disappeared."

" Rather an excessive meal, I should say."

" Yes, but they are large eaters, the Fijians. You might say that their appetites are, in a certain sense, robust."

" I should imagine that such was the case. But proceed."

" Well, when the little ones were gone, Blodgett whispered to the magnetized wardens that their fellow-vestrymen were also succulent propagators of Christianity; whereupon the unconscious wardens fell upon their colleagues, and in a few moments nearly the whole vestry was in the process of assimilation. There remained now but the two wardens, and Blodgett, having prevailed upon the younger and more vigorous of the two to eat the other, then seized the slumbering body of his converted

but erring brother and stood it on its head in the fire. The
Rev. Mr. Blodgett went away alone from
that picnic, and he went with a heavy
heart. When he got home, they asked
where the rest of the folks were, and he
said they were enjoying themselves up there
in the woods in their own quiet, innocent way,
but that he had to come away in order to
visit a sick friend who stood in need of his
ministrations. And then he packed his
trunk and borrowed a canoe and paddled
away to our ship, determined to seek some sunnier

clime, where the heathen rage less furiously, and where
the popular appetite for warm clergyman is not so intensely
vivid."

"That is a very remarkable narrative, lieutenant—very
remarkable indeed!"

"Yes. But poor Mott was not so lucky."

"Who was Mott?"

"Why the Rev. Peter Mott—he was a missionary engaged
upon one of the other islands. He knew nothing of mesmerism; and when his choir attacked him upon the way

home from church one day, he was unable to defend himself, and they ate him."

"How painful!"

"I had to carry the mournful news to Mrs. Mott, who lived in San Francisco. When we reached that port, I called upon her and performed the unpleasant duty. The manner in which she received the intelligence was, I conceive, in every way extraordinary. She

cried, of course, and I offered her what consolation I could under the circumstances. I alluded to the fact that all men must die at any rate, and dear Mott, let us hope, had gone to a better world than this one of sorrow and trouble and so forth.

"Mrs. Mott, in reply said, with a voice broken with sobs :

'It isn't that—oh, it isn't that. I know he is better off; I'm sure he is happier; but you know what a very particular man he was, and oh, Mr. Smiley, I fear that those brutal savages boiled him with cabbage.' There was no use trying to assuage her grief under such circumstances, so I shook hands with her and left. But it was an odd idea. Mott with cabbage! I thought as I came away that he would have tasted better with the merest flavor of onion."

When Lieutenant Smiley bade us good-night, I said,

"Mrs. Adeler, what do you think of that young man?"

"I think," she said, "that he tells the most dreadful falsehoods I ever listened to. It will be a burning shame if he succeeds in cutting out Robert with Miss Magruder."

"Mrs. Adeler, he shall not do that. Bob shall have Miss Magruder at all hazards. If he does not propose to her shortly, I shall go down and broach the subject to her myself. We must defeat Smiley even if we have to violate all the rules of propriety to achieve that result."

CHAPTER XII.

How the Plumber Fixed my Boiler—A Vexatious Busi-
ness—How he didn't come to Time, and what the Ul-
timate Result was—An Accident, and the Pathetic
Story of Young Chubb—Reminiscences of General
Chubb—The Eccentricities of an Absent-minded Man
—The Rivals—Parker versus Smiley.

E have had a great deal of
trouble recently with our
kitchen boiler, which is
built into the wall over the
range. It sprang aleak a
few weeks ago, and the assistance of a plumber had
to be invoked for the purpose of repairing it. I sent
for the plumber, and after
examining the boiler, he instructed the servant to let
the fire go out that night,
so that he could begin operations early the next morn-
ing. His order was obeyed, but in the morning the plumber
failed to appear. We had a cold and very uncomfortable
breakfast, and on my way to the dépôt I overtook the
plumber going in the same direction. He said he was sorry
to disappoint me, but he was called suddenly out of town on
imperative business, and he would have to ask me to wait
until the next morning, when he would be promptly on hand
with his men. So we had no fire in the range upon that

. 15 *
183

day, and the family breakfasted again upon cool viands without being cheered with a view of the plumber. Upon

calling at the plumber's shop to ascertain why he had not fulfilled his promise, I was informed by the clerk that he

had returned, but that he was compelled to go over to Wilmington. The man seemed so thoroughly in earnest in his assertion that the plumber positively would attend to my boiler upon the following morning that we permitted the range to remain untouched, and for the third time we broke our fast with a frigid repast. But the plumber and his assistants did not come.

As it seemed to be wholly impossible to depend upon these faithless artisans, our cook was instructed to bring the range into service again without waiting longer for repairs, and to give the family a properly prepared meal in the morning. While we were at breakfast there was a knock at the gate, and presently we perceived the plumber and his men coming up the yard with a general assortment of tools and materials. The range at the moment of his entrance to the kitchen was red hot; and when he realized the fact, he flung his tools on the floor and expressed his indignation in the most violent and improper language, while his attendant fiends sat around in the chairs and growled in sympathy with their chief. When I appeared upon the scene, the plumber addressed me with the air of a man who had suffered a great and irreparable wrong at my hands,  and he really displayed so much feeling that for a few moments I had an indistinct consciousness that I had somehow been guilty of an act of gross injustice to an unfortunate and persecuted fellow-being. Be-

fore I could recover myself sufficiently to present my side of the case with the force properly belonging to it, the plumbers marched into the yard, where they tossed a quantity of machinery and tools and lead pipe under the shed, and then left.

We had no fire in the range the next morning, but the plumbers did not come until four o'clock in the afternoon, and then they merely dumped a

cart load of lime-boxes and hoes upon the asparagus bed and
went home.   An interval of four days elapsed before we
heard of them again; and meanwhile the cook twice nearly
killed herself by stumbling over the tools while going out
into the shed in the dark.   One morning, however, the gang
arrived before I had risen; and when I came down to breakfast, I found that they had made a mortar bed on our best
grass plot, and had closed up the principal garden walk with
a couple of wagon loads of sand.   I endured this patiently

because it seemed to promise speedy performance of the
work.   The plumbers, however, went away at about nine
o'clock, and the only reason we had for supposing they had
not forgotten us was that a man with a cart called in the
 afternoon and shot a quantity of bricks down
upon the pavement in such a position that no-
body could go in or out of the front gate.   Two
days afterward the plumbers came and began
to make a genuine effort to reach the boiler.   It
was buried in the wall in such a manner that it was wholly
inaccessible by any other method than by the removal of the
bricks from the outside.   The man who erected the house
evidently was a party with the plumber to a conspiracy to

give the latter individual something to do. They labored right valiantly at the wall, and by supper-time they had removed at least twelve square feet of it, making a hole large enough to have admitted a locomotive. Then they took

cat the old boiler and went away, leaving a most discouraging mass of rubbish lying about the yard.

That was the last we saw of them for more than a week. Whenever I went after the plumber for the purpose of persuading him to hasten the work, I learned that he had been summoned to Philadelphia as a witness in a court case, or that he had gone to his aunt's funeral, or that he was taking a holiday because it was his wife's birthday, or that he had a sore eye. I have never been able to understand why the house was not robbed. An entire brigade of burglars might have entered the cottage and frolicked among its treasures without any difficulty. I did propose at first that Bob and I should procure revolvers and take watch and watch every

night until the breach in the wall should be repaired; but
Mr. Parker did not regard the plan with enthusiasm, and it

was abandoned. We had to
content ourselves with fastening
the inner door of the kitchen as
securely as possible, and we were
not molested. But we were
nervous. Mrs.
Adeler, I think,
assured me posi-
tively at least
twice every night

that she heard robbers on the stairs, and entreated me not to
go out after them; and I never did.

Finally the men came and began to fill the hole with new
bricks. That evening the plumber walked into my parlor
with mud and mortar on his boots, and informed me that

by an unfortunate mistake the
hole left for the boiler by the
bricklayers was far too small,
and he could not insert the
boiler without taking the wall
down again.

"Mr. Nippers," I said, "don't
you think it would be a good
idea for me to engage you permanently to labor upon that
boiler? From the manner in
which this business has been
conducted, I infer that I can

finally be rid of annoyance about such matters by employing
a perennial plumber to live for ever in my back yard, and
to spend the unending cycles of eternity banging boilers and
demolishing walls."

Mr. Nippers said, with apparent seriousness, that he thought it would be a first-rate thing.

"Mr. Nippers, I am going to ask a favor of you. I do not insist upon compliance with my request. I know that I am at your mercy. Nippers, you have me, and I submit patiently to my fate. But my family is suffering from cold, we are exposed to the ravages of thieves, we are deprived of the means of cooking our food properly, and we are made generally un-

comfortable by the condition of our kitchen. I ask you, therefore, as a personal favor to a man who wishes you prosperity here and felicity hereafter, and who means to settle your bill promptly, to fix that boiler at once."

Mr. Nippers thereupon said that he always liked me, and he swore a solemn oath that he would complete the job next day without fail. That was on Tuesday. Neither Nippers nor his men came again until Saturday, and then they put the boiler in its place and went away, leaving four or five cart loads of ruins in the yard. On Sunday the boiler began to leak as badly as ever, and I feel sure Nippers must have set the old one in again, although when he called early Monday morning with a bill for $237\frac{84}{100}$, which he wanted at once because he had a note to meet, he declared upon his honor that the boiler was a new one, and that it would not leak under a pressure of one thousand pounds to the square inch.

I am going to buy a cooking stove, and defy Nippers and the entire plumbing fraternity.

Cooley's boy has been in trouble again.   Yesterday morning Mrs. Adeler heard loud screaming in Cooley's yard, and in a few moments a servant came to say that Mrs. Cooley wished to see Mrs. Adeler at once. Mrs. A. hurried over there, supposing that something terrible had happened. She found Mrs. Cooley shaking her boy and crying, while the lad stood, the picture of misery and fright, his eyes protruding from his head and his hands holding his stomach. Mrs. Cooley explained in a voice broken with sobs that Henry had been playing with a small "mouth organ," and had accidentally swallowed it. The case was somewhat peculiar; and as Mrs. Adeler was not familiar with the professional methods which are adopted in such emergencies, she recommended simply a liberal use of mustard and warm water. The application was ultimately successful, and the missing musical instrument was surrendered by the boy. The incident is neither interesting nor remarkable, and I certainly should not have mentioned it but for the fact that it had a result which is perhaps worth chronicling here.

Last evening Bob came into the sitting-room and behaved in a manner which led me to believe that he had something on his mind. I asked him if anything was the matter. He said,

"Well, no; not exactly. The fact is I've been thinking about that accident to Cooley's boy, and it kind of suggested something to me."

"What was the nature of the suggestion?"

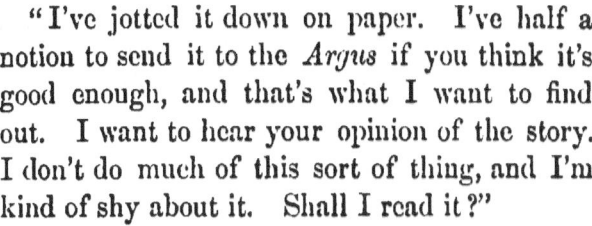

"I've jotted it down on paper. I've half a notion to send it to the *Argus* if you think it's good enough, and that's what I want to find out. I want to hear your opinion of the story. I don't do much of this sort of thing, and I'm kind of shy about it. Shall I read it?"

"Of course; let us hear it."

"I'm going to call it 'The Fate of Young Chubb.' I expect it'll make old Cooley mad as fury when he sees it. It is founded upon the catastrophe of which his boy was the victim."

THE FATE OF YOUNG CHUBB.

When Mr. Chubb, the elder, returned from Europe, he brought with him from Geneva a miniature musical box, long and very narrow, and altogether of hardly greater dimensions, say, than a large pocket-knife. The instrument played four cheerful little tunes for the benefit of the Chubb family, and they enjoyed it. Young Henry Chubb enjoyed it to such an extent that, one day, just after the machine had been wound up ready for action, he got to sucking the end

16

of it, and in a moment of inadvertence it slipped, and he swallowed it. The only immediate consequence of the accident was that a harmonic stomach-ache was organized upon the interior of Henry Chubb, and he experienced a restlessness which he well knew would defy peppermint and paregoric.

Henry Chubb kept his secret in his own soul, and in his stomach also, determined to hide his misery from his father, and to spare the rod to the spoiled child—spoiled, at any rate, as far as his digestive apparatus was concerned.

But that evening, at the supper-table, Henry had eaten but one mouthful of bread when strains of wild, mysterious

music were suddenly wafted from under the table. The family immediately made an effort to discover whence the sounds came, although Henry Chubb sat there filled with agony and remorse and bread and tunes, and desperately asserted his belief that the music came from the cellar, where the servant-girl was concealed with a harp. He well knew that Mary Ann was unfamiliar with the harp. But he was frantic with anxiety to hide his guilt. Thus it is that one crime leads to another.

But he could not disguise the truth for ever, and that very night, while the family was at prayers, Henry all at once began to hiccough, and the music box started off without warning with "Way down upon the Suwanee River," with variations. Whereupon the paternal Chubb arose from his knees and grasped Henry kindly but firmly by his hair and shook him up and inquired what he meant by such conduct. And Henry asserted that he was practicing something for a Sunday-school celebration, which old Chubb intimated was a singularly thin explanation. Then they tried to get up that music box, and every time they would seize Henry by the legs and shake him over the sofa cushion, or would pour some fresh variety of emetic down his throat, the instrument within would give a fresh spurt, and joyously grind out "Listen to the Mocking Bird" or "Thou'lt Never Cease to Love."

At last they were compelled to permit that musical box to remain within the sepulchral recesses of young Chubb. To say that the unfortunate victim of the disaster was made miserable by his condition would be to express in the feeblest manner the state of his mind. The more music there was in his stomach, the wilder and more completely chaotic became the discord in his soul. As likely as not it would occur that while he lay asleep in the middle of the night the works would begin to revolve, and would play "Home, Sweet Home" for two or three hours, unless the peg happened to slip, when the cylinder would switch back again to "Way down upon the Suwanee River," and would rattle out that tune with variations and fragments of the scales until Henry's brother would kick

him out of bed in wild despair, and sit on him in a vain effort to subdue the serenade, which, however, invariably proceeded with fresh vigor when subjected to unusual pressure.

And when Henry Chubb went to church, it frequently occurred that, in the very midst of the most solemn portion of the sermon, he would feel a gentle disturbance under the lower button of his jacket; and presently, when everything was hushed, the undigested engine would give a preliminary buzz and
then reel off "Listen to the Mocking Bird" and "Thou'lt Never Cease to Love," and scales and exercises, until the clergyman would stop and

glare at Henry over his spectacles and whisper to one of the deacons. Then the sexton would suddenly tack up the aisle and clutch the unhappy Mr. Chubb by the collar and scud down the aisle again to the accompaniment of "Home, Sweet Home," and then incarcerate Henry in the upper portion of the steeple until after church.

But the end came at last, and the miserable boy found peace. One day while he was sitting in school endeavoring to learn his multiplication table to the tune of "Thou'lt Never Cease to Love," his gastric juice triumphed. Something or other in the music box gave way all at once, the springs were unrolled with alarming force, and Henry Chubb, as he felt the fragments of the instrument hurled right and left among his vitals, tumbled over on the floor and expired.

At the *post mortem* examination they found several pieces of "Home, Sweet Home" in his liver, while one of his lungs was severely torn by a fragment of "Way down upon the Suwanee River." Small particles of "Listen to the Mocking Bird" were removed from his heart and breast-bone, and three brass pegs of "Thou'lt Never Cease to Love" were found firmly driven into his fifth rib.

They had no music at the funeral. They sifted the machinery out of him and buried him quietly in the cemetery. Whenever the Chubbs buy musical boxes now, they get them as large as a piano and chain them to the wall.

While Bob was engaged in reading the account of the melodious misery of the unhappy Chubb, Lieutenant Smiley came in, and the result was that both became uneasy. Bob disliked to subject himself to the criticism of a man whom he regarded as an enemy, and the lieutenant was so jealous of Bob's success that he began instantly to try to think of something that would enable him at least to maintain his reputation as a teller of stories.

"That is very good indeed, Bob," I said. "Bangs will be only too glad to publish it. It is very creditable. Put your name to it, however, if it goes into the *Argus*, or the colonel will persuade the community that he is the author of it."

"He will have to get a new brain-pan set in before he can write anything as good," said Bob.

"It is a very amusing story," remarked Mrs. Adeler. "I had no idea that you ever attempted such things. It is quite good, is it not, lieutenant?"

"Oh, very good indeed," said Smiley. "V-e-r-y good. Quite an achievement, in fact. Ha! ha! do you know that name 'Chubb' reminds me of a very comical incident."

"Indeed?"

"Ha! yes! Old General Chubb was the actor in it. Perhaps you knew him, Parker?"

"No, I didn't," growled Bob.

"Well, he was a very eccentric old man. Deuced queer,

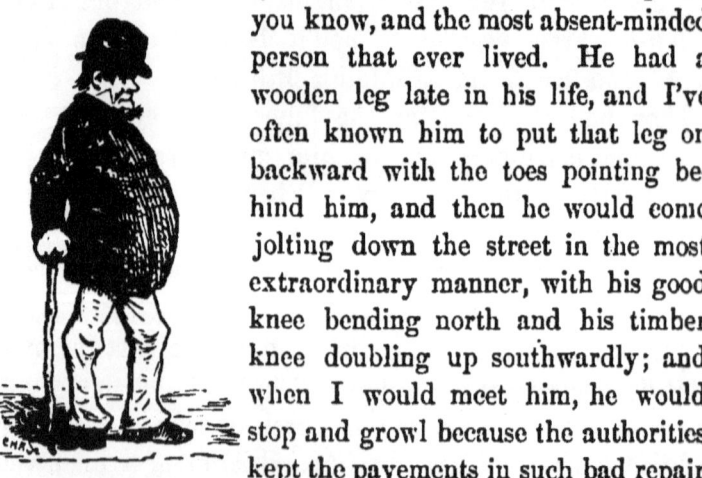

you know, and the most absent-minded person that ever lived. He had a wooden leg late in his life, and I've often known him to put that leg on backward with the toes pointing behind him, and then he would come jolting down the street in the most extraordinary manner, with his good knee bending north and his timber knee doubling up southwardly; and when I would meet him, he would stop and growl because the authorities kept the pavements in such bad repair that a man could hardly walk."

"I don't see anything very funny about that," said Bob, impolitely and savagely.

"Well, one day a few months ago," continued Smiley, without noticing Mr. Par-  ker's ill-nature, "he saunter- ed into the studio of the celebrated marine painter Hamilton, in Philadelphia. The artist was out at the moment, but standing upon the floor was a large and very superb picture of the sea-beach, with the surf roll- ing in upon it. The general stood looking at it for a while, until his mind wan- dered off from the present, and under the influence of the picture he was gradually impressed with a vague notion that he was at the seashore.

So, still gazing at the painting, he slowly removed his clothes, and finally stood in a revery without a stitch upon him. Then he clasped his nose with his fingers, bent his neck forward and plunged head foremost into the surf. The people on the floor below thought there was an earthquake. The artist came rushing in, and found General Chubb with his head against the washboard, one leg hanging from the ragged surf and the toes of his left foot struggling among the ruins of the lighthouse. Hamilton has that torn picture yet. He says that Chubb's dive is the highest tribute ever paid to his genius."

As the lieutenant finished the narrative, Bob rose and left the room with the suggestion, muttered as he passed me, that the story was tough.

"Mr. Parker don't seem well," remarked the lieutenant when Bob had gone.

"Oh yes, he is perfectly well. I imagine that he does not regard you with precisely the same amount of enthusiastic admiration that he might perhaps feel if you were not treading on his toes a little."

"Oh," laughed the lieutenant, "you refer, of course, to our relations with the Magruders? I don't like to talk much about that matter, of course; it is delicate, and you may think I am meddling with a business in which I have no concern. But perhaps I may as well tell you frankly that Parker has no earthly chance there—not the least in the world. The young lady won't smile on him. I am as certan of that as I am of death."

"You are positive of that, are you?"

"Yes, sir, you can rely upon my word. Parker might as well give it up. By the way, I wonder if he has gone down there now?"

"Very likely."

"Well, I must say good-night, then; I promised to call there at half-past eight, and it is time to be off."

So Lieutenant Smiley bade us adieu. Mrs. Adeler immediately asked:

"Do you believe what that man says?"

"Certainly not, my dear. I have as much faith as a dozen ordinary men, but it would require a grand army to believe him. He is foolish enough to hope to frighten Bob away. But Bob shall settle the matter to-morrow. If he doesn't, we will disown him. The end of the campaign has come. Now for victory or defeat!"

CHAPTER XIII.

HIS is St. Pillory's Day. It is the day upon which humane and liberal Delawarians hang their heads for shame at the insult offered to civilization by the law of their State. That law this morning placed half a dozen miserable creatures in the stocks, and then flogged them upon their naked flesh with a cat-o'-nine-tails. It was no slight thing to stand there wearing that wooden collar in this bitter November weather, with the north-east wind blowing in fierce gusts from the broad expanse of the river; and one poor wretch who endured that suffering was so benumbed with cold that he could hardly climb down the ladder to the ground. And when he had descended, they lashed his back until it was covered with purple stripes. He had stolen some provisions, and he looked as if he needed them, for he seemed hungry and forlorn and utterly desperate with misery. It would

200

have been a kindlier act of Christian charity if society, instead of mutilating his body, had fed it and clothed it properly, and placed him in some reformatory institution where his soul could have been taken care of. But that is not the method that prevails here.

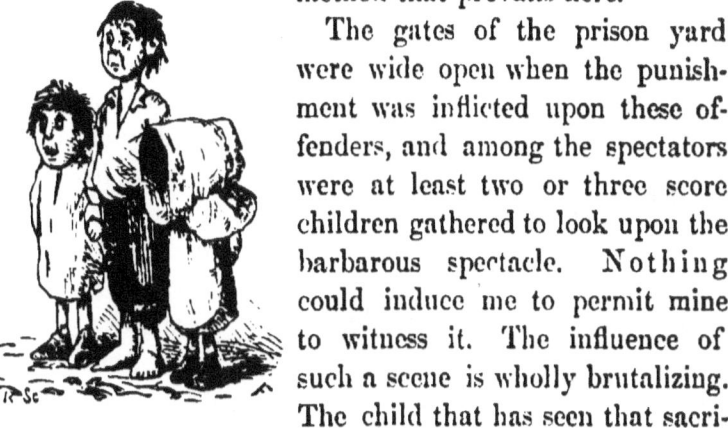

The gates of the prison yard were wide open when the punishment was inflicted upon these offenders, and among the spectators were at least two or three score children gathered to look upon the barbarous spectacle. Nothing could induce me to permit mine to witness it. The influence of such a scene is wholly brutalizing. The child that has seen that sacrifice has lost some of the sweetness and tenderness of its better nature.

The whipping-post and pillory is a sturdy bit of timber a foot square. Eight or nine feet from the ground it pierces a small platform, and five feet above this there is a cross-piece which contains in each of its two arms a hole for the neck and two holes for the wrists of the man who is to be pilloried. The upper half of the arm lifts to admit the victim, and then closes upon him, sometimes very tightly. It is fastened down with a wedge-shaped key, shot into the centre-post. Beneath the platform hangs

a pair of handcuffs in which the wrists of those who are to
be flogged are placed. The whole machine looks like a
gigantic cross. It is black with age, covered with patches
of green mold and moss, and shrunken and split until the
grain of the wood protrudes in ridges.

There was a time in the past when it stood, an instrument
of cruel torture, upon the public street. It was planted in
the green just at the end of the old market house, and there
the criminals were lashed by the sheriff. Any of the old

men who have
spent their lives in
this place can tell
how, when they
were boys, it was
the custom for the
urchins and the
loafers of the town
to pelt any poor
rogue who was pilloried with whatever missiles happened to
be at hand; and often the creatures thus abused were taken
down from the stocks and tied up to the post, there to have
their flesh lacerated with the leather thongs. They used to
flog women, too. They flogged women in the open street,
with their garments torn away from their bodies above the
waist, and the gaping crowd gathered about and witnessed
without shame that dreadful spectacle.

But that was more than half a century ago. Who shall
say that we do not advance in civilization? Who can assert
that these people have not acquired a higher sense of decency,
when public opinion has compelled the removal of this abominable relic of barbarism to the jail-yard, and the performance of the penalty in another place than before the doors
of the temple where a God of mercy is worshiped? I hope
that the day is not far distant when the whipping-post and

the infernal system that sustains it will go down together, and when the people of this State will learn that their first duty to a criminal is to strive to make him a better man.

They say here, in apologizing for the institution, that the punishment is not severe, because the sheriff never makes savage use of the lash. But it is a terrible infliction, no matter how lightly the blows are struck, for it is imposed in the presence of a multitude, and the sufferer feels that he is for ever to be known among men as a thief. The thongs do not always fall gently; the force of the lash depends upon the will of the sheriff, who may kill a man with the number of blows which in another case give no pain. I say that any law which places such discretionary power in the hands of an executive officer who may be bribed or frightened, or who may have some personal injury to avenge, defeats the true end of justice. The court should fix the penalty absolutely. They say here, also, that no man is ever flogged a second time. That is untrue. The same men do return again and again. Some do not; but where do they go? Why, to other communities, where they perpetrate other crimes and become a burden upon other people. We have no right to breed criminals and then to drive them into cities and towns that have already enough of their own. We are under a sacred obligation to place them in prisons supported by the money of the State, and there to attempt to teach them arts by which they may earn their bread if they will. In such a place a convict can be reached by those philanthropists who realize what society owes to its criminal classes. But as he is treated now, it is impossible that he should ever lift himself or be lifted to a purer and better life.

Fallen angels in Delaware never rise again. Law clips their wings and stamps upon them with its heel, and society shakes off the dust of its feet upon them and curses them in their degradation. The gates of mercy are shut upon them

17

hopelessly and for ever, and they walk abroad with the story of their shame blazoned upon them, as the women who wore the Scarlet Letter in the old Puritan times in New England, that all the world may read it. They know that their punishment has been fierce and terrible and out of all proportion to their offence, and they curse their oppressors and hate them with a bitter, unrelenting hatred. They know they will not be allowed to reform, and that the law which should have led them to a better future has cut them off from fellowship with their race, robbed them of their humanity and made pariahs and outcasts of them. They are turned to stone, and they come out of their prisons confirmed, hopeless criminals.

A certain judge who administered Delaware justice here once upon a time (we will say it was a thousand years ago) was a very peculiar man in certain of his methods. I do not know whether he was merely fond of listening to the music of his own voice, as too many less reverend and awful men are, or whether he really loved to torture the prisoners in the dock, when he sentenced them, by keeping them in suspense respecting his intentions, and by exciting hopes which he finally crushed. But he had a way of assuming a mild and benevolent aspect as he addressed a convicted man which was very reassuring to the unhappy wight, and then he usually proceeded to deliver a few remarks which were so ingeniously arranged, which expressed such

tender and affectionate sympathy, which were so highly charged with benevolence, so expressive, as it were, of a passionate yearning for the welfare of the victim, that the latter at last would be convinced that the judge was about to give him an exceedingly light sentence. Just as he had gotten himself into a frame of mind suitable to the unexpected brightness of his prospects, the judge's custom was to bring his observations suddenly to an end, and to hurl at the head of the convict, still with that philanthropic expression upon his countenance, the most frightful penalty permitted by the law.

On a certain day, while a certain historian was in court, he was engaged in exercising a youth named Busby in this fashion. Busby, it appears, was accused of stealing seventy-five cents' worth of old iron from somebody, and the jury had found him guilty.

Busby was ordered to stand up, and the judge, permitting a peculiarly bland smile to play upon his features, gazed tenderly at the prisoner, while he placed a small pinch of tobacco in his mouth; and then, drawing a long breath, he began:

"George Washington Busby, you have been found guilty by a jury of your fellow-countrymen of an offence against

society and against the peace and dignity of the commonwealth of Delaware, and I have now to impose upon you the penalties provided by the law. I am very, very sorry to see you here, George, and it grieves my heart to be compelled to fulfill the obligation devolving upon me as a judicial officer. Pause, I entreat you, at this the very outset of your career, and reflect upon what you are casting from you. You are a young man; you are, as it were, in the very morning of your life; a bright and happy home is yours, and around you are the kind parents and friends who have made you the child of their prayers, who have guided your footsteps from infancy, who have loved and cherished you and made for you mighty sacrifices.

"You have a mother"—and here the judge's voice faltered and he wiped away a tear—"a mother at whose knee

you were taught to lisp your earliest devotions, and who has watched over you and ministered to you with that tender and fervent love that only a mother can feel. You have a father who looked upon you with a heart swelling with pride, and who gave to you the heritage of his honest name. Up to the time when, yielding to the insidious wiles of the tempter, you committed this crime, your character had been irreproachable, and it seemed as if the brightest promises of your childhood were to have rich and beneficent fulfillment. For you the vista of the future appeared serene and beautiful; a pure and noble manhood seemed to await you, and all the blessings which may be gained by an unspotted reputation, by persistent energy and by earnest devotion to the right were to be yours."

Here Busby began to feel considerably better. He was

assured that such a kind old man as that could not treat him with severity, and he informed the tipstaff in a whisper that he calculated now on about sixty days' imprisonment at the furthest.

The judge shifted the quid in his cheek, blew his nose, and resumed:

"How difficult it is, then, for me to determine the precise measure of your punishment! Knowing that the quality of mercy is not strained, and that as we forgive so shall we be forgiven, how painful it is for me to draw the line between undue leniency and the demands of outraged law! Considering, I say, all these things, that are so much in your favor—your youth, your happy home, where the holiest influences are shed upon your path, where parental love covers you with its most gracious benediction, where your devoted mother lies stricken with anguish at the sin of her idolized son, where your aged father has his gray hairs brought down in sorrow to the grave, where you have been nurtured and admonished and taught to do right—"

"Certainly he can't intend to give me more than one month," said Busby to the tipstaff.

"Considering that this is your first offence; that your conduct hitherto has been that of an honest young man, and that the lesson you have learned from this bitter and terrible experience will sink deeply into your heart; that you have opening out to you in the possible future a life of usefulness and honor, with a prospect of redeeming this single error and winning for yourself a respected name—"

" He can't decently give me more than twenty days after that," suggested Busby.

The judge, after wiping the moisture from his eyes and borrowing a morsel of tobacco from the prosecuting attorney, continued:

"In view of all these extenuating circumstances, in view of the fact, fully recognized by this court, that justice is not revengeful, but exercises its highest prerogative in leading the fallen to reformation and moral improvement—in view, I say, of the fact that you are in the very spring-time of your existence, with the vista of the future opening out with alluring brightness before you and giving promise of higher and better things—in view of those sorrowing parents the child of whose prayers you are; of that mother who guided

your infant steps and cared for you with the yearning tenderness of maternal love, of that venerable father who looks upon you as the staff of his old age; considering, too, that this is your first misstep from the path of duty—"

" Two weeks as sure as death!" exclaimed Mr. Busby, joyfully, to the officer beside him.

" The path of duty," continued the judge, " and that up to the moment of the commission of the deed you had been above suspicion and above reproach,—in view of all this," remarked the judge, " I have thought it my duty, minister of the law though I am, and bound though I am by my oath to vindicate the insulted majesty of that law—"

"If he gives me more than one week, I will never trust signs again," murmured Busby.

"I say that although I am bound to administer justice with an impartial hand, I feel it to be incumbent upon me in this particular instance, in consequence of these extenuating circumstances, to mete it out so that, while the law will be vindicated, you may be taught that it is not cruel or unkind, but rather is capable of giving the first generous impulse to reformation."

"He certainly means to let me off altogether," exclaimed Busby.

"In view, then, of these mitigating circumstances of your youth, your previous good character, your happy prospects, your afflicted parents and your own sincere repentance, the sentence of the court is: That you, George Washington Busby, the prisoner at the bar, do pay seventy-five cents restitution money and the costs of this trial, and that on Saturday next you be whipped with twenty lashes on the bare back, well laid on; that you be imprisoned for six months in the county jail, and that you wear a convict's jacket in public for one year after your release. Sheriff, remove the prisoner from the court."

Then the judge beamed a mournful but sympathetic smile upon Busby, secured the loan of another atom of tobacco, spat on the floor and called up the next case.

Mrs. Adeler, you laugh and say that I have indulged in gross exaggeration in reproducing the sentence. Not so. I tell you that I have known a boy of thirteen to have that condemnation, couched in almost precisely those words, hurled at him from the bench of the New Castle court-house because he stole a bit of iron said to be worth seventy-five cents. And I was present among the spectators in the jail yard when the sheriff lashed the lad until he writhed with pain. It was infamous—utterly infamous. I cannot, perhaps, justly accuse the judge who imposed the sentence upon the boy of indulging in the lecture which has just been quoted. That, as I have said, may be attributed to a magistrate who lived ten centuries ago. But the sentence is genuine, and it was given recently. I do not blame the judge. He acted under the authority of statutes which were created by other hands. But the law is savagery itself, and the humane men of this State should sweep it from existence.

CHAPTER XIV.

HILE the scenes at the whipping-post on flogging-day are fresh in my mind, I have written down the story of Mary Engle. It is a Delaware legend, and the events of which it speaks occurred, I will say, seventy-odd years ago, when they were in the habit of lashing women in this very town of New Castle.

It was on Christmas day that a little party had assembled in the old Newton mansion to participate in the festivities for which, at this season of the year, it was famous all the country over. The house stood upon the river bank, three miles and more from New Castle, and in that day it was considered the greatest and handsomest building in the whole neighborhood. A broad lawn swept away from it down to the water's edge, and in summer-time this was covered with bright-colored flowers and bounded by green hedges. Now the grass was bleached with the cold; the hedges were brown and sere, and the huge old trees, stripped of their foliage, moaned and creaked and shivered in the wind, rattling their branches together as if seeking sympathy with each other in their desolation.

Inside the mansion the scene was as cheerful as life and fun and high spirits could make it.

Old Major Newton, the lord and master of all the wide estates, was one of the race of country gentlemen who introduced to this continent the manners, habits and large hospitality of the better class of English squires of his day. He was a mighty fox-hunter, as many a brush hung in his dining-hall could attest. A believer in the free use of the good things of life, his sideboard always contained a dozen de-canters, from which the coming, the remaining and the parting guests were expected to follow the major's example in drinking deeply. His table was always profusely supplied with good fare, and dining with him was the great duty and pleasure of the day. He was a gentleman in education, and to some extent in his tastes; but his manners partook of the coarseness of his time, for he swore fierce oaths, and his temper was quick, terrible and violent. His forty negro slaves were treated with indulgent kindness while they obeyed him implicitly, but any attempt at insubordination upon their part called down upon their heads a volley of oaths and that savage punishment which the major considered necessary to discipline.

To-day the major had been out of spirits, and had not joined heartily in the hilarity of the company, which, despite the gloom of the master, made the old house ring with the merriment and laughter due to the happiness of Christmas time.

At five o'clock dinner was done; and the ladies having withdrawn, the cloth was removed, the wine and whisky and apple-toddy, and a half dozen other beverages, were brought out, and the major, with his male guests, began the serious work of the repast. The major sat at the head of the table; Dr. Ricketts, a jolly bachelor of fifty, who neglected medicine that he might better spend his fortune in a life of ease and pleasure, presided at the lower end of the board, upon the flanks of which sat a dozen gentlemen from the neighboring estates, among them Tom Willitts, from the adjoining farm, and Dick Newton, the major's only son.

The conversation languished somewhat. The major was as gloomy as he had been earlier in the day. Dick seemed to sympathize with his father. Tom Willitts was impatient

to have the drinking bout over, that he might go to the parlor, where his thoughts already wandered, and where his *fiancée*, Mary Engle, the fair governess in the major's family, awaited him. The guests at last began to be depressed by the want of spirits in their host; and if it had not been for Doctor Ricketts, there would have been a dull time indeed. But the doctor was talkative, lively and wholly indifferent to the taciturnity of his companions. His weakness was a fondness for theorizing, and he rattled on from topic to topic, heedless of anything but the portly

goblet which he replenished time and again from the
decanter and the punch-bowl.

At last he exclaimed, in the hope of rousing his host
from his apparent despondency, "And now let's have a
song from the major. Give us the ' Tally Ho!' Newton."

"I can't sing it to-day, gentlemen," said the major; "the
fact is I am a good deal out of sorts. I have met with a
misfortune, and I—"

"Why, what's happened?" exclaimed the whole company.

"Why," said the major, with an oath, "I've lost my
famous old diamond brooch—a jewel, gentlemen, given to
my father by George II.—a jewel that I valued more than
all the world beside. It was the reward given to my father
for a brave and gallant deed at the battle of Dettingen, and
its rare intrinsic value was trifling beside that which it possessed as the evidence of my father's valor."

"How did you lose it, major?" asked the doctor.

"I went to my desk this morning, and found that the lock
had been picked, the inside drawer broken open and the
brooch taken from its box."

"Who could have done it?"

"I can't imagine," replied the major; "I don't think any
of those niggers would have done such a thing. I've searched
them all, but it's of no use, sir—no use; it's gone. But if I
ever lay hands on the scoundrel, I'll flay him alive—I will,
indeed, even if it should be Dick there;" and the old man
gulped down a heavy draught of port, as if to drown his
grief.

"My theory about such crimes," said the doctor, "is
that the persons committing them are always more or less
insane."

"Insane!" swore the major, fiercely. "If I catch the
man who did this, I'll fit him for a hospital!"

"We are all a little daft at times—when we are angry, in

love, in extreme want, or excited by intense passion of any
kind," said the doctor. "Extreme ignorance, being neglect
of one's intellectual faculties, is a kind of insanity, and so is
the perversion of the moral perceptions of those who are
educated to a life of crime from their childhood. My theory
is that punishment should be so inflicted as to restore reason,
not merely to wreak vengeance."

"And my theory is that every vagabond who breaks the
laws ought to be flogged and imprisoned, so that he may
know that society will not tolerate crime. Hang your fine-
spun theories about the beggars who prey upon the community!" said the major, rising and kicking back his chair ill-
naturedly.

The doctor had nothing more to say, and the company
withdrew to the parlor.

There, gathered around the great fireplace, sat Mrs. Newton, her daughters—both children—Mary Engle, their tutor,
Mrs. Willitts and the wives of the gentlemen who had come
from the dinner-table.

They rose as the men entered the room, and greeted them
cordially. Tom Willitts went quickly to Mary's side, and
while the others engaged in lively conversation he took her
hand gently and, as was their privilege, they walked slowly
up the room and sat by the window alone, Mary's face
brightening as she thanked Tom
heartily for the beautiful present
he had sent her the day before.

"Why don't you wear it now,
Mary?" asked Tom.

"Do you want me to? I will
get it and put it on, then, when I
go to my room," said Mary.

Mary Engle was the daughter
of a widow in humble circum-

18

stances who lived in the village. Talented and well-edu-
cated, she had determined no longer to be a burden upon
her mother, but to support herself. She had chosen to become a governess in Major Newton's family. Young, beautiful and of good social position, she was a valuable acquisi-
tion to that household, and was a universal favorite, although
the major could never quite rid himself of the notion that,
as she was a dependant and an employé, he was conferring
a favor upon her by permitting such intimate relations to
exist between her and his family. But he treated her
kindly, as all men must a pretty woman. She was a girl
with whom any man might have fallen in love upon first
acquaintance. Dick Newton loved her passionately before
she had been in his father's house a month. But she had
chosen rather to favor Tom Willitts, a constant visitor at
the Newton mansion, and as fine a fellow as ever galloped
across the country with the hounds. Dick had not had time
to propose before the game was up and Tom called the prize
his own. But Dick nursed his passion and smothered his
disappointment, while he swore that he would possess the
girl or involve her and her lover in common ruin with himself. Tom had been engaged for three months before this
Christmas day. He was to be married in the coming
spring.

There was to be a theatrical exhibition in the Newton
mansion this Christmas evening, in which the young people
were to participate. A temporary stage had been erected at
one end of the long room, and at an early hour seats were
placed in front of the curtain, and the guests took their
places, conversing with much merriment and laughter until
the bell gave the signal for the performance to begin.

It was a little play—a brief comedy of only tolerable merit,
and it devolved upon Mary Engle to enter first.

She tripped in smiling, and began the recitation with a

vivacity and spirit that promised well for the excellence of her performance throughout. Upon her throat she wore a diamond brooch which blazed and flashed in the glare of the foot-lights.

There was an exclamation of surprise on the part of the gentlemen present, and the sound startled Mary. She paused and looked around her inquiringly. Just then Major Newton caught sight of the brooch. With an ugly word upon his lips, he sprang from his seat and jumped upon the stage.

"Where did you get that?" he demanded, fiercely, pointing at the diamonds, his hand trembling violently.

There was absolute silence in the room as Mary, pale and calm, replied:

"Why do you ask, sir?"

"Where did you get that, I say? It was stolen from me. You are a thief!"

In an instant she tore it from her dress and flung it upon the floor.

The major leaped toward it and picked it up quickly.

Mary covered her face with her hands, and the crimson of her cheeks shone through her fingers.

"Where did you get it?" again demanded the major.

"I will not tell you, sir," said she, dragging down her hands with an effort and clasping them in front of her.

"Then leave this house this instant, and leave it for ever!" said the major, wild with passion.

Tom Willitts entered just as the last words were uttered. Mary seemed fainting. He flew to her side as if to defend her against her enemy. He did not know the cause of her trouble, but he glared at the major as if he could slay him.

But as he tried to place his arm around Mary, she shrank away from him; and giving him one look of scorn and contempt and hatred, she ran from the room.

From the room to the great door in the hall, which, with frantic eagerness, she flung open, and then, without any covering upon her fair head, hot with shame and disgrace, and maddened with insult, she fled out into the cold and dark and desolate winter's night.

Scarcely heeding the direction, she reached the river's shore; and choosing the hard sand for a pathway, she hurried along it. The tide swept up in ceaseless ripples at her feet, the waves breaking upon the icy fringe of the shore, each with a whisper that seemed to tell of her dishonor. The wind rustled the sedges upon the banks and filled them with voices that mocked her. The stars that lighted her upon her mad journey twinkled through the frosty air with an intelligence they had never before possessed. The lights, far out upon the river and in the distant town, danced up and down in the darkness as if beckoning her to come on to them and to destruction.

Her brain was in a whirl. At first she felt an impulse to end her misery in the river. One plunge, and all this anguish and pain would be buried beneath those restless waters. Then the hope of vindication flashed upon her mind, and the awful sin and the cowardice of self-destruction rose vividly before her. She would seek her home and the mother from whom she should never have gone out. She would give up happiness and humanity, and hide herself from the cold, heartless world for ever. She would have no more to do with false friends and false lovers, but would shut herself away from all this deceit and treachery and unkindness, and nevermore trust any human being but her own dear mother.

And so, over the sandy beach, through mire and mud,

through the high grass and the reeds of the water's edge, tangled and dead, and full of peril in the darkness, with

her hair disheveled and tossed about by the riotous wind, but with not a tear upon her white face, she struggled onward through the night, until, exhausted with her journey, her wild passion and her misery, she reached her mother's house, and entering, clasped her arms about her mother's neck, and with a sob fell fainting at her feet.

*   *   *   *   *

There was an end to merriment at the Newton mansion. When Mary ran from the room, the company stood for a moment amazed and bewildered, while the major, raging with passion, yet half ashamed of his furious conduct, walked rapidly up and down the stage, attempting to explain the theft to his guests and to justify his conduct. But Tom Willitts, shocked at the cruel treatment he had received from Mary, yet filled with righteous indignation at the major's violence, interrupted his first utterance.

18 *

"You are a coward and a brute, sir; and old as you are, I will make you answer for your infamous treatment of that young girl."

And before the major could reply he dashed out to pursue Mary and give her his protection. He sought her in vain upon the highway; and filled with bitterness, and wondering why she had so scorned him, he trudged on through the darkness, peering about him vainly for the poor girl for whom he would have sacrificed his life.

"Perhaps it was merely a jest," suggested Mrs. Willitts. "I think Mary wholly incapable of theft. She never could have intended seriously to keep the brooch."

"A pretty serious jest," said the major, "to break into my desk three days ago. It's the kind of humor that puts people in jail."

"My theory about the matter," said the doctor, "is this: She either was made the victim of a pretty ugly practical joke, or else some one stole the jewel from you and gave it to her to get her into trouble."

"I don't believe anything of the kind," said the major.

"It must be so. If she had stolen it, she certainly would not have worn it in your presence this evening. It is absurd to suppose such a thing. Taking this theory—"

"Hang theorizing!" exclaimed the major, seeing the force of this suggestion, but more angry that he was driven to admit it to his own mind. "She is a thief, and as sure as I live she shall either confess, tell how she got the jewel or go to prison."

"And as sure as I live," said the doctor, grown indignant and serious, "I will unravel this mystery and clear this innocent girl of this most infamous and wicked imputation."

"Do it if you can!" said the major, and turned his back upon him contemptuously.

The doctor left the house, and the company dispersed,

eager gossips, all of them, to tell the story far and wide throughout the community before to-morrow's noon.

*   *   *   *   *

When Mary had revived and told, in broken words, the story of her misery and disgrace, her mother soothed and comforted her with the assurance that she should never leave her again; and while she denounced Major Newton's conduct bitterly, she said he would find that he had made a mistake and would clear her of the charge.

" But he will not find it out, mother."

" Why? Where did you get the brooch, Mary?"

" Do not ask me, mother; I cannot, cannot tell you."

" Had you merely picked it up and put it on in jest?"

" No, no," said Mary, "it was given to me, I cannot tell by whom, and I thought it was mine. It was cruel, cruel!" and her tears came again.

" And who was it that did so vile a thing?" asked her mother.

" Mother, I cannot tell even you that."

" But, Mary, this is foolish. You must not, for your own sake, for mine, hide the name of this criminal."

" I will never, never tell. I will die first."

" Was it Tom Willitts?"

" You must not question me, mother," said Mary, firmly. "If the person who betrayed me is cowardly enough to place me in such a position, and then to stand coldly by and witness my shame, I am brave enough and true enough to bear the burden. I would rather have this misery than his conscience."

Tom Willitts knocked at the door.

" If it is Tom Willitts, mother," said Mary, rising, "tell him I will not see him. Tell him never to come to this house again. Tell him," she said, her eyes glowing with excitement, and stamping her foot upon the floor, "tell him I hate him—hate him for a false, mean villain!" and she fell back upon the chair in a wild passion of tears.

Mrs. Engle met Tom at the door. He was filled with anxiety and terror, but he rejoiced that Mary was safe. Mrs. Engle told him that Mary refused to see him. He was smitten with anguish, and begged for a single word with her.

"Do you know anything about this wicked business, Mr. Willitts?" asked Mrs. Engle, suspicious, because of Mary's words, that Tom was the criminal.

"Upon my honor I do not. I heard Major Newton's language, and saw the brooch upon the floor; and when Mary fled from me, I pursued her, wondering what it all meant."

"She evidently suspects you of having been the cause of the trouble. Prove that you were not. Until then she will not see you. I beg you, for yourself and her, to tell the truth about this, if you know it, or at least to persist till you discover it.

Tom went away distressed and confounded. She suspected him. No wonder, then, she had spurned him so rudely. He thought the matter over, and could arrive at no solution of the difficulty. He had sent her a bracelet which she had promised to wear, but she had not worn it. It was impossible that this brooch could have been substituted. No, his own servant had given it to her, and brought her thanks in return. Besides, who could be base enough to play such a dastardly trick upon a pretty young girl? He could not master the situation; and in his trouble he went the next morning to Dr. Ricketts.

The doctor was equally puzzled, but he was certain that there was foul play somewhere. He had pledged himself to unravel the mystery, and he began the work by visiting Mary. Alone, he went to her house. He found it in strange commotion. Mrs. Engle was sitting upon the sofa, crying bitterly; Mary, with pale, sad face, but with an air of determination, confronted an obsequious man, who, with many apologies and a manner that proved that he was ashamed of his business, extended a paper toward her, and requested her to accompany him.

It was a constable with a warrant for her arrest.

Nearly five weary months were to pass before the cruel time of the trial. Dr. Ricketts busied himself examining every one who could possibly have been connected with the affair of the brooch, but with no result but a deeper mystery. Tom's servant swore that he had given the bracelet into Mary's own hand. Two of the house servants at Major Newton's were present at the time, and they were certain the package was not broken. Mary's thimble had been found under the broken desk in which the brooch was kept, and the housemaid had discovered a chisel secreted behind some books in the bookcase in her room.

The evidence, slight though it was, pointed to Mary as the criminal, despite the absurdity of the supposition, in view of the manner in which she had worn the jewel. Mary herself preserved an obstinate silence, refusing to tell how or where or from whom she procured the fatal brooch. The doctor was bewildered and confounded, and he at last gave up his inquiries in despair, hoping for a gracious verdict from the jury at the trial.

Through all the weary time Mary kept closely at home, secluded from friends and acquaintances. Indeed, visitors were few in number now. She was in humble circumstances, and she was in disgrace. Society always accounts its members guilty until their innocence is proved. There were people in the town who had been jealous of her beauty, her popularity, her place in the affections of rich Tom Willitts, and these did not hesitate to hint, with a sneer, that they had always doubted the reported excellence of Mary Engle, and to assert their belief in her guilt.

Tom Willitts was nearly crazed about her treatment of him and the ignominy that was heaped upon her. With Dr. Ricketts and Dick Newton, who professed intense anxiety to help solve the matter, he strove valiantly to clear her of the charge, but without avail.

The day of the trial came. The court-room was crowded. Able lawyers on both sides sparred with each other, as able lawyers do, but the heart of the prosecuting attorney was evidently not with his work. His duty was clear, however, and the evidence was overwhelming. The defence had nothing to offer but Mary's good character and her appearance before the company with the brooch upon her person.

The judge was compelled to instruct the jury against the prisoner. An hour of anxious suspense, and they returned a verdict of "guilty."

Mrs. Engle began to sob violently. Mary drew her veil aside from a face that was ashen white, but not a muscle quivered until the judge pronounced the sentence :

"Costs of prosecution, a fine of one hundred dollars, twenty lashes upon the bare back on the Saturday following, and imprisonment for one year."

Mary fell to the floor insensible, and Dr. Ricketts, raising her in his arms, applied restoratives. She was removed to the jail to await her punishment.

The doctor mounted his horse and sped away in hot haste forty miles to Dover. He had influence with the governor. He would procure a pardon, and then have Mary taken away from the scene of her tribulation—where her suffering and disgrace would be forgotten, and she would be at peace. He was unsuccessful. The governor was a just, not a merciful, man. The law had been outraged. Twelve good men and true had said so. If people committed crimes, they must submit to the penalty. Society must be protected. The intelligence and social position of the criminal only made the demands of justice more imperative. If he pardoned Mary Engle, men would rightly say that the poor and friendless and weak were punished, while the influential and rich escaped the law. He must do his duty to Delaware and to her people. He could not grant the pardon.

But there was to be another appeal to executive mercy. It was the night before the punishment. The doctor sat in his parlor, before the glowing fire in the grate, and with his head resting upon his hand he thought sadly of the pitiful scene he had witnessed in the jail from which he had just come— of Mary, in the damp, narrow cell, bearing herself like a heroine through all this terrible trial, and still keeping a secret which the doctor felt certain would give her back her freedom and her good name if it could be disclosed; of Mrs. Engle, full of despair and terror, crying bitterly over the shame and disgrace that had come upon her child, and which would be increased beyond endurance on the morrow.

As the doctor's kind old heart grew heavy with these thoughts, and from the bewildering maze of circumstances he tried to evolve some theory that promised salvation, Dick Newton entered.

He was haggard and pale, and his eyes were cast down to the floor.

"Why, Dick, what's the matter?" asked the doctor.

"Dr. Ricketts, I have come to make a shameful confession. I—"

"Well?" said the doctor, suspiciously and impatiently, as Dick's voice faltered.

"I will not hesitate about it," said Dick, hurriedly; "I am afraid it is even now too late. I stole the diamond brooch."

"What?" exclaimed the doctor, jumping to his feet in a frenzy of indignant excitement.

"I am the cause of all this trouble. It was my fault that Mary Engle was accused and convicted, and it will be my fault if she is punished. Oh, doctor, cannot something be done to save her? I never intended it should go so far."

"You infamous scoundrel!" said the doctor, unable to restrain his scorn and contempt; "why did you not say this before? Why did you permit all this misery and shame to fall upon the defenceless head of a woman for whom an honest man should have sacrificed his very life? How was this villainy consummated? Tell me, quickly!"

The poor wretch sank upon his knees, and with a trembling voice exclaimed,

"I loved her. I hated Tom Willitts. He sent her a bracelet. I knew it would come. I broke open father's cabinet and took his brooch. With threats and money I induced Tom's servant to lend me the box for a few moments before he entered the house. I placed the brooch in it. She thought it came from Tom, and she resolved to die rather than betray him, although she thinks him the cause of her ruin. It was vile and mean and wicked in me, but I thought Tom would be the victim, not she; and when the trouble came, I could not endure the shame of exposure. But you will save her now, doctor, will you not? I will fly—leave the country—kill myself—anything to prevent this awful crime."

The miserable man burst into tears. Dr. Ricketts looked at him a moment with eyes filled with pity and scorn, and then said,

"So my theory was right, after all. Come, sir, you will go to the governor with me, and we will see if he will grant a pardon upon your confession."

"What, to-night?" asked Dick.

"Yes, to-night—now; and it will be well for you and your victim if fleet horses carry us to Dover and back before ten to-morrow morning."

In five minutes the pair were seated in a carriage, and through the black night they sped onward, the one with his heart swelling with hope, joy and humanity, the other cowering in the darkness, full of misery and self-contempt, and of horrible forebodings of the future.

* * * * * * *

Saturday morning—a cold, raw, gusty morning in May.

The town was in a small uproar. Men lounged on the porches of the taverns, in front of which their horses were hitched, talking politics, discussing crop prospects, tho prices of grain, the latest news by coach and schooner from Philadelphia. Inside the bar-room men were reading newspapers a month old, drinking, swearing and debating with loud voices.

But the attraction that morning was in another quarter. In the middle of the market street there was a common—a strip of green sod twenty feet wide fringed on either side with a row of trees. In the centre of this stood the whipping-post and pillory.

The hour of ten tolled out from the steeple down the street. It was the same bell that called the people together on Sunday to worship God and to supplicate his mercy. It

19

was a bell of various uses. It summoned the saints to prayer and the sinners to punishment.

At its earliest stroke the jailer issued from the prison with a forlorn-looking white man in his clutches. He hurried his prisoner up the ladder, and prepared to fasten him in the pillory. The boys below collected in knots, and fingered the missiles in their hands. The jailer descended. A boy lifted his hand and flung a rotten egg at the pilloried wretch. It hit him squarely in the face, and the feculent contents streamed down to his chin. That was the signal. Eggs, dead cats, mud, stones, tufts of sod and a multitude of filthy things were showered upon the prisoner, until the platform was covered with the *débris*. He yelled with pain, and strove vainly to shake from his face the blood that streamed forth

 from the cut skin and the filth that besmeared it. The crowd hooted at him and laughed at his efforts, and called him vile names, and jested with him about his wooden collar and cuffs, and no human heart in all that assembly had any pity for him. For an hour he stood there, enduring inconceivable torture. When the steeple clock struck eleven, he was taken out in wretched plight, almost helpless and sorely wounded. No more pillory that day. It was the turn of the whipping-post now. There were two women to be whipped, one of them white, the other black. We know who the white woman was.

The negro was to suffer first. She was dragged from the jail wild with fright and apprehension. Around her legs a soiled skirt of calico dangled. About her naked body, stripped for the sacrifice, a fragment of carpet was hung. The jailer brought her by main force to the post through the jeering crowd, and while she begged wildly, almost incoherently, for mercy, promising vague, impossible things, the officer of the law clasped the iron cuffs about her uplifted hands, so that

A FLOGGING SEVENTY YEARS AGO.

she was compelled to stand upon her toes to escape unendurable agony. The blanket was torn from her shoulders, and with dilated eyes glistening with terror, she turned her head half around to where the sheriff stood, ready to execute the law.

This virtuous officer felt the sharp thongs of his "cat" complacently as he listened with dull ear to the incessant prayers of the woman; and when the jailer said, "Forty lashes, sheriff," the cat was swung slowly up, and the ends of the lashes touched the victim's back, bringing blood at the first blow.

The crowd laughed and applauded. The sheriff accepted the applause with the calm indifference of a man who feels the greatness of his office and has confidence in his own skill.

As the lashes came thick and fast, the skin swelled up into thick purple ridges, and then the blood spurted out in crimson streams, flowing down upon the wretched skirt and staining it with a new and dreadful hue. The woman's piercing screams rang out upon the air and filled some kind hearts with tender pity. But as it was a "nigger," the tendency to human kindness was smothered.

Beneath the blows she writhed and contorted and shrank forward, until at last, faint with loss of blood, with terrible pain and nervous exhaustion, she sank helplessly down and hung by her arms alone. At first the sheriff thought he would postpone the rest of the punishment until she recovered. But there were only five more lashes to be given, and he concluded that it would be as well to finish up the job. They were inflicted upon the insensible form, and then the jailer came forward with a pair of shears. The sheriff took them coolly and clipped away a portion of the woman's ears. Her hands were then unshackled; and bleeding, mutilated, unconscious, she was carried into the prison.

Her agonized cries had penetrated those walls already and brought a whiter hue to the pale cheeks of the woman who by this ignominy had learned her sisterhood with the poor black. There were two other women in the cell, Mrs. Engle and Mrs. Willitts. The former controlled herself for her daughter's sake, but dared speak no word to her. Mrs. Willitts, through her tears, tried to comfort Mary as with hesitating hands she disrobed her for her torture:

"The day will come, Mary dear, when you will be vindicated, and these wicked men will hide their heads with bitter shame and humiliation. But bear up bravely, dear. Have good courage through it all. Perhaps it will not be so hard. 'Though there be heaviness for a night, joy cometh in the morning.' We will all be happy together yet some day."

Mary Engle stood there, speechless, statue-like, immovable, as they took away her garments, and her fair white skin glistened in the dim light.

It was almost time. The black woman was being dragged through the door to the next cell. The murmur of the crowd came up from the street. Mrs. Willitts placed the blanket upon those ivory shoulders, and Mary, turning to her mother, flung her arms about her and kissed her. In a whisper she said,

"I shall die, mother. I will not live through it. I will never see you again."

But there was not a tear in her eye. Wrapping the blanket tightly about her, with the calmness of despair she prepared to step from the cell at the call of the impatient jailer.

A great commotion in the streets. The noise of horse's hoofs. A din of voices; then a wild cheer.

Dr. Ricketts dashed in, flourishing a paper in his hand.

"She is pardoned! pardoned!" he shouted; "go back! take her back!" he said as the jailer laid his hand upon Mary. "See this!" and he flung the paper open in his face.

The long agony was over, and the reaction was so great that Mary Fngle, hardly conscious of the good thing that had happened to her, and not fully realizing the events by which her innocence was proved, stood stupefied and bewil-

dered. Then she felt faint, and laying her upon the low bed, they told her all the story; and when the doctor said that Tom was not a guilty man, she turned her face to the wall to hide the blinding tears, and she muttered:

"Thank God! thank God for that!"

As she came out of the prison doors, leaning on the doctor's arm, the crowd, now largely increased, hailed her with a hurrah, but Mary drew her veil over her face and shuddered as she thought how these very people had assembled to see her flogged.

19 *

"It is my theory, my dear," said the doctor, "that human beings are equally glad when their fellow-creatures get into trouble and when they get out of it."

Back once again in her old home, Mary was besieged by friends whose regard had suddenly assumed a violent form, and who were now eager to congratulate her upon her vindication.

Tom Willitts came to the door and inquired for Mrs. Engle.

"Can I come in now?" he inquired, with a glow upon his face.

He did go in, and there, before them all, he clasped Mary in his arms, while she begged him to forgive her for all the suffering she had caused him.

But Tom wanted to be forgiven, too; and as both confessed guilt, repentance and an earnest wish to be merciful, they were soon better friends than ever.

"I used to love you," said Tom, "but now I worship you for your heroism and your sacrifice for me."

There was another visitor. Old Major Newton entered the room, hat in hand, and with bowed head. The lines in his face were deeper and harder than usual, but he looked broken and sad.

He went up to Mary and said as he stood before her with downcast eyes:

"I have come to ask pardon for my brutality and cruelty. The injury I did to you I can never atone for. I shall carry my remorse to the grave. But if you have any word of pity for an old man whose son has fled from home a scoundrel and a villain, and who stands before you broken-hearted, ready to kiss your feet for your angelic goodness and your noble self-sacrifice, say it, that I may at least have that comfort in my desolation."

And Mary took the old man's hard hands in hers and

spoke kind and gentle words to him; and with tears coursing down his rough cheeks, he kissed her dainty fingers and went out, and back to his forlorn and wretched home.

There was another Christmas night a few months later, and this time the merry-making was going on in the Willitts mansion. There were two brides there. Mary and Tom Willitts were busy helping the children with their Christmas games, and keeping up the excitement as if no sorrow had ever come across their path; while seated at the upper end of the room, Dr. Ricketts and his wife (Mrs. Engle that had been), looking upon the younger pair with pride and pleasure, touched only now and then with a sad memory of the troubled times that were gone by for ever.

And when the games were all in full progress, Tom and his wife watched them for a while, and then he drew her arm through his, and they went to the porch and looked out upon the river beating up against the ice-bound shore, just as it did on that night one year ago. But it had a different language to Mary's ears now. It was full of music, but music that seemed in a minor key, as the remembrance of that wild flight along the shore came up vividly in her mind.

Neither spoke for a while, but each knew that the thoughts of the other went over all the misery and terror of the past, only to rest satisfied with the calm, sweet happiness of the present. Mary, clasping her husband's arm tighter in her grasp, looked with unconscious eyes out over the broad river, while her lips slowly repeated that grand old hymn of comfort and hope:

"There is a day of peace and rest
    For sorrow's dark and dreary night;
Though grief may bide an evening guest,
    Yet joy shall come with morning light.

"The light of smiles shall beam again
    From lids that now o'erflow with tears,
And weary days of woe and pain
    Are earnests of serener years."

CHAPTER XV.

AST evening, after waiting until eleven o'clock for Mr. Parker to come home, I went to bed. I had hardly composed myself for slumber when I thought I heard the door-bell ring; and supposing Bob had forgotten his latch-key, I descended for the purpose of letting him in. When I opened the door, no one was upon the porch; and although I was dressed simply in a night-shirt, I stepped out just beyond the doorway for the purpose of ascertaining if I could see any one who might have pulled the bell. Just as I did so the wind banged the door shut, and as it closed it caught a portion of my raiment which was fluttering about, and held it fast. I was somewhat amused at first, and I laughed as I tried to pull the muslin from the door; but after making very violent exertion for that purpose, I discovered that the material would not slip through. The garment was held so firmly that it could not possibly be re-

moved. Then I determined to reach over to the other side of the doorway and pull the bell, in the hope that some one would hear it and come to my assistance. But to my dismay I found that the doorway was so wide that even with the most desperate effort I could not succeed in touching the bell-knob with the tips of my fingers.

Meantime, I was beginning to freeze, for the night was very cold, and my legs and feet were wholly unprotected.

At last a happy thought struck me. I might very easily creep out of the shirt and leave it hanging in the door until I rang the bell, and then I could slip back again and await the result. Accordingly, I began to withdraw from the garment, and I had just freed myself from it and was about to pull the bell when I heard some one coming down the street. As the moon was shining brightly, I became panic-stricken,

and hurried into the garment again. In my confusion I got

it on backward, and found myself with my face to the wall; and then the person who was coming turned down the street

just above my house, and didn't pass, after all.

I was afraid to try the experiment again, and I determined to shout for help. I uttered one cry, and waited for a response. It was a desperately cold night. I think the air must have been colder than it ever was before in the history of this continent. I stamped my feet in order to keep the blood in circulation, and then I shouted again for assistance. The river lay white and glistening in the light of the moon, and so clear was the atmosphere, so lustrous the radiance of the orb above, that I could plainly distinguish the dark line of the Jersey shore. It was a magnificent spectacle, and I should have enjoyed it intensely if I had had my clothing on. Then I began to think how very odd it was that a man's appreciation of the glorious majesty of nature should be dependent upon his trousers! how strange it was that cold legs should prevent an immortal soul from having felicity! Man is always prosaic when he is uncomfortable. Even a slight

indigestion is utterly destructive of sentiment. I defy any man to enjoy the fruitiest poetry while his corns hurt him, or to feel a genuine impulse of affection while he has a severe cold in his head.

Then I cried aloud again for help, and an immediate response came from Cooley's new dog, which leaped over the fence and behaved as if it meditated an assault upon my

defenceless calves. I was relieved from this dreadful situation by Bob, who came up the street whistling and singing in an especially joyous manner. He was a little frightened, I think, when he saw a figure in white upon the porch, and he paused for a moment before opening the gate, but he entered when I called to him; and unlocking the door with his key, he released me, and went up stairs laughing heartily at my mishap.

I was about to retire when I heard a series of extraordinary sounds in Bob's room overhead, and I thought it worth while to go up and ascertain what was going on. Standing outside the door, I could hear Bob chuckling and making use of such exclamations as,

"Bul-l-*e-e-e!* Ha! ha! All right, my boy! All right! You've fixed that, I guess! Bul-l-*e-e-e-e!*"

Then he seemed to be executing a hornpipe in his stockings upon the carpet; and when this exercise was concluded, he continued the conversation with himself in such tones as these:

"How *are* you, Smiley! No chance, hadn't I? Couldn't make it, couldn't I? I know a thing or two, I reckon. How *are* you, Lieutenant Smil-*c-c-c-c!* Ha! ha! I've settled your case, I guess, my boy! Bully for you, Parker! You've straightened that out, anyhow. Yes, sir! Ha! ha! Fol de rol de rol de rol," etc., etc. (second performance of the hornpipe, accompanied by whistling and new expressions of intense satisfaction).

I went down stairs with a solemn conviction that Mr.

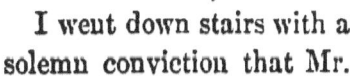

Parker had explained himself to Miss Magruder, and had received an answer from her that was wholly satisfactory. I did not reveal the secret to Mrs. Adeler, concluding that it would be better to permit Bob to do that himself in the morning.

Parker rose about two hours earlier than usual, and I entertain a suspicion that he expended a portion of the time in going down the street to examine the exterior of Mr. Magruder's house. It probably gave him some satisfaction merely to view the tenement wherein his fair enslaver reposed. He came to the breakfast-table with a radiant countenance, and it was evident that he would be unable to contain the news for many moments longer. In order to prepare the way for him, I asked him:

"Why were you so late last night, Bob?"

"Oh, I had some important business on hand. Big things have been happening ; I have some news to tell you."

"Another railroad accident?" I asked, carelessly, "or a riot in Philadelphia?"

"Riot? no! Thunder!" exclaimed Bob; "nothing of that kind. It's something more important. You know old Smiley—Fiji Island Smiley? Well, I've floored him; I've laid him out flat; I've knocked him into diminutive smith-ereens."

"Had a personal encounter with the lieutenant?" I asked, gravely.

"No, *sir!* better than that. I've cut him out down at Magruder's. Bessie and I are engaged! What do you think of that, Max?"

"Think of it? Why, I congratulate you heartily. You have secured a treasure."

"And I congratulate you, too," said Mrs. A. "Bessie is a very fine girl, and will make you a good wife."

"That's what I think about it," observed Mr. Parker.

"I am very glad Lieutenant Smiley didn't succeed there," said Mrs. A.

"Smiley! Smiley!" exclaimed Bob, scornfully. "Why, he never had the ghost of a chance. Bessie told me last night she despised him. She wouldn't look at such a man as he is."

"Not while such men as you are around, at any rate, I suppose?"

"When are you going to speak to Bessie's father?" asked Mrs. Adeler.

A cloud suddenly passed over Bob's face, and he said:

"I don't know. I have to do it, I s'pose, but I hate it worse than I can tell you. I believe I'd rather propose to a woman a dozen times than to broach the matter to a stern parent once. It's all well enough to express your feelings

to a woman who loves you; but when you come to explain
the matter to a cold-blooded, matter-of-fact old man who is
as prosy as a boiled turnip, it seems kind of ridiculous."

"Why don't you speak to Mrs. Dr. Magruder, then? She
is a power in that family."

"No; I'll talk to Mr. Magruder. It's hard, but it has to
be done. And see here, Max, don't you poke fun at Mrs.
Magruder. She's a first-rate woman, and those things Dr.
Jones told about her are the most rascally kind of lies. If
you'll excuse me, I'll go down and see the old man now. I
might as well settle the thing at once."

This evening, while we were waiting for tea, Bob made a
report. The paternal Magruder, it seems, had already considered the subject carefully, and was not by any means as
much surprised by Mr. Parker's statement as the latter expected he would be. Bob was amazed to find that although
the old gentleman during the courtship had appeared wholly
unconscious of the fact that his daughter was particularly
intimate with the youth, yet somehow he seemed now to
have had all the time a very clear perception of the state of
the case.

"I thought he would get excited and, maybe, show a little emotion," said Bob, "but blame me if he didn't sit there
and take it as coolly as if such things happened to him every
day. And you know, when I began to tell him how much I
thought of Bessie, he soused down on me and brought me
back to prose with a question about the size of my income.
But it's all right. He said he would be glad to have me a
member of his family, and then he called in Bessie, and gave
us a kind of a blessing and advised us not to be in a hurry
about getting married."

"Very good advice, too. There is no need of haste.
You ought to have plenty of time to think the matter
over."

"Think it over!" exclaimed Bob, indignantly. "Why, I *have* thought it over. You don't suppose I'd be such a fool as to engage myself to a girl without thinking seriously about it?"

"Certainly not; but marriage is a very solemn thing, and it should be undertaken advisedly. It is probable, I suppose, that you would never, under any circumstances, marry any woman but Bessie Magruder?"

"Nev-er; no, never!"

"You don't believe in second marriages, then?"

"Certainly not."

"They *do* get a man into trouble very often. Did I ever tell you about old Sparks, of Pencadder Hundred?"

"I think not," said Bob.

"Well, old Sparks was married four times; and several years after the death of his last wife they started a new cemetery up there at Pencadder. Sparks bought a lot, and determined to remove his sacred dust from the old graveyard.

Somehow or other, in taking the remains over to the cemetery in the wagon, they were hopelessly mixed together, so that it was utterly impossible to tell which was which. Any other man than Sparks would simply have taken the chances of having the reinterments properly made. But he was an extremely conscientious man; and when the sepulture was completed, he had a lot of new headstones set in, bearing such inscriptions as these: 'Here lies Jane (and probably part of Susan) Sparks;' 'Sacred to the memory of Maria (to say nothing of Jane and Hannah) Sparks.'

> "'Stranger, pause and drop a tear,
> For Susan Sparks lies buried here;
> Mingled, in some perplexing manner,
> With Jane, Maria and portions of Hannah.'"

"Don't it seem a little bit rough," said Bob, "to bring in such a story as that in connection with my engagement? I don't like it."

"Pardon me, Bob. Perhaps it was neither gracious nor in good taste, but somehow I just happened to think of old Sparks at that moment. I am sure, though, you won't object to another narrative which I am going to read to you upon the subject of too frequent marriage. It is the story of Bishop Potts. Do you feel like hearing it?"

"Well, no," said Bob, gloomily, "to tell you the truth, I don't; but I suppose I will have to hear it, so go ahead."

"Yes, I am going to inflict it upon you whether you want it or not. A man who is meditating matrimony, and is in a hurry, needs the influence of a few 'awful examples' to induce him to proceed slowly. Here is the story. The hero was a dignitary in the Mormon Church, and his sufferings were the result of excessive marriage. The tale is entitled

"BISHOP POTTS.

"Bishop Potts, of Salt Lake City, was the husband of three wives and the father of fifteen interesting children.

20 *

Early in the winter the bishop determined that his little ones should
have a good time on Christmas, so
he concluded to take a trip down
to San Francisco to see what he
could find in the shape of toys with
which to gratify and amuse them.
The good bishop packed his carpet-
bag, embraced Mrs. Potts one by one
and kissed each of her affectionately,
and started upon his journey.

"He was gone a little more than
a week, when he came back with
fifteen brass trumpets in his valise
for his darlings. He got out of the train at Salt Lake,
thinking how joyous it would be at home on Christmas
morning when the fifteen trumpets should be in operation
upon different tunes at the same moment. But just as he
entered the dépôt he saw a group of women standing in the

ladies' room apparently waiting for him. As soon as he
approached, the whole twenty
of them rushed up, threw
their arms about his neck
and kissed him, exclaiming:

"'Oh, Theodore, we are
so, so glad you have come
back! Welcome home!
Welcome, dear Theodore, to
the bosom of your family!'
and then the entire score of
them fell upon his neck and
cried over his shirt front and
mussed him.

" The bishop seemed surprised and embarrassed. Struggling to disengage himself, he blushed and said :

" ' Really, ladies, this kind of thing is well enough—it is interesting and all that; but there must be some kind of a —that is, an awkward sort of a—excuse me, ladies, but there seems to be, as it were, a slight misunderstanding about the—I am Bishop Potts.'

" ' We know it, we know it, dear,' they exclaimed, in chorus, ' and we are glad to see you safe at home. We have all been very well while you were away, love.'

" ' It gratifies me,' remarked the bishop, ' to learn that none of you have been a prey to disease. I am filled with serenity when I contemplate the fact; but really, I do not understand why you should rush into this railway station and hug me because your livers are active and your digestion good. The precedent is bad; it is dangerous !'

" ' Oh, but we didn't !' they exclaimed, in chorus. ' We came here to welcome you because you are our husband.'

" ' Pardon me, but there must be some little—that is to say, as it were, I should think not. Women, you have mistaken your man !'

" ' Oh no !' they shouted; ' we were married to you while you were away !'

" ' What !' exclaimed the bishop; 'you don't mean to say that—'

" ' Yes, love. Our husband, William Brown, died on Monday, and on Thursday, Brigham had a vision in which he was directed to seal us to you ; and so he performed the ceremony at once by proxy.'

" ' Th-th-th-th-under !' observed the bishop.

"'And we are all living with you now—we and the dear children.'

"'Children! children!' exclaimed Bishop Potts, turning pale; 'you don't mean to say that there is a pack of children, too?'

"'Yes, love, but only one hundred and twenty-five, not counting the eight twins and the triplet.'

"'Wha-wha-wha-what d'you say?' gasped the bishop, in a cold perspiration; 'one hundred and twenty-five! One hundred and twenty-five children and twenty more wives! It is too much—it is awful!' and the bishop sat down and groaned, while the late Mrs. Brown, the bride, stood around in a semicircle and fanned him with her bonnets, all except the red-haired one, and she in her trepidation made a futile effort to fan him with the coal-scuttle.

"But after a while the bishop became reconciled to his new alliance, knowing well that protests would be unavailing, so he walked home, holding several of the little hands of the bride, while the red-haired woman carried his umbrella

and marched in front of the parade to remove obstructions and to scare off small boys.

"When the bishop reached the house, he went around among the cradles which filled the back parlor and the two second-story rooms, and attempted with such earnestness to become acquainted with his new sons and daughters that he set the whole one hundred and twenty-five and the twins to crying, while his own original fifteen stood around and swelled the volume of sound. Then the bishop went out

and sat on the garden fence to whittle a stick
and solemnly think, while Mrs. Potts distrib-
uted herself around and soothed the children.
It occurred to the bishop while he mused, out
there on the fence, that he had not enough
trumpets to go around among the children as the family
now stood; and so, rather than seem to be partial, he determined to go back to San Francisco for one hundred and
forty-four more.

"So the bishop repacked his carpet-bag, and began again
to bid farewell to his family. He tenderly kissed all of the
Mrs. Potts who were at home, and started for the dépôt,
while Mrs. Potts stood at the various windows and waved
her handkerchiefs at him—all
except the woman with the
warm hair, and she, in a fit
of absent-mindedness, held one
of the twins by the leg and
brandished it at Potts as he
fled down the street toward the
railway station.

"The bishop reached San
Francisco, completed his purchases, and was just about to
get on the train with his one
hundred and forty-four trum-
pets, when a telegram was handed him. It contained information to the effect that the auburn-haired Mrs. Potts
had just had a daughter. This induced the bishop to
return to the city for the purpose of purchasing an additional trumpet.

"On the following Saturday he returned home. As he
approached his house a swarm of young children flew out
of the front gate and ran toward him, shouting, 'There's pa!

Here comes pa! Oh, pa, but we're glad to see you! Hurrah for pa!' etc., etc.

"The bishop looked at the children as they flocked around him and clung to his legs and coat, and was astonished to perceive that they were neither his nor the late Brown's. He said, 'You youngsters have made a mistake; I am not your father;' and the bishop smiled good-naturedly.

"'Oh yes, you are, though!' screamed the little ones, in chorus.

"'But I say I am not,' said the bishop, severely, and frowning; 'you ought to be ashamed of yourselves. Don't you know where little story-tellers go? It is scandalous for you to violate the truth in this manner. My name is Potts.'

"'Yes, we know it is,' exclaimed the children—'we know it is, and so is ours; that is our name now, too, since the wedding.'

"'Since what wedding?' demanded the bishop, turning pale.

"'Why, ma's wedding, of course. She was married yesterday to you by Mr. Young, and we are all living at your house now with our new little brothers and sisters.'

"The bishop sat down on the nearest front-door step and wiped away a tear. Then he asked,

"'Who was your father?'

"'Mr. Simpson,' said the crowd, 'and he died on Tuesday.'

· "'And how many of his infernal old widows—I mean how many of your mother—are there?'

"'Only twenty-seven,' replied the children, 'and there are only sixty-four of us, and we are awful glad you have come home.'

"The bishop did not seem to be unusually glad; somehow, he failed to share the enthusiasm of the occasion. There appeared to be, in a certain sense, too much sameness about these surprises; so he sat there with his hat pulled over his eyes and considered the situation. Finally, seeing there was no help for it, he went up to the house, and forty-eight of Mrs. Potts rushed up to him and told him how the prophet had another vision, in which he was commanded to seal Simpson's widow to Potts.

"Then the bishop stumbled around among the cradles to his writing-desk. He felt among the gum rings and rattles for his letter-paper, and then he addressed a note to Brigham, asking him as a personal favor to keep awake until after Christmas. 'The man must take me for a foundling hospi tal,' he said. Then the bishop saw clearly enough that if he

 gave presents to the other children, and not to the late Simpson's, the bride would make things warm for him. So he started again for San Francisco for sixty-four more trumpets, while Mrs. Potts gradually took leave of him in the entry— all but the red-haired woman, who was up stairs, and who had to be satisfied with screeching good-bye at the top of her voice.

"On his way home, after his last visit to San Francisco, the bishop sat in the car by the side of a man who had left Salt Lake the day before. The stranger was communicative. In the course of the conversation he remarked to the bishop:

"'That was a mighty pretty little affair up there at the city on Monday.'

"'What affair?' asked Potts.

"'Why, that wedding; McGrath's widow, you know—married by proxy.'

"'You don't say?' replied the bishop. 'I didn't know McGrath was dead.'

"'Yes; died on Sunday, and that night Brigham had a vision in which he was ordered to seal her to the bishop.'

"'Bishop!' exclaimed Potts. 'Bishop! What bishop?'

"'Well, you see, there were fifteen of Mrs. McGrath and eighty-two children, and they shoved the whole lot off on old Potts. Perhaps you don't know him?'

The bishop gave a wild shriek and writhed upon the floor as if he had a fit. When he recovered, he leaped from the train and walked back to San Francisco. He afterward took the first steamer for Peru, where he entered a monastery and became a celibate.

" His carpet-bag was sent on to his family. It contained the balance of the trumpets. On Christmas morning they were distributed, and in less than an hour the entire two hundred and eight children were sick from sucking the brass upon them. A doctor was called, and he seemed so much interested in the family that Brigham divorced the whole concern from old Potts and annexed it to the doctor, who immediately lost his reason, and would have butchered the entire family if the red-haired woman and the oldest boy had not marched him off to a lunatic asylum, where he spent his time trying to arrive at an estimate of the number of his children by ciphering with an impossible combination of the multiplication table and algebra."

" And now that that's over," said Bob, as I folded up the manuscript, " will you please to tell me what the suffering of old Potts has to do with my engagement?"

" Well, to tell the truth, nothing in particular, I thought

21

perhaps you might feel a sort of general interest in the mere subject of matrimony just now; and at any rate, I wanted your opinion of the merit of the story."

"Well, I think it is a pretty poor story. The humor of

the Mormon business is stale, anyhow, and in your hands it becomes absolutely dismal. I can write a better Mormon story than that myself, and I don't even profess to be a scribbler."

Then Mr. Parker swaggered out with the air of a man whose opinions have the weight of a judicial decision. I think he has acquired, since his engagement, a much greater notion of his importance than he had before. It is remarkable how a youth who has succeeded in a love affair immediately begins to cherish the idea that his victory is attributable to the fact that he possesses particularly brilliant qualities of some kind. Bob was the humblest man in Delaware a week ago; to-day he walks about with such an air as he might have had if he had just won the battle of Waterloo.

CHAPTER XVI.

HEN the people of our village are in the mood to reflect upon antiquity, when they feel as if they would like to meditate upon the heroic deeds that have been achieved in this kindly old place by the mighty men of valor who swaggered and swore and fought here a hundred years before the war of the Revolution was dreamed of, they turn from the street down the gentle slope of the highway which runs by the river; and when they have wandered on a brief distance beyond the present confines of the town, they reach old Fort Lane. It is but a little stretch of greensward, gashed by the wheels of vehicles and trodden by the feet of wayfarers. It extends from the road eastward for a hundred yards, and then it dips downward and ends upon the sandy beach of the stream. Here, right upon the edge of the water.

once stood brave old Fort Kasimir, with its guns threatening destruction not only to unfriendly vessels which sailed up the bay, but absolutely menacing the very town itself. The village then was called New Stockholm. That was the name given to it by the Swedes, who perceived what a superb site for a city lay here, and who went to work and built a swarm of snug wooden houses. It has had half a dozen other names since. When the Dutchmen conquered it, they dubbed it Sandhoec, then New Amstel and then Fort Kasimir. Afterward it was known as Grape Wine Point, then as Delaware-town and finally as New Castle. But twenty years after the Swedes had settled here, the Dutchmen at New York coveted the place and the command of the river; and as an earnest of what they intended to do, they came right here under the very noses of the villagers and built Fort Kasimir.

I can imagine how the old Swedes in the village stood over there on the Battery and glowered at the Dutchmen as they labored upon the fort; and it is not difficult to conceive the terror and dismay that filled those humble little homes in New Stockholm when the intruder placed his queer brass cannon in the embrasures of the fort after its completion, and when he would hurl a ball across the bows of a Swedish ship coming up to the town, or would send a shot whistling over the roofs of the village itself merely to gratify a grim humor. I would give a great deal, Mrs. Adeler, to have but one day of that distant past recalled; to see New Stockholm and its people as they were; to watch the Dutch chieftain and his handful of men parading about in the fort in the panoply of war, and boasting of the prowess that dared thus to defy the enemy upon his own threshold. But, alas! look! not one vestige of the ancient battlements remains. The grass has grown over the spot whereon they stood, and the rolling river has long since buried beneath the sand of its shores whatever timbers of the structure touched its waters.

THE SITE OF FORT KASIMIR.

It would have been forgotten, perhaps, but that Irving, with the humorous pen which traced the history of the Knickerbockers, has given it immortality in the lines that tell how the exasperated Swedes seized the fort and held the Dutchmen prisoners, and how, when the news came to Manhattan island, the Dutch sent forth a valiant army, which not only retook the fortress, but carried away nearly all the villagers.

There was wild lamentation in the little community upon that day as the unhappy people were torn from their homes and sent into exile; and though the historian tells his tale sportively, the story always seemed to me to be full of pathos.

This place was thronged with strange figures, and it witnessed some very sad scenes in that far-off time. And if the traditions of the neighborhood may be believed, those tough old warriors even yet have not bid farewell for ever to the spot. There is no more fighting here, unless when some of the village urchins come out to have a tussle upon the sward, and the chimneys of the town are unmolested by hostile shot. But they do say that sometimes we may look upon the shadowy outline of the ancient Hollanders who made this their battleground. The venturesome wight who comes to old Fort Lane at certain seasons after nightfall may see headless Dutchmen in strange and ghostly  attire marching up and down the shore, and he may hear the cry of sentinels, uttered in an unknown tongue, borne past him on the wind. There are those who have listened to the noise of cannon balls rolling in the dusk over floors which no mortal eye can ever see, and often, when there

is a tempest, the booming of guns will be heard above the roar of the storm, and from spectral ships floating upon the bosom of the river will come the wailing voices of women and children who are still sorrowing for their lost homes.

I do not say that this is so, Mrs. Adeler; I merely assert the existence of a popular theory to that effect. I have private doubts if the goblin Dutchmen ever have been seen, and I know of no reason why, if a ghost of that kind really comes back to earth, he should return without his head.

Judge Pitman has a field that is bounded upon one side by the lane, and in this enclosure we found, upon our visit to the historic spot, a meditative cow with a blindboard upon her forehead. There was nothing especially remarkable about the board, and yet it has caused a great deal of trouble. In a recent interview with me the judge sought to console himself for the misery created by that blindboard by relating the story of his sorrow.

"Adeler," he said, "you know I j'ined the temp'rance society a couple o' months ago, not because I was much

afeared of gittin' drunk often, but just to please the old
woman. You know how women
are—kinder insane on the subject
of drinkin'. Well, my cow had
a way o' jumpin' the fence, an' I
couldn't do nothin' to stop her.
She was the ornariest critter that
way that I ever see. So at last I
got a blind-board an' hung it on
her horns. That stopped her.

But you know she used to come jam up agin' the fence an'
stand there for hours; an' one day one o' them vagabone
advertisin' agents come along—one o' them fellers that daubs
signs all over the face of natur'—an' as soon as he seen that
blind-board he went for it."

" A patent medicine man, I suppose ?"
" No, he was advertisin' some kind o' stomach bitters; and

he painted on that board the follerin': ' *Take Brown s Bitters for your Stomach's Sake. They make the Best Cocktails.'* "

"The temperance society didn't like that, of course ?"

"No, *sir!*   The secretary happened to see it, and he brought out the board of directors; and the fust thing I knowed, they hauled me up an' wanted to expel me for circulatin' scand'lous information respectin' bitters an' cocktails."

"That was very unjust."

"Well, sir, I had the hardest time to make them fellers understand that I was innercent, an' to git 'em to let up on me. But they did. Then I turned the blind-board over; and now the first man I ketch placin' any revolutionary sentiments on the frontispiece of that cow, why, down goes his house; I'll knock the stuffin' out o' him; now mind *me!*"

"I am usually not in favor of resort to violence, judge; but I must say that under the circumstances even such severity would be perfectly justifiable."

"This bitters business is kinder fraudulent anyway," continued the judge, meditatively. "I once had a very cur'ous experience drinkin' that stuff. Last winter I read in one of the papers an advertisement which said— But hold on; I'll read it to you. I've got 'em all. I kep' 'em as a cur'osity. Let's see; where d' I put them things? Ah! yes; here they are;" and the judge produced some newspaper cuttings from his pocketbook. "Well, sir, I read in the *Argus* this parergraph:

" 'The excessive moisture and the extreme cold and continuous dampness of winter are peculiarly deleterious to the human system, and colds, consumption and death are very apt to ensue unless the body is braced by some stimulating tonic such as Blank's Bitters, which give tone to the stomach, purify the blood, promote digestion and increase the appetite. The Bitters are purely medicinal, and they contain no intoxicating element.'

"I'd been kinder oneasy the winter afore about my health, and this skeered me. So I drank them Bitters all through the cold weather; an' when spring come, I was just about to knock off an' begin agin on water, when I was wuss frightened than ever to see in the *Argus* the followin':

" 'The sudden changes of temperature which are characteristic of the spring, and the enervating influence of the increased heat, make the season one of peculiar danger to the human system, so that ague, fever and diseases resulting from impurities clogging the circulation of the blood can only be avoided by giving tone to the stomach and increasing the powers of that organ by a liberal use of Blank's Bitters.'

"I thought there wa'n't no use takin' any risks, so I begun agin; but I made up my mind to stop drinkin' when summer come an' danger was over."

"Your confidence in those advertisements, judge, was something wonderful."

"Jes so. Well, about the fust of June, while I was a-finishin' the last bottle I had, I seen in the *Argus* this one. Jes lissen to this:

"'The violent heat of summer debilitates and weakens the human system so completely that, more easily than at any other time, it becomes a prey to the insidious diseases which prevail during what may fairly be called the sickly season. The sacrifice of human life during this dangerous period would be absolutely frightful had not Nature and Art offered a sure preventive in Blank's Bitters, which give tone to the stomach,' etc., etc.

"This seemed like such a solemn warnin' that I hated to let it go; an' so I bought a dozen more bottles an' took

another turn. I begun to think that some mistake 'd been made in gittin' up a climate for this yer country, and it did seem astonishin' that Blank should be the only man who knew how to correct the error.

Howsomdever, I determined to quit in the fall, when the sickly season was over, an' I was jes gittin' ready to quit when the *Argus* published another one of them notices. Here it is:

"'The miasmatic vapors with which the atmosphere is filled during the fall of the year break down the human system and destroy life with a frightful celerity which is characteristic of no other season, unless the stomach is strengthened by constant use of Blank's Bitters, which are a sure preventive of disease,' etc., etc.

"But they didn't fool me that time. No, sir. I took the chances with those asthmatic vapors, and let old Blank rip. I j'ined the temperance society, an' here I am, hearty as a buck."

"You look extremely well."

"But, Adeler, I never bore no grudge agin the bitters men for lyin' until they spread their owdacious falsehoods on the blind-board of my cow. Then it did 'pear 's if they was crowdin' me too hard."

"Judge, did you ever try to convert Cooley to temperance principles? It seems to me that he would be a good subject to work upon."

"Well, no; I never said nothin' to him on the subject. I'm not a very good hand at convertin' people; but I s'pose I ought ter tackle Cooley too. He's bin a-carryin' on scan-d'lus lately, so I hear."

"Indeed! I hadn't heard of it."

"Yes, sir; comin' home o' nights with a load on, an' a-snortin' at that poor little wife of his'n. By gracious, it's rough, isn't it? An' Mrs. Cooley was tellin' my old woman that some of them fellers rubbed Cooley's nose the other night with phosphorous while he was asleep down at the tavern; an' when he went home, it 'peared 's if he had a locomotive headlight in front of him."

"A very extraordinary proceeding, judge."

"Well, sir, when he got in the hall it was dark, an' he ketched a sight o' that nose in the lookin'-glass

on the hat-rack, an' he thought Mrs. Cooley had left the gas burnin'. Then he tried to turn it off, an' after fumblin' around among the umbrellers an' hat-pegs for a while for the stop-cock, he concluded the light must come from a candle, an' he nearly bu'sted his lungs tryin' to blow it out. Then he grabbed his hat an' tried to jam her down over that candle; an' when he found he couldn't, he got mad, picked up an um-breller an' hit a whack at it, which broke the lookin'-glass all to flinders; an' there was Mrs. Cooley a-watchin' that old lunatick all the time, an' afraid to tell him it was his own nose. I tell you, Adeler, this yer rum drinkin' 's a fearful thing any way you take it, now, ain't it?"

I am glad to say that the *Argus* has been fully repaid for its attempts to beguile the judge into the use of bitters. The *Argus* is in complete disgrace with all the people who attend our church. Some of the admirers of Rev. Dr. Hopkins, the clergyman, gave ñim a gold-headed cane a few days ago, and a reporter of the *Argus* was invited to be present. Nobody knows whether the reporter was temporarily insane, or whether the foreman, in giving out the "copy," mixed it accidentally with an account of a patent hog-killing machine which was tried in Wilmington on that same day, but the appalling result was that the *Argus* next morning contained this somewhat obscure but very dreadful narrative:

"Several of Rev. Dr. Hopkins's friends called upon him yesterday, and after a brief conversation the unsuspicious hog was seized by the hind legs and slid along a beam until he reached the hot-water tank. His friends explained the object of their visit, and presented him with a very handsome gold-headed butcher, who grabbed him by the tail, swung him around, slit his throat from ear to ear, and in less than a minute the carcass was in the water. Thereupon he came forward and said that there were times when the feelings overpowered one, and for that reason he would not attempt to do more than thank those around him, for the manner in which such a huge animal was cut into fragments was simply astonishing. The doctor concluded his remarks, when the machine seized him, and in less time than it takes to write it the hog was cut into fragments and worked up into delicious sausage. The occasion will long be remembered by the doctor's friends as one of the most delightful of their lives. The best pieces can be procured for fifteen cents a pound; and we are sure that those who have sat so long under his ministry will rejoice that he has been treated so handsomely."

The *Argus* lost at least sixty subscribers in consequence of this misfortune, and on the following Sunday we had a very able and very energetic sermon from Dr. Hopkins upon "The Evil Influence of a Debauched Public Press." It would have made Colonel Bangs shiver to have heard that discourse. Lieutenant Smiley came home with us after church, and I am sorry to say he exulted over the sturdy blows given to the colonel.

"I haven't any particular grudge against the man," he said, "but I don't think he has treated me exactly fair. I sent him an article last Tuesday, and he actually had the insolence to return me the manuscript without offering a word of explanation."

"To what did the article refer?"

"Why, it gave an account of a very singular thing that happened to a friend of mine, the son of old Commodore

Watson. Once, when the commodore was about to go upon a voyage, he had a presentiment that something would occur

to him, and he made a will leaving his son Archibald all his property on condition that, in case of his death, Archibald would visit his tomb and pray at it once every year. Archibald made a solemn vow that he would, and the commodore started upon his journey. Well, sir, the fleet went to the Fiji Islands, and while there the old man came ashore one day, and was captured by the natives. They stripped him, laid him upon a gridiron, cooked him and ate him."

"That placed Archibald in a somewhat peculiar position?"

"Imagine his feelings when he heard the news! How could he perform his vow? How could he pray at the commodore's tomb? Would not the tomb, as it were, be very apt to prey upon him, to snatch him up and assimilate him? There seemed to be an imminent probability that it would

But he went. That noble-hearted young man went out to the islands in search of the savage that ate the commodore, and I have no doubt that he suffered upon the same gridiron."*

"You don't mean to say that Bangs declined to publish that narrative?"

"He did, and he offered no explanation of his refusal."

"He is certainly a very incompetent person to conduct a newspaper. A man who would refuse to give such

* I have reasons for believing that Smiley did not construct this story. I remember having seen it in a French newspaper long before I met the lieutenant, and I am sure he borrowed it from that or some other publication.

a story to a world which aches for amusement is worse than a blockhead."

"By the way," said the lieutenant, changing the subject suddenly, "I hear Parker has taken a class in the Sunday-school. He is sly—monstrous sly, sir. Miss Magruder teaches there, too. Parker seems to be determined to have

her, and I hope he may be successful, but I don't think he will be, I'm sorry to say."

It was evident that Smiley had not heard the news, and I did not enlighten him.

"Some men have a fitness for that kind of work, and some haven't. There was poor Bergner, a friend of mine. He took a class in a Sunday-school at Carlisle while we were stationed there. The first Sunday he told the scholars a story about a boy named Simms. Simms, he said, had climbed a tree for the purpose of stealing apples, and he fell and killed himself. 'This,' said Bergner, 'conveys an impressive warning to the young. It teaches an instructive lesson which I hope will be heeded by all you boys. Bear in mind that if Simms had not gone into that tree he would probably now be alive and well, and he might have grown up to be a useful member of society. Remember this, boys,' said Bergner, 'and resolve firmly now that when you wish to steal apples you will do so in the only safe way, which is to stand on the ground and knock them down with a pole.' A healthy moral lesson, wasn't it? Somebody told the su-

pcrintendent about it, and they asked Berguer to resign.
Yes, a man has to have a peculiar turn for that kind of
thing to succeed in teaching Sunday-school. I
don't know how Parker will make out."
   Then the lieutenant shook hands and left in
order to catch the last boat for the fort.
   "Mrs. Adeler," I said, as I lighted a fresh
cigar, "we may regard it as a particularly fortunate thing that Smiley is not entrusted with the religious
education of any number of American youth. Place the
Sunday-schools of this land in the hands of Smiley and
others like him, and in the next generation the country
would be overrun with a race of liars."

   I am not aware that Bob Parker has ever made any very
serious attempt to write poetry for the public. Of course
since he has been in love with the bewildering Magruder he
has sometimes expressed his feelings in verse. But fortunately these breathings of passion were not presented to a cold
and heartless world; they were reserved for the sympathetic
Magruder, who doubtless read them with delight and admiration, and locked them up in her writing-desk with Bob's letters
and other precious souvenirs. This, of course, is all right.
Every lover writes what he considers poetry, and society
permits such manifestations without insisting upon the con-
finement of the offenders in lunatic asylums. Bob, however,
has constructed some verses which are not of a sentimental
kind. Judge Pitman's story of the illumination of Cooley's
nose suggested the idea which Bob has worked into rhyme
and published in the *Argus*. As the poet has not been permitted to shine to any great extent in these pages as a
literary person, it will perhaps be fair to reproduce his
poem in the chapter which contains the account of Cooley's
misfortune. Here it is:

   22 *

TIM KEYSER'S NOSE.

TIM KEYSER lived in Wilmington;
 He had a monstrous nose,
Which was a great deal redder than
 The very reddest rose,
And was completely capable
 Of most terrific blows.

He wandered down one Christmas day
 To skate upon the creek,
And there, upon the smoothest ice,
 He slid around so quick
That people were amazed to see
 Him do it up so slick.

The exercise excited thirst;
  And so, to get a drink,
He cut an opening in the ice
  And lay down on the brink.
He said, "I'll dip my lips right in
  And suck it up, I think."

And while his nose was thus immersed
  Six inches in the stream,
A very hungry pickerel was
  Attracted by its gleam;
And darting up, he gave a snap,
  And Keyser gave a scream.

Tim Keyser then was well assured
  He had a splendid bite.
To pull his victim up he jerked
  And tugged with all his might;
But that disgusting pickerel had
  The better of the fight.

And just as Mr. Keyser thought
  His nose was cut in two,
The pickerel gave its tail a twist
  And pulled Tim Keyser through,
And he was scudding through the waves
  The first thing that he knew.

Then onward swam that savage fish
  With swiftness toward its nest,
Still chewing Mr. Keyser's nose;
  While Mr. Keyser guessed
What sort of policy would suit
  His circumstances best.

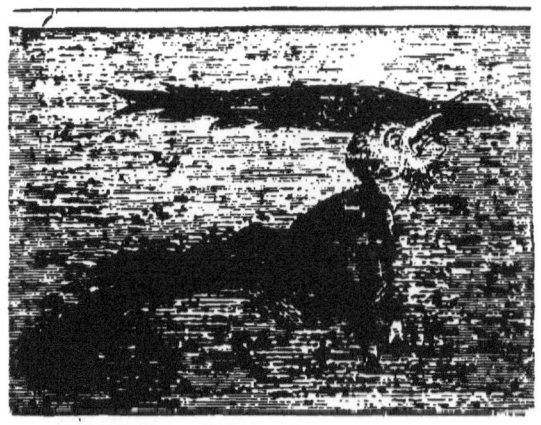

Just then his nose was tickled with
  A spear of grass close by;
Then came an awful sneeze, which knocked
  The pickerel into pi,
And blew its bones, the ice and waves
  Two hundred feet on high!

Tim Keyser swam up to the top
  A breath of air to take;
And finding broken ice, he hooked
  His nose upon a cake,
And gloried in a nose which could
  Such a concussion make.

And thus he drifted slowly on
  Until he reached the shore;
And creeping out all dripping wet,
  He very roundly swore
To use that crimson nose as bait
  For pickerel no more.

His Christmas turkey on that day
  He tackled with a vim,
And thanked his stars as, shuddering,
  He thought upon his swim,
That that wild pickerel had not
  Spent Christmas eating him!

CHAPTER XVII.

T is difficult to imagine anything more dismal than a
rainy day at New Castle,
particularly at this late
period in the year. The
river especially is robbed of
much of its attractiveness.
The falling drops obscure the
view, so that the other shore
is not visible through the
gray curtain of mist, and
the few vessels that can be
seen out in the channel
struggling upward with the
tide or beating slowly downward to the bay look so
drenched and cold and utterly forlorn that one shivers as he
watches them, with their black sails and their dripping cord-
age, and sees the moist sailors in tarpaulins and sea-boots hurrying over the slippery decks. The grain schooner lying at
the wharf has all her hatches down, and there is about her
no other sign of life than one soaked vagabond, who sits

upon the bowsprit angling in a most melancholy fashion for
fish which will not bite. He may be seeking for his supper,
poor, damp sinner! or he may be an infatuated being who
deceives himself with the notion that he is having sport.
There is a peculiar feeling of comfort on such a day to
stand in a room where a bright fire blazes in the grate, and
from the window to watch this solitary fisherman as the fit-
ful gusts now and then blow
the rain down upon his head in
sheets, and to observe the few
people who remain upon the
streets hurrying by under their
umbrellas, each anxious to reach
a place of shelter. The water
pours in yellow torrents through
the gutter-ways, the carriages
which go swiftly past have their
leathern aprons drawn high up in
front of the drivers, the stripped
branches of the trees are black
with moisture, and from each
twig the drops trickle to the earth; the water-spout upon the
side of the house continues its monotonous song all day long,
drip, drip, drip, until the very sound contributes to the gloom-
iness of the time; there is desolation in the yard and in the
garden, where a few yellow corn-stalks and headless trunks
of cabbage remain from the summer's harvest to face the
 wintry storms, and where the chickens gath-
ered under the woodshed are standing with
ruffled feathers, hungry, damp and miserable,
some on one leg and some on two, and with an
expression upon their faces that tells plainly
the story of their dejection at the poor prospect of having
any dinner,

23

It is a good time, Mrs. Adeler, to offer a few remarks upon that subject of perennial interest, the weather, and especially to refer to some facts in reference to that useful but uncertain implement, the umbrella. I do not know why it is so, but by common agreement the umbrella has been permitted to assume a comic aspect. No man, particularly no journalist, can be considered as having wholly discharged his duty to his fellow-creatures unless he has permitted himself to make some jocular remarks concerning the exception of umbrellas from the laws which govern other kinds of property. The amount of facetiousness that has attended the presentation of that theory is already incalculably great, and there is no reason for believing that it will not be increased to an infinite extent throughout the coming ages. It is perhaps a feeble idea upon which to erect so vast a structure; but if it makes even a dismal sort of merriment,

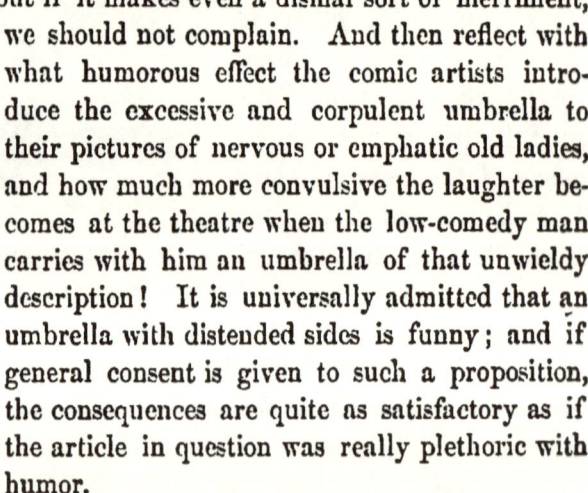

we should not complain. And then reflect with what humorous effect the comic artists introduce the excessive and corpulent umbrella to their pictures of nervous or emphatic old ladies, and how much more convulsive the laughter becomes at the theatre when the low-comedy man carries with him an umbrella of that unwieldy description! It is universally admitted that an umbrella with distended sides is funny; and if general consent is given to such a proposition, the consequences are quite as satisfactory as if the article in question was really plethoric with humor.

There are occasions when the simple elevation of an umbrella is grotesquely absurd, as when a group of British guardsmen sheltered themselves in this fashion from the rain during a certain battle, to the infinite disgust of Wellington, who ordered the

tender warriors to put their
umbrellas down lest the service should be made ridiculous. It was a Frenchman,
Émile Girardin, I think, who
brought an umbrella with him
to the dueling-ground, and insisted upon holding it over his
head during the combat. "I
do not mind being killed," he

said, "but I object decidedly to getting wet." They gave
him much credit for admirable coolness; but I cherish a
private opinion that he was scared, and hoped, by making the
affair ridiculous, to bring it to a conclusion without burning
powder; and he succeeded, for the combatants shook hands
and went away friends.

And there was the case of Colonel Coombs—Coombs of
Colorado. He had heard that the most ferocious wild beast
could be frightened and put to flight if an umbrella should
suddenly be opened in its face, and he determined to test
the matter at the earliest opportunity. One day, while
walking in the woods, Coombs perceived a panther crouch-
ing, preparatory to making a spring at him. Coombs held
his umbrella firmly in his hand, and presenting it at the
panther, unfurled it. The result was not wholly satisfac-

tory, for the next mo-
ment the animal leaped
upon the umbrella,
flattened it out and
began to lunch upon
Coombs. Not only did
the beast eat that anx-
ious inquirer after
truth, but it swallowed

the hooked handle of the umbrella, which was held tightly in Coombs's grasp, and for two or three weeks it wandered  about with its nose buried among the ribs of the umbrella. It was very handy when there was rain, but it obstructed the animal's vision, and consequently it walked into town and was killed.

In some countries the umbrella is the symbol of dignity and power. One of the magnates of Siam is proud to begin his list of titles with "Lord of Thirty-seven Umbrellas." Conceive, if you can, the envy and hatred with which that bloated aristocrat must be regarded by a man who is lord of only fifteen umbrellas! Among certain African tribes the grandeur of the individual increases with the size, and not with the number, of the umbrellas. Did I ever tell you the story of the African chieftain who determined to surpass all his rivals in this respect?

He made up his mind to procure the largest umbrella in the world, and he induced a trader to send his order to London for the article. Its ribs were forty feet in length, and its handle was like a telegraph pole. When it was distended, the effect was sublime. The machine resembled a green gingham circus tent, and it was crowned with a ferule as large as a  barrel. When the umbrella arrived, there was great rejoicing in the domestic circle of that dusky sovereign, and so impatient was the owner to test its qualities that he fairly yearned for the arrival of a rainy day. At last, one morn-

!ng, he awoke to find that his opportunity had come. The rain was pouring in torrents. Exultingly he called forth his vassals, and the work of opening the umbrella began in the presence of an awestricken multitude. Two entire days

were consumed by the effort to elevate the monster, and at the end of the second day, as the task was done, the storm ceased, and there was a general clearing up. The disappointed chieftain waited a day or two in vain for another shower, and finally, sick at heart, he commanded the umbrella to be closed. The work occupied precisely forty-eight hours, and just as the catch snapped upon the handle a thunder-gust came up, and it rained furiously all day. The frenzied monarch then consulted with his medicine man, and was assured that there would certainly be rain on the following Wednesday. The king therefore ordered the gingham giant up again. While the
swarthy myrmidons were struggling with it there were at least
sixty or seventy violent showers,
but just as it was fairly open
the clouds drifted away, and the
sun came out with terrific force.
And it remained out. There was
not a drop of rain or so much as
a fragment of cloud in the sky
for two hundred and seventy-
three days, and the umbrella remained open during all the time,

while the potentate who owned it went dancing about daily

23 *

in an ecstasy of rage. At the end of the period he sought the medicine man and slew him upon the spot. Then he ordered the umbrella down. The very next morning after it was closed the rain began, and it has been raining ever since.

Mrs. Adeler, that unfortunate savage thus became intimately familiar with one of the most striking of meteorological phenomena.

The influence of the umbrella upon the weather is a subject that has engaged the attention of millions of mankind. The precise laws by which that influence is exerted and governed have not yet been defined, but the fact of the existence of the influence is universally recognized. If there seems to be a promise of rain in the morning when I leave home, and I carry my umbrella with me, the sky clears before noon; but if I neglect to take my umbrella, I will certainly be drenched. If I carry an umbrella forty days in order to be prepared in case of sudden showers, there will be perfect dryness during that period; but if I forget the umbrella on the forty-first day, the floodgates of heaven will assuredly be opened. Sometimes the conduct of the elements is peculiarly aggravating. When I have been caught in town by a rain-storm and I had no umbrella, I have sometimes darted through the shower to a store to purchase one, but always, just as the man has given me the change, the rain has stopped. And when I have kept one umbrella at the house and another at the office, in order to be prepared at both ends of the line, all the storms have begun and expended their fury while I was passing between the two points.

This experience is not peculiar. It is that of every man who uses an umbrella. I am persuaded, Mrs. Adeler, that the time will come when science, having detected the character of the mysterious sympathy existing between umbrellas and the weather, will be able to give to a suffering world sunshine or rain as we want it. Whether we shall then be any better off is another matter.

In the mean time, while we are waiting for science to penetrate the hidden secrets of the umbrella, let me unfold to you a plan which I have devised for the better management of the weather bureau at Washington. I confided the scheme, once upon a time, to Old Probabilities himself, through the medium of a newspaper at the capital, but he did not deign to express an opinion concerning it. Perhaps it contained too much levity to entitle it to the consideration of a man who meditates upon the thunder and tries to trace the pathway of the cyclone. I have called it

The Improved Weather System.

The Probability man who meddles with our great American weather means well, and tries conscientiously to do his best, but his system is radically defective, and the consequence is that his conjectures are despicably incorrect quite half the time. The inconvenience caused by these mistakes, not only to the people generally, but to me personally, is inconceivably great, and it is not to be endured any longer.

For instance, if I read in the morning that this Probability person entertains a conviction that we shall have a clear day in my neighborhood, I place confidence in his assurance. I remove the roof from my house in order to dry the garret thoroughly, and I walk down town with a new umbrella under my arm. Now, it is plainly evident that if, after all, it does begin to rain, and I am obliged to unfurl that umbrella and ruin it with the wet, and I am compelled, when I arrive at home, to witness my family floating around in the dining-room upon a raft constructed out of the clothes-horse and a few bed-slats and pie-boards, the government for which Washington died is a failure.

Or suppose that our friend at the weather office asserts

that a thunder-storm is certain to strike my section of the country upon a given day. I believe him. I bring out my lightning-rods and buckle them to the chimneys and set them around on the roof and plant them out in the yard and rivet them upon my hired girl; and I place my family safely in feather beds in the middle of the room, and drink all the milk in the neighborhood, and prevail upon the tax collector to go and stand an hour or two under a tree where he will be almost certain to be struck by lightning. And when all these arrangements are completed, so that I feel equal to the promised emergency, suppose that thunder-storm does not come? When I watch that tax collector sally out and begin to assess my property, counting in all those lightning-rods at double their cost, is there any reason to wonder that I sit down and sigh for some responsible despot who will give us a Probability man who grasps the subject of the weather, as it were, in a more comprehensive manner?

But I lost all faith in him after his ill-treatment of Cooley. He said that a cyclone would sweep over this district upon

 a certain morning, and Cooley was so much alarmed at the prospect that he made elaborate preparations to receive the storm. He arose before daybreak and went into the middle of his garden, where he filled his pockets with pig lead, fettered himself to the apple tree and fixed the preserving kettle securely upon his head with a dog chain in order to preserve his hair. Cooley stayed there until five o'clock in the afternoon waiting for the simoom to swoop down upon him.

But it was a failure—a disgraceful failure. And when Cooley looked out from under the kettle in the afternoon, he was surprised to observe that the fence was filled with men and boys who were watching him with intense interest. Then the boys began to whistle upon their fingers and to make unpleasant remarks, and finally Cooley was obliged to cut loose and go into the house to avoid arrest by a policeman upon a charge of lunacy.

Now, this is all wrong. The feelings of American citizens ought not to be trifled with in such a manner, and I propose to arrange a plan by which meteorological facts and conditions can be observed with something like certainty.

The basis of my system is Corns. The marvelous accuracy with which changes in the weather can be foretold by a man whose feet are decorated with those excrescences is so well known that it is hardly worth while to consider at length, at this particular crisis, the human corn in its meteorological characteristics. It is quite certain, however, that it will be impossible to expect the Probability being to walk around the country once or twice every day for the purpose of submitting his corns to the diverse atmospheric influences which exist between the Atlantic and Pacific Oceans. It would wear out any man. It will be better, therefore, to have him kept stationary. I propose, in that event, that he should buy up any available corn that is in the market in any given State, and have it transplanted and grafted upon his own toe. Doubtless there are patriotic citizens in every portion of the land who would be willing to lay upon the altar of their beloved country their most cherished corns.

The Probability official then might obtain, let us assume, one corn from each State and a reliable bunion to represent each Territory. When these were engrafted upon his feet in a healthful condition, each one would, as a matter of course, be peculiarly susceptible to the atmospheric influences which prevail in its native clime. All we have to do, then, is to compel the weather man to wear exceptionally tight boots while he is not attending to business, so that his barometers will acquire the requisite amount of sensibility. Then I should have pipes laid from each State to the office in Washington for the purpose of conveying the different varieties of atmosphere to the foot of the Probability person. Suppose, then, he desired to make a guess in regard to the weather in Louisiana. I should have a man stationed at the end of the pipe in New Orleans with a steam fan, and he could waft zephyrs, as it were, upon the Louisiana corn, which would respond instantly, and we should have the facts about the weather in that State with precision and accuracy. When we admitted a new State, our friend could weld on a new corn; or if the Mormons succeeded in procuring the admission of their Territory as a State, we could plough up the Utah bunion and plant a corn, so as to preserve the proprieties.

Of course this system of excrescences would be of no value as an indicator of the movements of thunder-storms and hurricanes. But in order to acquire information concerning the former, how would it do to build up stacks of lightning-rods in every portion of every State, and to connect each State group, if I may be allowed the expression, with a wire which shall be permanently fastened to the arm or leg of the Probability man in Washington? Because, in such a case, whenever a thunder-gust appeared in any portion of the country, some one out of all those bunches of lightning-rods would certainly be struck, and our conjectural friend at the weather office would be likely to know about it right soon.

As for hurricanes, I am in favor of putting an end to them at once, instead of telegraphing around the country to warn people to look out for them. When I reorganize the weather service, I shall have men stationed everywhere with machines fixed up like the wind sails that are used on ship-board for sending air into the hold. I should make the mouth of each one a mile wide, construct it of stout canvas, and run the lower end into a coal-mine, or a mammoth cave, or a volcano. Then, when a tornado approached, I should place a man at each side of the sail, put the men into bal-loons, send them up, and spread the sail directly across the route of the approaching cyclone. When it arrived, it would strike the sail, of course; there would be a momentary flap-ping and jerking around, and in a minute or two I should have that hurricane comfortably packed away in the vol-cano, suppose we say. A man would then be upon the spot, of course, to drive a plug into the crater, so as to make everything tight and snug, and one more nuisance is taken off the face of the earth.

"Is that the whole of the article?" inquired Mrs. Adeler.

"Yes, that is all of it."

"Well, I am not surprised that no notice was taken of it. It is perfectly nonsensical."

"I admit the fact, but still I shall not smother the article. It will not do to take all the nonsense out of the world. While thousands of learned fools are hard at work trying to stupefy mankind, we must be permitted sometimes to in-dulge in absurdities of a less weighty kind in order to coun-teract them."

And while we are discussing the weather, let me not forget to allude to the most remarkable of Judge Pitman's pecu-liarities. He is the only man in the world of whom I know anything who is always satisfied with the weather. No mat-ter what the condition of the atmosphere, he is contented and happy, and willing to affirm that the state of things at any given moment is the very best that could have been devised.

In summer, when the mercury bolted up among the nineties, the judge would come to the front door with beads of perspiration standing out all over his red face, and would look at the sky and say, "Splendid! perfectly splendid! Noble weather for the poor and for the ice companies and the washerwomen! I never saw sich magnificent weather for dryin' clothes. They don't shake up any such climate as this in Italy. Gimme me my umbreller, Harriet, while I sit out yer on the steps and enjoy it."

In winter, when the mercury would creep down fifteen degrees below zero, and the cold was nearly severe enough to freeze the inside of Vesuvius solid to the centre of the globe, Pitman would sit out on my fence and exclaim, "By gracious, Adeler! did you ever see sich weather as this? I like an atmosphere that freezes up yer very marrer. It helps the coal trade an' gives us good skeetin'. Don't talk of summer-time to me. Gimme cold, and give it to me stiff."

When there was a drought, Pitman used to meet me in the street and remark, "No rain yet, I see! Magnificent, isn't it? I want my weather dry, I want it with the dampness left out. Moisture breeds fevers and ague, an' ruins yer boots. If there's anything I despise, it's to carry an umbreller. No rain for me, if you please."

' When it rained for a week and flooded the country, the judge often dropped in to see me and to observe, "I dunno how you feel about this yer rain, Adeler, but it allers seems to me that the heavens never drop no blessin's but when we

have a long wet spell. It makes the corn jump an' cleans
the sewers an' keeps the springs from gittin' too dry. I
wouldn't give a cent to live in a climate where there was no
rain. Put me on the Nile, an' I'd die in a week. Soak me
through an' through to the inside of my bones, and I feel
as if life was bright and beautiful, an' sorrer of no
account."

On a showery day, when the sun shone brightly at one
moment and at the next the rain poured in torrents, the
judge has been known to stand at the window and exclaim,
"Harriet, if you'd 've asked me how I liked the weather, I'd
've said, just as it is now. What I want is weather that is
streaked like a piece of fat an' lean bacon—a little shine an'
a little rain. Mix 'em up an' give us plenty of both, an'
I'm yer man."

The judge is always happy in a thunder-storm, and one
day, after the lightning had knocked down two of his best
apple trees and splintered them into fragments, and the wind
had torn his chimney to pieces,
I went over to see him. He was
standing by the prostrate trees,
and he at once remarked, "Did
you ever know of a man havin'
sich luck as this? I was goin'
to chop down them two trees to-
morrer, an' as that chimney
never draw'd well, I had concluded to have it rebuilt. An'
that gorgeous old storm has fixed
things just the way I want 'em.
Put me in a thunder-storm an'

let the lightnin' play around me, an' I'm at home. I'd
rather have one storm that 'd tear the bowels out of the
American continent than a dozen of yer little dribblin'

24

waterin'-pot showers. If I can't have a rippin' and roarin storm, I don't want none."

They say here in the village, but I do not believe it, that one day the judge was upon his roof fixing a shingle, when a tornado struck him, lifted him off, carried him a quarter of a mile, and dashed him with such terrible force against a fence that his leg was broken. As they carried him home, he opened his eyes languidly and said, "Immortal Moses! what a storm that was! When it does blow, it suits me if it blows hard. I'd give both legs if we could have a squall like that every day. I—I—" Then he fainted.

If contentment is happiness, then the life of Pitman is one uninterrupted condition of bliss.

CHAPTER XVIII.

E had been talking of asking
the Magruders to come to
take tea with us, so that the
two families, which were now
to be brought into close relations, might become better
acquainted. But one even-
ing, just as I had settled
myself for a comfortable
perusal of the paper, Miss
Magruder was ushered into
the room by the servant. It
was plainly evident from her
appearance that she was in
distress from some cause.
We should have guessed from her visit at such an hour un-
accompanied by any one that all was not right, even if her
countenance had not manifested extreme agitation. After
the usual salutation she asked,

"Is Mr. Parker not at home?"

"He has not yet returned from the city," I said. "I suppose he has been detained for some reason. It is probable
that he will be here presently."

"I wanted to see him," she said, hesitatingly. "I am
afraid you'll think it very queer for me to come here at such

a strange time; but—but "—and here her voice quavered a little—" but oh, something dreadful has happened—something very, very dreadful."

Then the tears began to come into her pretty brown eyes, and the little maid, after striving desperately to restrain them and to retain her composure, buried her face in her hands and began to sob. There was a woman by her side in a moment to comfort her and to seek her confidence; but it was very awkward for me. I was not quite certain whether I ought not to fly from the room and permit the two to be alone. But I remained with mingled feelings of sympathy and curiosity, and with an indistinct notion that the forlorn damsel before me regarded me as a flinty-hearted brute because I didn't express violent indignation at her ill-treatment. I should have done so if I had had any conception of the nature of the wrong endured by her. At last, when she had obtained relief in a good cry—and it is surprising how much better a troubled woman feels when she has cried and wiped her weeping eyes—Bessie told us the story.

"Father came to me to-day," she said, "and told me that he had heard some dreadful things about Robert; and he said he could not consent to my marriage with such a man, and that our engagement must be broken off."

"What kind of things?" indignantly demanded Mrs. Adeler, whose family pride was aroused; "what did he hear?"

"Oh, something perfectly awful!" exclaimed Bessie, looking up with fresh tears in her eyes. "He said Robert drank a great deal and that he was very often intoxicated."

"What an outrageous falsehood!" exclaimed Mrs. Adeler.

"I told father it was," said Bessie; "but he said he knew it was true, and, worse than that, that Robert not only kept very bad company in the city, but that he was an atheist—that he only came to church in order to deceive us."

If the late Mr. Fahrenheit had had to indicate the warmth of Mrs. Adeler's indignation at this moment, he would have given 215° as the figure. "I declare," she said, "that is the wickedest falsehood I ever heard. I will call upon Mrs. Magruder to-morrow morning and tell her so."

"And father insisted," said Bessie, "that I should write a formal note to Robert, breaking our engagement and asking him to discontinue his visits to our house. I did so, but I could not bear to have him think me so heartless, and I felt as if I must come here and tell him about it before the note reached him. Please don't think it strange that I came, and don't let any one know it." Then Bessie began to sob again.

"Certainly, Bessie," I replied, "it was very proper for you to do as you have done. Your father has been unjust to you and to Bob. Robert shall see him and demand an explanation. But who do you suppose told your father these things?"

"I have no idea. But it must have been somebody who was opposed to our marriage, and who hated Robert. I can't believe that any one would have invented such stories without a very malicious motive."

"Well, Bessie, the only thing we can do now is to permit the matter to rest as it is until we have an opportunity to disprove these slanders. Let me go home with you; and when Bob comes in, I will tell him all about it. He shall call upon your father. I will do so myself to-morrow. Bob has been unfairly used. He is as proper a youth as any in the land, and worthy of the love of any woman."

Then I escorted Bessie to her home, and upon my way back I met Bob coming in hot haste toward me. He arrived at the house just after our departure; and a few words from Mrs. Adeler having placed him in command of the situation, he started off at once with the hope to overtake us and to

24*

have a few words with Bessie. He was breathless and in a condition of frenzy. He at first insisted upon storming the  castle of the Magruders at once for the purpose of assailing the dragon that guarded his fair lady. But I showed him that it would perhaps injure Bessie if he should excite suspicion that she had visited him, and that it would be ridiculous at any rate to attack old Magruder at that time of night and while he was in such a state of excitement. It was finally agreed that we should wait until morning, and that then I should first visit Mr. Magruder and obtain an explanation from him, so that Bob could go there afterward fully prepared to vindicate himself.

"I'll bet anything," said Bob, as we walked home, "I know who is the author of these slanders. It is Cooley. He don't like you or any of your family, and he has taken this means of injuring us. If it is he, I'll give him an aggravated case of assault and battery to settle. I'll thrash him within an inch of his life."

"I don't believe Cooley did it," I replied. "It is not the kind of business that he would care to trouble himself with. It is some one who has an interest in separating you and Bessie."

"I don't know of any such person," said Bob.

"Perhaps Smiley did it."

"That may be," replied Bob; "he has little enough principle, but I hardly think he would display so much malice. Besides, he knows very well Bessie would not accept him under any circumstances."

"Well, let us wait patiently for further developments. It

is not worth while to denounce any one until we can ascertain who the offender is."

Bob had been delayed in the city by a visit to his parents, who were going north for a week or two, and they consigned to his care his younger brother, who came with him to our house to remain during the absence of his father and mother. The boy was at the house when we reached it; and when the time came for him to go to bed, it was arranged that he should sleep with Bob. The consequences of this were some-
what peculiar. The youngster, it appears, has a habit of walking in his sleep, and he was so afraid that he would do so on this night, in a strange house, that Bob tied a strong piece of twine about the lad's waist and fastened the other end to his own body, so that he would be roused by any

attempt on the part of his bro-ther to prowl about the room. It turned out, however, that Bob was the restless one. According to his own account, he got to dreaming of his troubles. He imagined that he was engaged in a frightful combat with Mr. Magruder, and that, at the last, that amiable old gentleman pursued him with a drawn dagger with the intent to butcher him. In his alarm Bob pushed over to Henry's side of the bed, and finally, as the visionary Magruder still appeared to be thirsty
for his blood, he climbed over Henry, got upon the floor and hid himself beneath the bed. When the apparition of the

sanguinary parent disappeared, Bob, still soundly asleep,
must have emerged from his hiding-place
upon the side of the bed opposite that at
which he entered it.   At any rate, the cord
ran from Henry's body beneath the bed
clear around until it connected with Bob.
Early in the morning Bob moved over suddenly toward his
brother; and although he was more than half asleep, he was
amazed to see Henry drop over upon the floor.   Bob in-

stantly jumped out after him, and as he did so, he was even
more surprised to perceive the child dart under the bed.
He followed Henry; and at the first movement in that direc-

tion, Henry shot
up off the floor,
and was heard
rolling swiftly
across the mattress
above, only to dis-
appear again over
the side as Bob
came once more to
the surface.   By
this time both of them were wide awake and able to com-

prehend the phenomenon. This is Mr. Parker's version. It
is probably exaggerated slightly. My private impression is
that Henry was pulled out upon the floor and under the bed,
and that the exercise ended immediately. Henry does not
remember the particulars with sufficient distinctness to be
considered a thoroughly reliable witness. His mind is clear
upon only one
point: he is fully
persuaded that he
will not sleep in
harness with Bob
again.

Upon the day
following Bessie's
visit I called at
Magruder's, in accordance with my agreement with Bob.
The servant said Mr. Magruder had gone out, but that he
would probably be home in a few moments. I declined an
invitation to go in the house. It was a fine day, and I pre-
ferred to walk up and down the porch while waiting. When
a considerable time had elapsed and Magruder did not come,
I threw myself upon one of the chairs on the porch and began to read the *Argus*.

While I was sitting there Magruder's dog came bounding
up the yard, and when he saw me instantly manifested a desire to investigate me. I have never liked Magruder's dog;
he is very large, and he has an extremely bad reputation.
When he approached me, he looked at me savagely, and
growled in such a manner that cold chills began to run up
and down my back. Then the dog walked up and sniffed
my legs with an earnestness of purpose that I had never
expected to see displayed by a dumb animal. During this
operation I maintained a condition of profound repose. No

man will ever know how quiet I was. It is doubtful if any human being ever before became so thoroughly still until his immortal soul went to the land of everlasting rest.

When the ceremony was ended, the dog lay down close to the chair. As soon as I felt certain that the animal was asleep, I thought I would go home without seeing Mr. Magruder; but when I attempted to rise, the dog leaped up and growled so fiercely that I sat down again at once. Then I thought perhaps it would be better *not* to go home. It occurred to me, however, that it would be as well to call some one to remove the dog, in case circumstances should make it desirable for me to depart. But at the very first shout the animal jumped to his feet, gave a fiendish bark and began to take a few more inquisitorial smells at my legs. And whenever I shuffled my feet, or attempted to turn the *Argus* over in order to continue an article on to the following page, or made the slightest movement, that infamous dog was up and

at me. Once, when I was positive-
ly compelled to sneeze, I thought,
from the indignation boisterous-
ly manifested by the dog, that
my hour at last had come.

, Finally, Cooley's dog, which
happened to be in the neighborhood, became engaged in an
angry controversy with another
dog in the street in front of me.
Magruder's dog was wide awake in a moment; and after
turning a regretful glance at me, as if he knew he was delib-

 erately and foolishly throwing away a chance
of obtaining several glorious bites, he dashed
down the walk and over the fence for the
purpose of participating in the discussion between his two friends.

I did not actually run, because that would not have been
dignified, and the servant-girl, looking from the kitchen
window, and not understanding the nature of the emergency,
might have suspected me of
emotional insanity. But I walk-
ed rapidly—very rapidly—to the
rear fence of the yard, and climbed over it. As I reached the
top of the fence, I saw the dog
coming at full gallop down the
yard. He was probably cha-
grined, but I did not remain to
see how he bore it. I went directly home. Mr. Parker may
manage his own love affairs in
the future. I shall not approach
Mr. Magruder upon this disagree-

able subject again. I have enough to do to attend to my own business.

　　When I reached home, I found Judge Pitman waiting for me. He came in for the purpose of borrowing my axe for a few moments. As we went around to the rear of the house to get it, the judge said:

"I reckon you don't use no terbacker, do you?"

"I smoke sometimes; that is all."

"Well, I was jist feelin' 's if I wanted a chaw, an' I thought p'rhaps you might have one about you. Seein' Cooley over there on his porch put me in mind of it."

"That is rather a singular circumstance. Why should a view of Cooley suggest such a thing?"

"'Tis kinder sing'lar; but you see," said the judge, "Cooley was a-tellin' me yesterday mornin' about somethin' that occurred the day before at his house. The old woman is opposed to his chawin', an' she makes it stormy for him when he does. So he never uses no terbacker 'round home, an' he told her he'd given it up. The other day, just as he was goin' in to supper, he pulled out his handkercher, an' out come a plug of terbacker 'long with it. He didn't know it, but directly Mrs. Cooley lit on it, an' she walked up to him an' wanted to know if it was his. It was a little rough, you understand, but he had presence of mind enough to turn to his boy and say, 'Great

Heavens! is it possible you've begun to chaw this ornary
stuff? What d'you mean by sich conduct?
Haven't I told you often enough to let terbacker alone? Commere to me this minute,
you rascal!' Cooley licked him like the nation,
an' then threw the terbacker out the winder
onto the porch, where he could git it agin in
the mornin'. "

"That was pretty severe treatment of the
boy."

" An' Cooley says to me, ' By gracious, judge! s'pose'n my
children had all been girls! It makes an old father's heart
glad when he thinks he has a boy he can depend upon at
sich times!' Healthy old parent, ain't he?"

" The word 'healthy' hardly expresses with sufficient vigor
the infamy of his conduct."

"Cooley never did treat that there boy right," said the
judge, as he seated himself on the saw-horse in the woodshed
and locked his hands over one of his knees, evidently with
the intention to have some sociable conversation. "He
never behaved like a father to him. He brought up that
there child to lie. That echo business, f'r instance; it was
scand'lus in him."

"To what do you refer?"

" Why, afore Cooley come yer to live he kep' a hotel up
in the Lehigh Valley—a fashionable kinder tavern, I reckon;
an' there was another man about two miles furder up who
had a bigger hotel. You could stand on this other man's
porch an' make a splendid echo by whistlin' or hollerin'.
You could hear the noise agin a dozen times. Leastways,
Cooley told me so. Well, Cooley, you know, hated like pisin
to be beaten on that echo, an' so he kinder concluded to git
one up for himself. He made that there boy of his'n go
over on the mountain across the river an' hide among the

25

bushes, an' then he would take people up on the roof of the house and holler, an' the boy would holler back agin. He told everybody that the echo could only be heard on the roof, an' he kep' the trap door locked, so's nobody would find him out."

"That was a poor kind of a swindle."

"Yes, sir. Well, that boy, you 'bserve, gradually got rusty in the business an' tired of it, an' sometimes he'd take another boy over with him, an' they'd git to playin' an' forgit to answer. It was embarrassin' for Cooley, an' the secret begun to leak out. But one day the whole concern was bu'sted. Cooley took a lot of folks from the city, among 'em some o' them newspaper people, an' for a while the boy worked all right. But he had another feller with him, and he kep' a-repeatin' things that no-body said. Cooley stood it for a while, though he was mad as fury; an' at last, when somebody tried to start the echo, there was no answer. They all thought it was mighty queer, but after callin' a good many times, the boy come out in full view an' yelled back, 'I'm not a-goin' to answer any more. Bill Johnson won't gimme my knife, an' I won't holler till I git it; blamed if I do.' Cooley

tells me that the manner in which he sailed across the

creek after that child was someth'n' awful to behold. But
it knocked him, sir. It closed him up. Them newspaper
men started the thing on him, an' they run him so hard
that he had to quit. He sold out and come yer to live. But
is it any wonder that boy's spiled? Cooley 'd spile a blessed
young angel the way he goes on. But I must say good-
mornin'. Much obleeged for the axe. Good-bye."

And the judge went home meditating upon Cooley's unfit-
ness for the duties of a parent. I would like to know if that
echo story is true. I have no doubt the judge received it
from Cooley, but it sounds as if the latter ingenious gentleman might have wreuched it from his imagination.

CHAPTER XIX.

I HAVE been the victim of a somewhat singular persecution for several weeks past. When we came here to live, Judge Pitman was partially bald. Somebody induced him to apply to his head a hair restorative made by a Chicago man named Pulsifer. After using this liquid for a few months, the judge was gratified to find that his hair had returned; and as he naturally regarded the remedy with admiration, he concluded that it would be simply fair to give expression to his feelings in some form. As I happened to be familiar with all the facts of the case, the judge induced me to draw up a certificate affirming them over my signature. This he mailed to Pulsifer. I have not yet ceased to regret the weakness which permitted me to stand sponsor for Judge Pitman's hair. Of course, Pulsifer immediately inserted the certificate, with my name and residence attached to it, in half the papers in the country, as a displayed advertisement, beginning with the words, "HOPE FOR THE BALDHEADED; THE MOST REMARKABLE CURE ON RECORD," in the largest capital letters.

I have had faith in advertising since that time. And Pulsifer had confidence in it too, for he wrote to me to know what I would take to get him up a series of similar certificates of cures performed by his other patent medicines. He had a corn-salve which dragged a little in its sales, and he was prepared to offer me a commission if I would write him a strong letter to the effect that six or eight frightful corns had been eradicated from my feet with his admirable preparation. He was in a position, also, to do something handsome if I could describe a few miraculous cures that had been effected by his Rheumatic Lotion, or if I would name certain ruined stomachs which had, as it were, been born again through the influence of Pulsifer's Herb Bitters; and from the manner in which he wrote, I think he would have taken me into partnership if I had consented to write an assurance that his Ready Relief had healed a bad leg of eighteen years' standing, and that I could never feel that my duty was honorably performed until he sent me a dozen bottles more for distribution among my friends whose legs were in that defective and tiresome condition. I was obliged to decline Pulsifer's generous offer.

I heard with singular promptness from other medical men. Fillemup & Killem forwarded some of their Hair Tonic, with a request for me to try it on any bald heads I happened to encounter, and report. Doser & Co. sent on two packages of their Capillary Pills, with a suggestion to the effect that if Pitman lost his hair again he would get it back finally by following the enclosed directions. I also heard from Brown & Bromley, the agents for Johnson's Scalp Awakener. They sent me twelve bottles for distribution among my bald friends; then Smith & Smithson wrote

25 *

to say that a cask of their Vesuvian Wash for the hair would be delivered in my cellar by the express company; and a man called on me from Jones, Butler & Co. with a proposition to pump out my vinegar barrel, and fill it with Balm of Peru for the gratuitous use of the afflicted in the vicinity.

But this persecution was simply unalloyed felicity when compared with the suffering that came in other forms. I

will not attempt to give the number of the letters I received. I cherish a conviction that the mail received at our post-office doubled the first week after Judge Pitman's cure was announced to a hairless world. I think every bald-headed man in the Tropic of Cancer must have written to me at least twice upon the subject of Pulsifer's Renovator and Pitman's hair. Persons dropped me a line to inquire if Pitman's baldness was hereditary; and if so, if it came from his father's or his mother's side. One man, a phrenologist, sent on a plaster head mapped out into town-lots, with a suggestion that I should ink over the bumps that had been barest and most fertile in the case of Pitman. He said he had a little theory which he wanted to demonstrate. A man in San Francisco wrote to inquire if my Pitman was the same Pitman who came out to California in 1849 with a bald head; and if he was, would I try to collect two dollars Pitman had borrowed from him in that year? The superintendent of a Sunday-school in Vermont forwarded eight pages of foolscap covered with an argument supporting the theory that it was impious to attempt to force hair to grow upon a head which had been made bald, because, although Elisha was bald, we find no record in the Bible that he used renovator of any kind. He warned Pitman to beware of Absalom's fate, and to avoid riding mules out in the woods. A woman in Snyder county, Penna., sent me a poem inspired by the incident, and entitled "Lines on the Return of Pitman's Hair." A party in Kansas desired to know whether I thought Pulsifer's Renovator could be used beneficially by a man who had been scalped. Two men in New Jersey wrote, in a manner totally irrelevant to the subject, to inquire if I could get each of them a good hired girl. I received a confidential letter from a man who was  willing to let me into a "good thing" if I had five hundred dollars cash capital. Mrs. Singerly, of Frankford, related that she had shaved her dog, and shaved him too close, and she would be relieved if I would inform her if the Renovator would make hair grow on a dog. A devoted mother in Rhode Island said her little boy had accidentally drank a bottle of the stuff, and she would go mad unless I could assure her that there was no danger of her child having his stomach choked up with hair. And over eleven hundred boys inquired what effect the Renovator would have on the growth of whiskers which betrayed an inclination to stagnation.

But the visitors were a more horrible torment. Bald men came to see me in droves. They persecuted me at home and abroad. If I went to church, the sexton would call me out during the prayers to see a man in the vestibule who wished to ascertain if Pitman merely bathed his head or rubbed the medicine in with a brush. When I went to a party, some bald-headed miscreant would stop me in the midst of the dance to ask if Pitman's hair began to grow in the full of the moon or when it was new. While I was being shaved, some one would bolt into the shop and insist, as the barber held me by the nose, upon knowing whether Pitman wore ventilators in his hat. If I attended a wedding, as likely as not a bare-headed outlaw would stand by me at the altar and ask if Pitman ever slept in nightcaps; and more than once I was called out of bed at night by wretches who wished to learn, before they left the town, if I thought it hurt the hair to part it behind.

It became unendurable. I issued orders to the servants to admit to the house no man with a bald head. But that very day a stranger obtained admission to the parlor; and when I went down to see him, he stepped softly around, closed all the doors mysteriously, and asked me, in a whisper, if any one could hear us. Then he pulled off a wig; and handing me a microscope, he requested me to examine his scalp and tell him if there was any hope. I sent him over to see Pitman; and I gloat over the fact that he bored Pitman for two hours with his baldness.

I am sorry now that I ever wrote anything upon the subject of his hair. A bald Pitman, I know, is less fascinating than a Pitman with hair; but rather than have suffered this misery, I would prefer a Pitman without an eye-winker, or fuzz enough on him to make a camel's-hair pencil. But I shall hardly give another certificate of cure in any event. If I should see a patent-medicine man take a mummy which died the year Joseph was sold into Egypt, and dose it until it kicked off its rags and danced the polka mazourka while it whistled the tune, I would die at the stake sooner than acknowledge the miracle on paper. Pitman's hair winds me up as far as medical certificates are concerned.

Bob has succeeded in obtaining from Mr. Magruder an explanation of the interference of that stern parent with the progress of his love affair, and we hope now to secure a happy adjustment of the difficulty.

"When I entered the room," said Bob, "the old man looked gloomy and stiff, as if he regarded me as a totally depraved being, too far gone in iniquity to be worth an effort to effect a reform. I went right at him. I told him I had heard that some one had made certain charges against me which were likely to hurt my reputation, and that it was because of these that he had refused to permit me to marry his daughter.

"He said I had stated the case correctly. Then I asked him to give me the name of the person who had made these accusations. He hesitated for a few moments, and I then declared that the charges were false and slanderous, and asserted that I had a right to know who the author of them was.

"After thinking over the matter for a while, he said,

"'Well, Mr. Parker, I believe you have that right. I have thought lately that I did not perhaps treat you very fairly in not bringing you face to face in the first place with the man who accused you. But I almost pledged myself to regard his statements as confidential; and as the evidence seemed to be overwhelming against you, I concluded not to offer you the opportunity. Mrs. Magruder takes a different view of the matter. She thinks you should not be condemned without a hearing, and she distrusts your accuser. His name is Smiley—Lieutenant Smiley.'

"Then the old man went on," said Bob, "and told me that Smiley had sought a private interview with him, at which Smiley had declared that I was not only a debauchee, but an atheist. He made this statement, he told Mr. Magruder, with reluctance and regret, but he felt that as a friend of the family he had a duty to perform which was imperative. Smiley declared that he had frequently seen me under the influence of liquor, and that I had often attacked him for professing to believe in the Christian religion. A splendid old professor of religion he is!" exclaimed Mr. Parker. "And then," continued Bob, "Mr. Magruder said Smiley produced two letters, one from a man named Dewey who pretended to be the pastor of a church in Philadelphia, from which he said I was dismissed for expressing atheistical opinions, and the other from a certain Samuel Stonebury, wherein Samuel gave me a dreadful character for honesty and sobriety.

"Thereupon I informed Mr. Magruder that I knew of no clergyman named Dewey, and that I didn't believe such a man existed in Philadelphia; that I never belonged to any

church, and certainly was never kicked out of one because of
my atheistical opinions, for I never entertained such views.
I informed him also that Mr. Stonebury was a youth who was
once employed in our store, and who was discharged because
I discovered that he had been stealing. How Smiley found
him I can't imagine. They must have had a natural tendency to gravitate toward each other as children of the same
old father of lies.

"Then Mr. Magruder said that if I could prove these facts
he would not only hand Bessie over to me again, but he
would also make me a very humble apology. I promised to
accomplish these results, and to-morrow I will set about the
work. I have no doubt at all that Stonebury wrote the letter
signed 'Dewey,' and that Smiley suggested that playful little
dodge to him. I will move on Smiley's works when I meet
him. He is the wickedest kind of a scoundrel."

And so the case of Parker *versus* Smiley stands at present.
I should have a higher respect for Magruder if he had acted
more justly with Bob in the first place. If Mrs. Magruder's
instinct and common sense had not induced her to regard
Smiley with suspicion, I am afraid that Bob's wrongs would
never have been righted. The
doctor is evidently the wiser and
better person of the two, and I
am not surprised now that she
keeps her husband a little in the
background.

Some relatives of the Magruders
named Kemper came to the village
to live a few weeks ago, and they
rented a house not far from mine.
We have a life insurance agent in
the town named Benjamin P.

Gunn, and he is decidedly the most enterprising and in-
defatigable of the fraternity of which he is a member. He
has already bored everybody in the county nearly to death,
and it is easy to imagine the delight he feels when a new
victim comes within his reach. The Kempers were hardly
fixed in their new home when Gunn, who had been awaiting with impatience a chance to attack them, one morning called for the purpose of ascertaining if he could induce
Mr. Kemper to take out a policy of insurance upon his life.
In response to his summons Mrs. Kemper came into the
parlor to see him. The following conversation then ensued:

"I suppose," said Gunn, "Mr. Kemper has no insurance
on his life?"

"No," said Mrs. Kemper.

"Well, I'd like to get him to take a policy in our company. It's the safest in the world—the largest capital,
smallest rates and biggest dividends."

"Mr. Kemper don't take much interest in such things
now," said Mrs. K.

"Well, madam, but he ought to, in common justice to
you. No man knows when he will die; and by paying a
ridiculously small sum now, Mr. Kemper can leave his
family in affluence. I'd like to hand you, for him, a few
pamphlets containing statistics upon the subject; may I?"

"Of course, if you wish to."

"Don't you think he can be induced to insure?" asked
Gunn.

"I hardly think so," replied Mrs. Kemper.

"He is in good health, I suppose? Has he complained
lately of being sick?"

"Not lately."

"May I ask if he has any considerable wealth?"

"Not a cent."

"Then, of course, he must insure. No poor man can

afford to neglect such an opportunity. I suppose he travels sometimes—goes about in railroad cars and other dangerous places?"

"No, he keeps very quiet."

"Man of steady habits, I s'pose?"

"Very steady."

"He is the very man I want," said Gunn. "I know I can sell him a policy."

"I don't think you can," replied Mrs. Kemper.

"Why? When will he be home? I'll call on him. I don't know of any reason why I shouldn't insure him."

"I know," replied Mrs. K.

"Why?"

"He *has been dead twenty-seven years!*" said the widow.

Then Mr. Gunn said "good-morning," and returned to his office. The widow must have told the story to some one, probably to Magruder, for it was soon known all over town, and those who had suffered from an excess of Gunn gloried in his discomfiture. As this was the first time in his career that he had ever been down, it is not surprising that several of his enemies should improve the opportunity by giving him  a few vigorous kicks. The most venomous attack upon him, however, appeared in the *Argus*. It came, I think, from that remarkable medical man Dr. Tobias Jones, who dislikes Gunn because he employs a rival physician, Dr. Brindley, to examine persons who apply for policies. He called the article

A LIFE INSURANCE AGENT.

His name was Benjamin P. Gunn, and he was the agent for a life insurance company. He came around to my office fourteen times in one morning to see if he could not persuade me to take out a policy. He used to waylay me on the street, at church, in my own house, and bore me about that policy. If I went to the opera, Gunn would buy the seat next to me, and sit there the whole evening talking about sudden death and the advantages of the ten-year plan. If I got into a railway car, Gunn would come rushing in and sit by my side, and drag out a lot of mortality tables and begin to explain how I could gouge a fortune out of his company. If I sat down to dinner in a restaurant, up would come Gunn; and seizing the chair next to me, he would tell a cheering anecdote about a man who insured in his company for $50,000 only last week, and was buried yesterday. If I attended the funeral of a departed friend, and wept as they threw the earth upon his coffin, I would hear a whisper; and turning around, there would be the indomitable Benjamin P. Gunn, bursting to say, "Poor Smith! Knew him well. Insured for ten thousand in our company. Widow left in comfortable circumstances. Let me take your name. Shall I?"

He followed me everywhere, until at last I got so sick of Gunn's persecutions that I left town suddenly one evening and hid myself in a distant city, hoping to get rid of him. At the end of two weeks I returned, reaching home at one o'clock in the morning. I had hardly got into bed before there was a ring at the door-bell. I looked out, and there was Gunn with another person. Mr. Gunn observed that he expected my return, and thought he would call around about that insurance policy. He said he had the doctor with him, and if I would come down he would take my name and have me examined immediately. I was too indignant to reply. I shut the window with a slam and went to bed again. After breakfast in the morning I opened the front door, and there was Gunn sitting on the steps with his doctor, waiting for me. He had been there all night. As I came out they seized me and tried to undress me there on the pavement in order to examine me. I retreated  and locked myself up in the garret, with orders to admit nobody to the house until I came down stairs.

But Gunn wouldn't be baffled. He actually rented the house next door and stationed himself in the garret adjoining mine. When he got fixed, he spent his time pounding on the partition and crying, "Hallo! I say! how about that policy? Want to take it out now?" And then 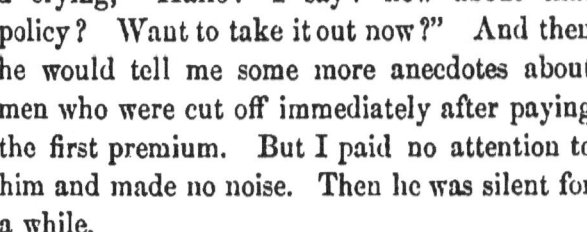 he would tell me some more anecdotes about men who were cut off immediately after paying the first premium. But I paid no attention to him and made no noise. Then he was silent for a while.

Suddenly the trap-door of my garret was wrenched off; and upon looking up, I saw Gunn, with the doctor and a crowbar and a lot of death-rates, coming down the ladder at me. I fled from the house to the Presbyterian church close by, and paid the sexton twenty dollars to let me climb up to the point of the steeple and sit astride of the ball. I promised him twenty more if he would exclude everybody from that steeple for a week. Once safely on the ball, three hundred feet from the earth, I made myself comfortable with the thought that I had Gunn at a disadvantage, and I determined to beat him finally if I had to stay there for a month. About an hour afterward, while I was looking at the superb view to the west, I heard a rustling sound upon the other side of the steeple. I looked around, and there was Benjamin P. Gunn creeping up the side of the spire in a balloon, in which was the doctor and the tabular estimates of the losses of his company from the Tontine system. As soon as Gunn reached the ball he threw his grappling-iron into the shingles of the steeple, and asked me at what age my father died, and if any of my aunts ever had consumption or liver complaint.

Without waiting to reply, I slid down the steeple to the ground and took the first train for the Mississippi Valley. In two weeks I was in Mexico. I determined to go to the interior and seek some wild spot in some elevated region where no Gunn would ever dare to come. I mounted a mule, and paid a guide to lead me to the summit of Popocatapetl. We arrived at the foot of the mountain at noon. We toiled upward for about four hours. Just before reaching the top I heard the sound of voices; and upon rounding a point of rocks, whom should I see but Benjamin P. Gunn, seated on the very edge of the crater,

explaining the endowment plan to his guide and stupefying him with a mortality table, while the doctor had the other guide a few yards off, examining him to see if he was healthy! Mr. Gunn arose and said he was glad to see me, because now we could talk over that business about the policy without fear of interruption. In a paroxysm of rage I pushed him backward into the crater, and he fell a thousand feet below with a heavy thud. As he struck the bottom I heard a voice screaming out something about "non-forfeiture;" but there was a sudden convulsion of the mountain, a cloud of smoke, and I heard no more.

But on the following Thursday an eruption began, and the first thing that was thrown out was Benjamin P. Gunn, scorched, with his hair singed off and in a profuse perspiration, but still active and ready for business. If I should be killed, I verily believe Gunn would commit suicide in order that he might follow me into the next world.

Of course this is mere burlesque and it is hardly fair treatment of Gunn. But I am gratified to learn that such ridicule does not hurt his feelings. On the day the article appeared he called to see Colonel Bangs. The colonel apprehended an assault; and rallying his clerks and reporters around him, he

seized a club and gave orders that Gunn should be admitted. But Benjamin did not intend war. He grasped the colonel's hand; and after thanking him for such a handsome gratuitous advertisement, he pulled a schedule out of his pocket and argued with Bangs until the latter in despair agreed to take out another policy for ten thousand dollars in Gunn's company.

We do not regard Lieutenant Smiley as a very entertain- ing person at present, and of course he is not quoted with enthusiasm. But during the prevalence of the excitement created by the victory over Pitman's baldness, Smiley related an anecdote bearing upon the subject of hair which combined instruction with amusement in a remarkable degree, and it may be profitable to reproduce it here as an illustration of the demoralizing tendencies of the red man.

During the recent visit of a party of Indians to the East, one of the number, Squatting Bear, was observed to behave himself in a very remarkable and mysterious manner. He separated himself from his companions on one occasion for several hours, and was then seen returning dragging a huge Saratoga trunk behind him through the streets with a string. When he reached his lodgings with the trunk, the other Indians were puzzled. Some of them believed the trunk to be a model for a new kind of wigwam with a Mansard roof, while others conceived the idea that it was a patent bath-tub of some peculiar sort, and that Squatting Bear, in a moment of mental aberration, had been seized with an inexplicable and unprecedented desire to wash himself. The souls of the savages burned with fiery indignation as they contemplated the possibility of the adoption of this revolutionary, enervating and demoralizing practice of the pale faces by the noble red man. But when they questioned Squatting Bear and remonstrated with him, that incomprehensible brave merely placed his copper-colored finger upon his burnt-umber nose and winked solemnly with his right eye.

The trunk was carried through to the wigwam of Squatting Bear unopened, and within the precincts of his home it was hidden finally from view, and was soon entirely forgotten.

In the tribe the brave who killed the largest number of enemies in any given year and secured the usual trophies of victory was entitled to occupy the position as chief. Squatting Bear was known to have ardent aspirations for the office, and he worked hard to win it. For a while after his return he was always foremost in every fight; and when the scalps were counted around the camp-fire, he invariably had secured the greatest number. Gradually, however, certain of the braves were impressed with the notion that Squatting's trophies sometimes did not bear a very correct proportion to the ferocity of the contest or to the number of the slain. Several times, after a brief skirmish in which ten or fifteen men were killed, Squatting would come sidling home with as many scalps as there were dead men ; and at the same time the other warriors would together have nearly as many more.

The braves thought it was queer, but they did not give the subject very serious attention until after the massacre of a certain band of emigrants which had passed close by the camp of the tribe. There were just twenty persons in the company, and after the butchery several Indians took the trouble to count the bodies and to keep tally with a butcher-knife upon the side of a chip. That night, when the scalps were numbered, each brave had one or two apiece, but Squatting Bear handed out exactly forty-seven of the most beautiful bunches of human hair that had ever been seen west of the Mississippi. The braves looked cross-eyed at each other and cleared their throats. Two of their number stole out to the battlefield for the purpose of counting the bodies again, and of ascertaining if this had been a menagerie with a few double-headed persons in the party.

Yes, there lay exactly twenty corpses, and, to make matters worse, one of them was a bald-headed man who, for additional security to his scalp, had run a skate-strap over his head and buckled it under his chin.

When they returned, the entire camp devoted itself to meditation and calculation.

Twenty men killed and forty-seven scalps in the possession of a single Indian, without counting those secured by other participants in the contest! The more the warriors pondered over this fact, the more perplexing it became. A brave, while eating his supper and reflecting upon the problem, would suddenly imagine he saw his way clear, and he would stop, with his mouth full of baked dog, and fix his eyes upon the wall and think desperately hard. But the solution invariably eluded him. Then all of them would glide behind their wigwams and perform abstruse mathematical calculations upon their fingers, and they would get sticks and jam the points into the sand and do hard sums out of their aboriginal arithmetic. And they would tear around through the Indian rule of three, and struggle through their own kind of vulgar fractions, and wrestle with something that they believed to be a multiplication table. But in vain. Forty-seven scalps off twenty heads! It seemed incredible and impossible.

They tried it with algebra, and let the number of heads equal x and the number of scalps equal y, and they multiplied x into y and subtracted every letter in the alphabet in succession from the result until their brains reeled; but still the mystery remained unsolved.

At last a secret council was held, and it was determined that Squatting Bear must have some powerful and wonderful charm which enabled him to perform such miracles, and all hands agreed to investigate the matter upon the first opportunity. So the next week there was another fight, in which four persons were killed, and that night Squatting actually had the audacity to rush out one hundred and eighty-seven scalps, and to ask those benighted savages, sitting around their fire, to believe that he had snatched all that hair from those four heads.

It was too much—much too much; they seized him and drove a white oak stake through his bosom to hold him still, and then they proceeded to his wigwam to ascertain how that scalp business was conducted by the Bear family. They burst open the Saratoga trunk the first thing, and there they found fifteen hundred wigs and a keg of red paint, purchased by the disgraceful aboriginal while in Philadelphia.

That concluded his career. They buried him at once in the Saratoga trunk, and the wigs with him; and ever since that time they have elected annually a committee on scalps, whose business it is to examine every hirsute trophy with a double-barreled microscope of nine hundred diameters.

CHAPTER XX.

WHILE I was helping one of my youngsters a night or two ago to master a tough little problem in his arithmetic, I picked up the history that he had been studying, and as he went off to bed with the other tiny travelers up the hill of knowledge, I looked through the volume. It was Goodrich's History of the United States, for the use of beginners; and it had a very familiar appearance. I gained my first glimpse of the past from this very book; and not only could I remember the text as I turned over the leaves, but the absurd pictures of General Washington and the surrender of Cornwallis, the impossible portraits of John Smith and Benjamin Franklin, and the unnatural illustration of the manner in which the Pilgrim Fathers landed, seemed like respectable old acquaintances whom I had known and admired in happier days.

The man who can find one of the books that he studied

324

when he was a child at school will experience a pleasant
sensation if he will open it and look over its pages. It will
recall some delightful memories, and bring him very close
again to the almost forgotten time when that wretched
little book was to him the mightiest literary achievement in
existence. For this reason I love Goodrich's History; and
I will continue to regard it with affection even though my
judgment may not give it approval as a work of very remarkable excellence.

When Mrs. Adeler descended, after tucking the weary
scholars comfortably in bed, I directed her attention to
these facts, and to some of the peculiarities of Goodrich's
effort:

"This little book, Mrs. A., first unlocked for me the door
of history. It is a history of the United States; and as it was
written by a man who lived in Boston and believed in Boston, it is hardly necessary to say that in my childhood I
obtained from the volume the impression that our beloved
native land consisted chiefly of Boston. I do not wish to
revile that city. It is in many respects a model municipality.
It is, I think, better governed than any other large community in the land, it has greater intellectual force than any
of our cities, and its people have a stronger and more demonstrative civic pride. In Boston the best men are usually
at the front, and the conduct of public affairs is not entrusted, as it is in Philadelphia and other cities, to black-
guardly politicians whom a respectable man would not admit to his house, and who maintain themselves in power by
fraudulent elections and by stealing the people's money.
Every Boston man believes in the greatness of his city, and
is proud of it. That is an excellent condition of public sentiment, and we may pardon it even if it does sometimes produce results that are slightly ridiculous.

"Goodrich was what might be called an excessive Boston

man, and his little history is very apt, unintentionally, to convey erroneous impressions to the infant mind. In my early boyhood, being completely saturated with Goodrich, I entertained an indistinct idea that the eye of Columbus rested upôn Boston long before any other object appeared above the horizon, and somehow I cherished a conviction that the natives who greeted him and bowed down at his feet were men who inhabited Bunker Hill Monument and disported themselves perpetually among the chambers of Faneuil Hall. I never doubted that every important event in our annals, from the landing of those unpleasant old Puritans of the Mayflower down to the election of Andrew Jackson, occurred in Boston, and was attributable entirely to the remarkable superiority of the people of that city. I scoffed at the theory that John Smith was in Virginia at the time of his salvation by Pocahontas, and I was even disposed to regard the account of the signing of the Declaration of Independence at Philadelphia as a sort of an insignificant 'side show' which should have been alluded to briefly in a foot-note. I honestly believed that the one great mistake of George Washington's life was that he was born elsewhere than in Boston, and I felt that, however hard such retribution might appear, he deserved to be considered a little less great on account of that error.

"As for the war of the Revolution, I could not doubt, while I maintained my faith in Goodrich, that it was begun by the high-spirited citizens of Boston in consequence of the wrongs inflicted upon them by that daring and impious monarch King George III. It was equally clear that the conflict was carried on only by the people of Boston, and that the victory was won at last because of the valor displayed by the citizens of that community.

"In my opinion, and apparently in the opinion of Good-rich, the leading event of the war was that related in chapter eighty-five. The story occupies the whole chapter. The historian evidently intended that the youthful mind, while meditating upon the most important episode of the dreadful struggle, should not be disturbed by minor matters. Chapter eighty-five relates that certain British soldiers demolished snow hills that had been constructed by some boys upon Boston Common, a hallowed spot which Goodrich taught me to regard as the pivotal point of the universe. The boys determined to call upon General Gage, and to protest against this brutal outrage committed by the hireling butchers of a bloated despot. Now listen while I read the account of that interview as it is given by Goodrich:

"General Gage asked why so many children had called upon him. 'We come, sir,' said the tallest boy, 'to demand satisfaction.' 'What!' said the general; 'have your fathers been teaching you rebellion, and sent you to exhibit it here?' 'Nobody sent us, sir,' answered the boy, while his cheek reddened and his eye flashed. 'We have never injured nor insulted your troops; but they have trodden down our snow-hills and broken the ice on our skating-ground. We complained, and they called us young rebels, and told us to help ourselves if we could. We told the captain of this, and he laughed at us. Yesterday our works were destroyed the third time, and we will bear it no longer.' General Gage looked at them a moment in silent admiration, and then said to an officer at his side, 'The very children here draw in a love of liberty with the air they breathe.'

"The story of this event, which shaped the destinies of a great nation and gave liberty to a continent, I learned by heart. Many and many a night have I lain awake wishing that Philadelphians would organize another war with Great Britain, so that British soldiers could come over and batter down a snow hill that I would build in Independence Square. I felt certain that I should go at once, in such an event, to see the general, and should overwhelm him with another

27

outburst of fiery indignation. It seemed rather hard that Philadelphia boys should never have a chance to surpass the boys of Boston. But still I could not help admiring those young braves and regarding them as the real authors of American independence. I was well assured that if that 'tallest boy' had not entered the general's room and flashed his eye at Gage all would have been lost; the country would have been ground beneath the iron heel of the oppressor, and Americans would have been worse than slaves. Perhaps it did me no harm to believe all this; but it seems to me that we might as well instruct children properly to begin with. Therefore I shall give our boy, Agamemnon, some private lessons in history to supplement the wisdom of Goodrich."

Just as I had concluded my remarks, Judge Pitman came in to ask me to let him look at the evening paper which I had brought with me from the city. I explained to him the nature of the subject that had been considered, and the judge, as usual, had something to say about it.

"Do you know," he observed, "that them school-books that they make now-a-days is perfectly bewilderin' to a man like me? When I went to school, we learned nothin' but readin', writin' and arithmetic. But now—well, they've got clear past me. I could no more rassle with the learnin' they have at the schools, now than a babe unborn."

"To what special department of learning do you refer?" I inquired.

"Oh, all of 'em, all of 'em. I had a very cur'ous experience with one o' them books once," said the judge, with a laugh. "Some years ago I took a notion to jine the church, an' they give me the catechism to learn afore I could git in. When I got home, I laid the book away on the shelf, an' didn't go for it for two or three days. When I was ready to study it up, I reached down what I thought was the catechism, an'

I was kinder surprised to see that it was called 'Familiar Science.' You understand it was a book my daughter had been learnin' at school. But I knowed no better. I never paid no 'tention to religion afore; an' although it struck me as sorter queer that a catechism should have such questions and answers in it, I thought the church people that give me the book must know what was right, so I said nothin' an' went to work at it."

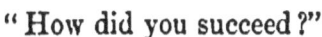

"How did you succeed?"

"Oh, putty good. I learned three or four pages by heart, an' I thought that was 'bout enough. So after while the minister an' the rest come 'round an' begun examinin' me. I noticed that the questions kinder didn't fit in, but I did my best; an' when they'd ask me about the Scripters, I'd jam in somethin' about carbonic acid gas, an' when they inquired about the whole duty of man, I desp'rately give 'em somethin' relatin' to the functions of lightnin'-rods."

"You must have astonished them."

"You never seen men wuss bewildered," replied the judge; "but I think I really skeered 'em when they asked me about Solomon's temple, an' I lit out with an answer referrin' to smoky chimneys. They thought I was insane. But when

I pulled out the book an' showed it to 'em, the preacher laughed an' told me about the mistake. Then we hunted up the catechism an' got the thing straight. The church folks had the laugh on me for a while, but I didn't mind it. An' it *was* pretty fair for a joke, wasn't it ?"

"Excellent."

"But I got a better one on at least one of them fellers. Doctor Brindley was on the examinin' committee, an' he run me harder than any of 'em about it. Well, sir— Do you know old Hillegass?"

"No; I never heard of him."

"He lives out yer on the Wilmington road. Well, sir,

some time afore that Hillegass was putty near dead. He was the wust case I ever seen. Broken down, thin an' pale, with no appetite, his lungs weak, his liver good for nothin', his legs full of rheumatics, his heart affected an' his head achin' with neuralger, I really believe that man was the sickest human bein' that ever breathed the breath of life. All the doctors in the country had a shy at him one time an' another; an' as he kep' a-gettin' wuss an' wuss, they made him mad, an' he wouldn't pay their bills."

"He was not much to blame for that."

"Certainly not. Well, one day them doctors met, an' after talkin' the thing over they agreed not to go to Hillegass's again unless he settled up, you understand. They said, ' Now we'll let Hillegass die ; we've fooled with him long enough. He's either got to pay or perish. No more Hillegass for us unless we see some cash.' So for about a year they let him alone; an' whenever one of 'em would drive past the house, he would pull up for a minute, look to see if there was crape on the door, an' then go on, shakin' his head an' sayin', 'Poor Hillegass! the stingy old fool's not long for this world.'"

"Did he die?"

"Die! One day Dr. Brindley felt kinder sorry for Hillegass, an' he weakened on his resolution. So he called at the house to see how he was gittin' on. As he went in the yard he seen a stoutish man liftin' a bar'l of flour in a waggin. When the man got the bar'l in, he seen the doctor an' come for'ard. The doctor thought he knew the scar on the man's nose, but he couldn't believe it. Howsomedever, it *was* old Hillegass, well an' hearty as a buck, an' able to h'ist the roof off the barn if he'd a mind to. You understand that I had a very soft thing on Brindley jes' then; an' he

27 *

never seemed to take no furder interest in the catechism
business when he met me.   An' they don't encourage
doctors much out that way now; no, sir. They trust to luck
an' natur', which in my opinion is the best way, anyhow."

"A great many remarkable things seem to have happened
in this place," I said.

"Yes," responded the judge. "You'd hardly think it of
such a quiet town as this 'pears to be; but somehow there's
'most always somethin' lively goin' on.   There was that fuss
'round at Dr. Hopkins's a couple o' year ago; did you hear
'bout that?"

"Not that I know of."

"Well, we'd jes' got a new fire-engine in the
town, an' the men that run her thought they'd
play a little joke on the chief of the department by rushin' 'round to his house an'
pretendin' it was afire. By a most unfort'nit
circumstance, the chief moved out of the
house that mornin', and Dr.
Hopkins—the preacher, you
know—moved in.   Them fellers come a-peltin' 'round with
the engine, an' they run up
their ladders an' begun a-
playin' on the roof in a manner that skeered the Hopkinses
nearly to death.   But the
other fire company thought

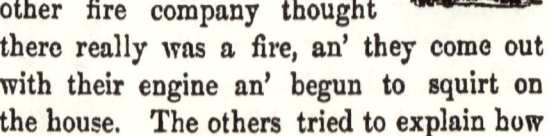

there really was a fire, an' they come out
with their engine an' begun to squirt on
the house.   The others tried to explain how
it was, but the new-comers wouldn't believe 'em, an' they
kep' a-pourin' water into the winders an' a carryin' on like
mad. So at last they got up a fight, an' they fought all

over the house an' on the stairs an' up an' down the

entries, until Dr. Hopkins was putty near insane; an' when they went home, he counted up about two hundred dollars damages, which them fellers had to pay. Yes, it is astonishin' how they used to keep things a-movin' in this town. An' now I really must be goin'. I'll send back the paper the fust thing in the mornin', for certain."

The judge then went home; and just as he passed out of the door Bob Parker came in with a radiant countenance. He had succeeded in obtaining the evidence that was needed for his vindication.

CHAPTER XXI

SETTLING THE BUSINESS—VINDICATION OF MR. BOB PARKER—
A COMPLETE RECONCILIATION—THE GREAT COOLEY IN-
QUEST—THE UNCERTAINTY IN REGARD TO THOMAS COOLEY
—A PHENOMENAL CORONER—PROFITABLE INVESTIGATIONS—
HOW THE PEOPLE PROSPERED—THE SOLUTION OF THE
MYSTERY.

R. PARKER had good rea-
son for exultation. He had
in his possession testimony
which exposed and com-
pletely defeated the wretched little conspiracy organized against him by Smiley.

"It was a very easy
thing to settle this business," said Bob. "I ex-
plained the matter to the
members of our firm, and
they not only gave me a letter containing very strong
expressions of confidence in
me and denouncing Stone-
bury as a wholly untrustworthy and disreputable person, but
they insisted that I should make Stonebury confess. Accordingly, a member of the firm accompanied me while I
hunted him up. We found that he had a clerkship in one
of the municipal offices, and we called to see him. He
turned absolutely white when he saw me, and looked as if
he would like to beat a retreat. But we went at him, and

334

threatened that if he did not acknowledge in writing that he had maligned me we would prosecute him for the theft committed while he was engaged at the store, and have him ousted from his present position.

"He came down at once, and began to excuse his conduct upon the ground that Smiley had compelled him to do as he did. Then he made a written confession that his statements concerning me were lies, and that he was the real author of the letter which professed to come from Rev. Dr. Dewey. Here it is—here are both letters; and I propose to enlighten the Magruder intellect with them this very night."

"Wouldn't it be better to wait until to-morrow? It is rather late now."

"No, sir. I intend to settle the affair finally and for ever before I go to bed. I have been waiting long enough. Now I am going to enjoy my victory without further delay. Let's go around there at once."

So Bob and I started for the Magruder mansion; and when we reached the street, he strode along at such a rapid gait that I could hardly keep up with him. As we approached the house I ventured to suggest that the dog might perhaps be at large, in which event I thought I would rather remain in the drug store on the other side of the street until he returned.

"I would go into the house," exclaimed Bob, "if there were a million bloodhounds tearing around the front yard."

"Well, I believe I wouldn't. I have less enthusiasm than you. I am growing old and cautious. A much smaller quantity of bloodhound would restrain what little impetuosity I have. Only one vigorous bloodhound stationed in that yard and betraying a disposition to exclude me would dampen my ardor. I should go home at once."

"Magruder's dog won't bite," said Bob. "He knows me well, and we needn't be a bit afraid of him."

"Very well, I will run the risk; but if any accident occurs, I shall blame you for it. I would rather you should lose your lady-love than that I should be deprived of the use of my legs."

"And, of course, I wouldn't. But come along, and never mind the dog."

As we entered the gate the dog was there, and he followed  us upon the porch, still manifesting intense eagerness to sniff our trowsers. It is remarkable with what carefulness and steadiness a man walks under such circumstances. I would not have made a sudden jump or a quick movement of any kind for a valuable consideration.

When we entered the house, Mr. Magruder met us, and we went with him into the library, where Mrs. Magruder was sitting with a book in her hand. We obtained a glimpse of Bessie as she vanished through the other door into the next room; and Bob seemed to feel a little disappointed that she had not remained. Mr. Magruder began the conversation :

"Well, Mr. Parker, I trust you have been successful in your efforts?"

"Yes, sir," replied Bob. "I have accomplished all that I hoped for. I have, I think, procured evidence which will vindicate me completely and prove that I have been grossly slandered."

"I hope this is the case," said Mr. Magruder. "What is the nature of your—"

"Here are two letters. This one is from one of my employers. The other is written by Samuel Stonebury, a man whose name at least is known to you."

Magruder took the papers and read them aloud, so that

his wife might obtain the information supplied by them. Then, as he slowly folded them up, he said:

"Mr. Parker, this does indeed seem to be conclusive. I blame myself very much for having reposed confidence in Smiley and in his villainous friend, but more than all because I treated you as if you were guilty before I heard you in your own defence. I owe you a very humble apology, sir, and I now make it. I hope you will forgive me;" and Magruder extended his hand.

"I believed in you from the first," said Mrs. Magruder.

"And I thank you for it," replied Bob.

"I suppose Bessie might as well come in now, my dear," said Mr. Magruder.

"Certainly," replied his wife, and she called Bessie.

Bessie had evidently been listening upon the other side of the door, for she entered instantly, with her smiling face rosy with blushes. Bob merely took her hand, and stood by her looking as if he would like to indulge in a tenderer demonstration. Then I announced my intention to go home, and as I did so Bob said he believed he would stay a little longer. Mr. and Mrs. Magruder came out with me into the hall to say good-bye, and as the library-door closed I thought I heard the sound of a kiss. I hope the old people went into the parlor or retired to bed after my departure. There had been a cruel separation of the two lovers, and a good deal of genuine suffering, at least upon Bessie's part, and it was but fair that they should have a chance to enjoy to the very utmost, without the intrusion of another person, the bliss of that reunion.

Upon the day following this reconciliation Smiley was in town, and he called at Magruder's. The old gentleman saw him coming, and met him at the door. In reply to Smiley's salutation Magruder looked sternly at him, and after telling him that his villainy had been exposed, the indignant man ordered the lieutenant to leave his house and never to enter it again. Smiley turned upon his heel and slunk away. We have probably seen the last of him; and just as he has disappeared we have learned that he is likely to be cashiered from the army for bad conduct. His brother officers at the fort have discovered his true character just as it has been revealed to us.

This rambling narrative would not deserve to be received as a faithful record of events that have occurred in our neighborhood if it should fail to include an account of the extraordinary circumstances attending what is known here as "The Great Cooley Inquest." The story of that remarkable business must be given even if it shall be introduced with abruptness.

My neighbor William Cooley had a brother named Thomas, who lived at a place called Vandyke, in New Castle county. Thomas Cooley was in some respects a very remarkable man. He was gifted with genius, but it was genius of an impracticable kind. He was an inventor, and during the later years of his life he devoted all his time to the work of constructing surprising machines which would never do anything when they were constructed.

Down at the patent-office they got so at last that when a new model and specifications would come along from Cooley, the commissioner and clerks would grant him a patent on the spot, for they knew, from a rich and generous experience, that when Cooley invented anything it was perfectly certain to be unlike any other contrivance ever conceived by the mind of fallen man; and they were aware, at any rate, that nobody who was sane enough to be at large would ever want to interfere with Cooley's exclusive right to pin together such a bewildering and useless lot of cranks and axles and wheels. I think Cooley had about two hundred patents of various kinds; and besides the machines and dodges thus protected by the law, he owned scores of others which were never heard of in Washington or anywhere else but at Cooley's home.

Cooley had a kind of "den" of his own in the garret. He used to shut himself up in this for hours together while he perfected his inventions or conducted his chemical investigations. His last idea was that he could put together a compound which would rule gunpowder out of the market, and make the destruction of armies and navies comparatively easy. And so, for a time, Mrs. Cooley, while bustling about in the vicinity of the den, instead of hearing the buzz and hum of wheels and the click of the hammer, would sniff terrific smells, evolved by the irrepressible Cooley from the contents of his laboratory. And one day there came a fearful explosion. The roof was torn off and reduced to splinters, and Thomas Cooley had disappeared.

Vandyke, as I have said, is in New Castle county, Delaware, but it is also close to the boundary line between Delaware and the counties of Cecil and Kent, in Maryland.

And so it was not surprising when, a few minutes after the explosion, persons in all three of the counties perceived fragments of a demoralized and disintegrated human being tumbling from the air. The pieces of the unhappy victim of the disaster were unevenly distributed between New Castle, Cecil and Kent. The first named got twelve of the fragments. There were persons who thought Cooley might have showed even greater partiality for his own county, but I do not blame him; he was in a measure controlled by circumstances.

I think the friends of the coroner complained with greatest bitterness. He was an enthusiastic coroner. He had been known, when one of Dr. Tobias Jones's relatives returned from Egypt with a mummy embalmed fifteen hundred years before the Christian era, to seize that ancient subject of Pharaoh and summon a jury, and sit upon it, and brood over it and think. And it is rumored that he put that jury up to bringing in a verdict, "The death of the deceased ensued from cause or causes unknown, at the hands of persons also unknown." His enemies at the next election openly asserted that he charged the county with the usual fee, with compound interest from the time of Moses.

So of course when Thomas Cooley went up, *he* wasn't sorry; and the more Cooley was scattered over New Castle county, the more serene and affable the coroner felt. When he had selected his jury and looked around him a little in order to command the situation, he perceived that Cooley had put into his hands a tolerably good thing. The coroner spent the next three days holding an inquest upon each of the twelve fragments of the deceased. He empaneled a new jury every time, and then proceeded cautiously and deliberately in each case.

There was by no means complete unanimity of opinion. The first jury decided that "the deceased met his death by being struck by something sudden." The second one advanced the theory that "Thomas Cooley was surreptitiously and insidiously blowed apart." The others threw out suggestions respecting the probability that the trouble came from Cooley's well-known weakness for flying machines, or from his being lifted out and cut up by some kind of a hurricane. Once the jury decided not to bring in a verdict, but merely to pass resolutions of regret.

And the coroner would sit there over the particular piece of Cooley in question, and smile and permit these manifestations of generous feeling to have full play. It didn't perplex *him* that all the verdicts differed. "Truth," he remarked to a friend, "is well enough. But as Cooley is certainly dead, what's the odds if we can't agree as to what killed him? Let us collect our fees and yield with Christian resignation to destiny."

It was always interesting to me to hear that coroner converse upon the subject of resignation. He would rather have died than to have resigned while any of the Cooleys were in town inventing explosive compounds.

The Cecil county coroner discovered six pieces of the deceased within his jurisdiction, but his pride would not permit him to yield the supremacy in such a matter to his rival over the line. The New Castle man had twelve inquests, and so would he, with more besides. And his juries used to go out and consult and come in after a while with a majority report, declaring, perhaps, that deceased was killed by fooling with some sort of a gun, and a minority report insisting that he had been murdered and dissected by a medical student or students unknown.

And then the coroner would disband the inquest and drum up a fresh jury, which would also disagree, until out of those six fractions of poor old Cooley the coroner got thirty-seven deliberations, with the attendant fees. And every time the doctors would testify that *post-mortem* examinations revealed the fact that the inside of the deceased was crammed with fragments of the Latin language; and invariably the jurors would sit there and try to look as if they understood those terms, although a dim impression prevailed most of the time that the physicians were indulging recklessly in profanity.

And when a relative of Cooley's testified before the thirty-seventh jury that "Thomas Cooley was a man of marked idiosyncrasies, and his brain was always excited by his irresistible fondness for chimeras of various kinds," the jury looked solemn and immediately brought in a verdict that "death was caused by idiosyncrasies forming on his brain in consequence of excessive indulgence in chimeras, thus supplying an awful warning to the young to refrain from the use of that and other intoxicating beverages."

Only two pieces fell in Kent county, but the coroner was animated by even greater professional enthusiasm than his neighbors across the border. He spent the entire season over as much of Cooley as he could reach. All his juries but one disagreed, and he had eighty-four. The sixth would have been unanimous but for an obstinate man named Selfridge. All the others were for a verdict of mysterious butchery, but Selfridge insisted upon attributing the disaster to nitro-glycerine. So earnest was he that he fought over

the subject with a fellow-juryman named Smith; and he held Smith down and remonstrated with him, and showed him the matter in different lights, and bit his nose to convince Smith that

the nitro-glycerine hypothesis was correct. And when the
jury was dismissed, Selfridge, true to his solemn convictions,
carried the war into the papers, and published an obituary
poem entitled " A Monody on the Death of Thomas Cooley,"
in which he presented his views in this fashion :

" When Cooley got his glycerine all properly adjusted,
  He knocked it unexpectedly, and suddenly it busted;
  And when it reached old Thomas C., he got up quick and dusted,
  And left his wife and family disheartened and disgusted."

It was discovered that one of the bones of the deceased had
fallen directly across the boundary line between Cecil and
Kent. As soon as the fact was reported, the coroner of
Kent rallied a jury upon his end; and just as the proceedings were about to begin, the Cecil coroner arrived with a
jury for the purpose of attending to his share of the work.
While the authorities of Kent mused at one end of the bone,
the jurymen of Cecil reflected at the other end, and the re-

sult was that each brought in an entirely different verdict.
But they were unanimous on the question of the collection
of fees.

In all there were thirteen or fourteen conflicting verdicts
rendered, and so some uncertainty prevailed as to the precise cause of Cooley's death. Men's minds were unsettled,
and their conclusions were demoralized, in the presence of
so much official authority of an indecisive kind. But nobody mourned over these differences. They were a blessing
for the people of the counties. Almost every man in the

neighborhood had had a turn at Cooley's remains, and some of them had served on the juries six or seven times. The farmers all bought new mowing-machines that spring with their fees. The doctors collected more money for *post-mortem* examinations than they would have done in a time of an epidemic of small-pox and sudden death. People fixed up their houses and paid off mortgages and laid in their pork and started grocery stores and gave hops out of the profits of Cooley's explosion. And there were men who cherished a wish that Cooley could be put together again and exploded once a month for the next decade. But that of course was impossible.

One day, when the tide of prosperity was at its height, the widow Cooley perceived a wagon driving up to her door. The man within the vehicle dismounted, and unloaded four pieces of iron pipe sixty feet long. Presently another wagon arrived, and this driver also unloaded the same quantity of pipe. Then a third driver arrived and did the same thing. Then a fourth came, and Mrs. Cooley saw a man in it with a queer-looking object by him. It proved to be Thomas Cooley himself. Thomas had been up to the city at a machine-shop getting up a working model of a new kind of a patent duplex elliptic artesian pump; and now he was home again. The remains scattered over the counties were—so Cooley said—merely a lot of beef with which he had been trying to make a new kind of patent portable soup and an improved imperishable army sausage; and the explosion, he thought, must have been caused by spontaneous combustion.

Thomas Cooley would have been happy, after all, but for one thing—everybody outside of his own family refused to recognize him as a living man. If he was willing to move about in the community in the character of an unburied corpse, the people would agree not to interfere and not to insist upon his burial; but that was as far as they could go conscientiously. Their duty to society, their obligations to the law, compelled them to reject the idea that he was anything more than inanimate remains. He was officially dead. The fact had been declared under oath by hundreds of jurymen, and it was registered in the records of two States and three counties. The testimony was overwhelmingly against him. To admit that he was still alive would be dangerous, it would be revolutionary. The foundations of society would be shaken, the majesty of the law would suffer insult, the fabric of republican government would be undermined. If a being who was legally only a mere cadaver was to be permitted to strut out into daylight, and to urge incendiary theories about the condition of his vital spark, nothing would be safe; there would be no guarantee that the cemeteries would not unload, and that all of the departed would not be crowding out and wanting to vote. Besides, if it was admitted that Cooley was yet alive, all the money that had been earned by the jurymen, all the fees that had been charged by the coroners, would have to be returned to the county treasuries. The people were aghast at the thought. The coroners entered into a solemn compact to persist in ignoring Cooley or to regard him merely as an absurd and very indelicate goblin who had behaved in a manner wholly unworthy of a ghost with gentlemanly instincts. They declared publicly that they could not admit that Cooley was alive unless there should be a general resurrection in the States of Delaware and Maryland, and until that time arrived, they considered that the best thing Cooley could do would be to select a sepulchre somewhere and creep into it and behave.

I do not know that I can find a better place than this to insert a bundle of rhymes which I have at hand. The wholesale slaughter in which the hero and heroine indulge seems to entitle the poem to association with the three coroners above mentioned. And I may venture to remark that not one of the officials in question will read the lines without a feeling of profound regret that such magnificent opportunities for inquests are hardly likely to be presented in Maryland and Delaware. Our New Castle coroner would accumulate millions in the shape of fees if he could have the privilege of summoning juries to investigate such a butchery as this.

A HINDOO LEGEND.

There was a Hindoo maiden once on India's coral strand
Who had some forty suitors for her coffee-colored hand.
Her father was a Brahmin of aristocratic caste
Who much internal revenue in dry goods had amassed.

These lovers thought it would be nice the dusky maid to wed,
And spend the rupees lavishly when her papa was dead.
But she turned up her nose at them—a very pretty pug—
Because clandestinely she loved an elegant young Thug.

This Thug, in his profession, was a very active man;
He strangled eighty men the year to practice he began.
But as the maiden's father had no taste for art at all,
He foolishly disliked the Thug, and wouldn't let him call.

And then she loved him better still, as always is the case,
And so she met him daily at a certain trysting-place.
Hand in hand amid the verdant fields deliciously they strayed,
Now culling flowers, now strangling little children as they played.

And this young Thug, one afternoon, he kissed the maid and said,
"It really seems to me, my dear, high time that we should wed.
And as your guardians to me so seriously object,
'Twould be as well to kill them; I can do it, I expect."

Then said the lovely maiden, with a sweet, confiding smile:
"I go for chopping of them up in most effectual style.
And as my marriage simply on my papa's death depends,
Why, just for fun we'll butcher all my relatives and friends."

The Thug procured a hatchet, and the maiden got a knife;
They cut and slashed the Brahmin till he was bereft of life;
Then they seized the loving mother, though she desperately fought,
And crunched her aged bones beneath the car of Juggernaut.

A consecrated lasso, thrown with admirable skill,
Swiftly roped her brother in and choked him 'gainst his will.
Her sister's fair young form was hooked upon the sacred swing;
And flying 'round until she died, she screamed like everything.

The maiden jabbed the knife into the colored coachman's brain,
And stabbed her uncle William and her aunt Matilda Jane.
The Thug he steeped his hatchet in the chambermaiden's gore,
And with a skewer pinned the cook against the cellar door.

The maiden cut her grandpa up in little tiny bits,
And scared her grandma so she died in epileptic fits.

The dry nurse with the clothes-line was serenely strangled, while
They tossed the little baby to the sacred crocodile..

And when the fuss was over, said the maiden to the Thug:
"You'd better have a hole within the cemetery dug;
And let the undertaker take extraordinary pains
To decently inter this lot of mangled-up remains."

And when the usual bitter tears were at the funeral shed,
The lovers to the temple went, in order to be wed.
The priest had barbecued a man that day for sacrifice;
They cooked him with the cracklin' on; with gravy brown and nice.

The chief priest asked the maiden, when the services began,
If her papa had said she might annex this fine young man?
"Oh no," she said, "my loving wish he foolishly withstood,
So him and all the family we slaughtered in cold blood."

"You shock me!" said the pious priest; "your conduct makes me
          sad;
You never learned at Sunday-school to be so awful bad.
I've told you often, when you killed a person anywhere,
To bring the body to that old nine-headed idol there;

"The great Vishnu is suffering for victims every day,
And here you go and cut them up and throw the bones away!
Extravagance is sinful; I must really put it down;
I've half a mind to pull the string and make the idol frown.

"I must punish you with rigor; and I order that you two
Instead of getting married shall severest penance do."
So on a piece of paper then he scribbled a brief word;
The lovers as they left, of course, felt perfectly absurd.

The Thug then read the order o'er, and bursting into tears,
He said, "This paper realizes my unpleasant fears.
Upon my word, my sweetest one, it really chills my blood;
I've got to suffocate you in the Ganges' holy mud."

And so he sadly led her down unto the river's bank,
And like a stone into the cold, religious slime she sank.
And there she stuck the livelong day, and all the following night,
Until an alligator came and ate her at a bite.

The Thug he felt exceeding hurt at her untimely fate,
But his, though not so dreadful, was not nice, at any rate.
The priest, in his fierce anger, had condemned him, it appears,
To stand alone upon one leg for forty-seven years!

CHAPTER XXII

An Arrival—A Present from a Congressman—Meditations upon his Purpose—The Patent Office Report of the Future—A Plan for Revolutionizing Public Documents and Opening a New Department of Literature —Our Trip to Salem—A Tragical Incident—The Last of Lieutenant Smiley.

VERY mysterious package came to me through the post-office yesterday. I brought it home unopened, and, as is usual in such cases, we began to speculate upon the nature of the contents before we broke the seals. Everybody has a disposition to dally for a while with a letter or a package from an unknown source. Mrs. Adeler felt the parcel carefully, and said she was sure it was something from her aunt—something for the baby, probably. Bob imagined that it was an infernal machine forwarded by the revengeful Stonebury, and he insisted that I should put it to soak in a bucket of water for a few hours before removing the wrapper. The children were hopeful that some benign fairy had adopted this method of supplying the Adeler

350

family with supernatural confectionery; and for my part, I had no doubt that some one of my friends among the publishers had sent me half a dozen of the latest books.

We opened the bundle gradually. When the outside casing was torn away, another envelope remained, and as this was slowly removed the excitement and curiosity reached an almost painful degree of intensity. At last all the papers were taken off, and I lifted from among them a large black volume. It was only a patent-office report sent to me by that incorruptible statesman and devoted patriot, the Congressman from our State.

I have endeavored to conjecture why he should have selected me as the object of such a demonstration. Certainly he did not expect me to read the report. He knows that I, as a man of at least ordinary intelligence, would endure torture first. I cannot think that he hoped to purchase my vote by such a cheap expedient. Congressmen do, I believe, still cherish the theory that the present of a patent-office report to a constituent secures for the donor the fealty of the recipient; but it is a delusion. Such a gift fills the soul of an unoffending man with gloomy and murderous thoughts. Every one feels at times as if he would like to butcher some of his fellow-men; and my appetite for slaughter only becomes keen when I meet a Congressman who has sent me a patent-office report. Neither can I accept the suggestion that my representative was deceived by the supposition that I would be grateful for such an intimation that an eminent man, even amid the oppressive cares of State, has not forgotten so humble a worm as I. He knows me well; and although I am aware that there is in Washington a prevalent theory that a wild thrill of exultation agitates the heart of a constituent when he receives a public document or a flatulent oration from a lawmaker, my Congressman is better informed. He would not insult me in such a manner. I can only account for his conduct upon the theory that he misdirected the volume, which he intended for some one else, or upon the supposition that he has heard me speak of the necessity for the occasional bombardment of Cooley's dog at night, and he conceived that he would be helping a good cause by supplying me with a new and formidable missile. I have never attacked a dog with a patent-office report, but I can imagine that the animal might readily be slain with such a weapon. A projectile should have ponderosity; and a patent-office report has more of that quality to the cubic inch than any other object with which I am familiar. Still, I do not care to tax the treasury of the United States for material with which to assail Cooley's dog. I would rather endure the nocturnal ululations, and have the money applied to the liquidation of the national debt.

It is, however, apparent that Congressmen will never surrender the patent-office report; and if this is admitted, it seems to me that the man who succeeds in infusing into those volumes such an amount of interest that people will be induced to read them will have a right to be regarded as a great public benefactor. I suppose no human being ever did read one of them. It is tolerably certain that any man who would deliberately undertake to peruse one from beginning to end would be regarded as a person who ought not to be at large. His friends would be justified in placing him in an asylum. I think I can suggest a method by which a reform can be effected. It is to take the material that comes to hand each year and to work it up into a continuous story, which may be filled in with tragedy and sentiment and humor.

For instance, if a man came prowling around the patent-

office with an improvement in hayrakes, I should name
that man Alphonso and start him off in the story as the

abandoned villain; Alphonso lying in wait, as it were, behind a dark corner, for the purpose of scooping his rival with
that improved hay-rake. And then the hero
would be a man, suppose we say, who desired
an extension of a patent on accordeons. I
should call such a person Lucullus, and plant
him, with a working model of the accordeon,
under the window of the boarding-house where
the heroine, Amelia, who would be a woman
who had applied for a patent on a new kind
of red flannel frills, lay sleeping under the
soothing influence of the tunes squeezed from
the accordeon of Lucullus.

In the midst of the serenade, let us suppose, in comes a
man who has just got out some extraordinary kind of a fowling-piece about which he wants to interview the head of the

department. I should make this being Amelia's father and call him Smith, because that name is full of poetry and sweetness and wild, unearthly music. Then, while Lucullus was mashing out delicious strains, I might make Alphonso rush on Smith with his hay-rake, thinking he  was Lucullus, and in the fight which would perhaps ensue Smith might blow out Alphonso's brains somehow on the spot by a single discharge, we might assume, of Smith's extraordinary fowling-piece, while Lucullus could be arrested upon the suit of the composer who had a copyright on the tune with which he solaced Amelia.

If any ingenious undertaker should haunt the patent-office at this crisis of the story with a species of metallic coffin, I might lay Alphonso away comfortably in one of them and have a funeral, or I might add a thrill of interest to the narrative by resuscitating him with vegetable pills, in case any benefactor of the race should call to secure his rights as the sole manufacturer of such articles. In the mean time, Lucullus, languishing in jail, could very readily burst his fetters and regain his liberty, provided some man of inventive talent called on the commissioner to take out searches, say, on some kind of a revertible crowbar.

Then the interest of the story would be sustained, and a few more machines of various kinds could be worked in, if, for instance, I should cause this escaped convict of mine to ascertain that the musical composer had won the heart of Amelia, in the absence of her lover, by offering to bring her flannel frills into market, and to allow her a royalty. we will assume, of ten cents a frill. When Lucullus hears of this, I should induce him to try to obtain the influence of Amelia's parents in his behalf by propitiating old Mr. Smith with the latest variety of bunion plaster for which a patent was wanted, while Mrs. Smith could be appeased either with a gingham umbrella with an improvement of six or seven extra ribs, or else a lot of galvanized gum rings, if any inventor brought such things around, for her grandchildren.

Then, for the sake of breaking the monotony of these intrigues, we could have a little more of the revivified Alphonso. I could very readily fill the heart of that reanimated corpse with baffled rage, and cause him to sell to old Smith one of McBride's improved hydraulic rams. Smith could be depicted as an infatuated being who placed that ram down in the meadow and caused it to force water up to

his house. And Alphonso, of course, with malignant hatred in his soul, would meddle with the machine, and fumble around until he spoiled it, so that Smith could not stop it,

29 *

and it would continue to pump until the Smiths had a cascade flowing from their attic window. Mrs. Smith, in her despair, might impale herself on a variety of reversible toasting-fork, and die mingling the inventor's name with maledictions and groans, while Smith, in the anguish of his soul, could live in the barn, from whence he could use an ingenious kind of breech-loading gun—patent applied for—to perforate artists who came around to sketch the falls.

In the mean time, Lucullus might come to the rescue with a suction pump and save the Smith mansion, only to find that Amelia had flown with the composer, and had gone to sea in a ship with a patent copper bottom, and a kind of a binnacle for which an extension had been granted by Congress on the 26th of February. It would then be well, perhaps, to have that copper-bottomed ship attacked by pirates, and after a bloody hand-to-hand contest, in which the composer could sink the pirate craft with the model of a gunpowder pile-driver which he has in the cabin, the enraged corsairs should swarm upon the deck of the other ship for the purpose of putting the whole party to the sword. And, of course, at this painful crisis it would be singularly happy to cause it to turn out that the chief pirate is our old friend Alphonso, who had sold out his interest in his hay-rake, discontinued his speculations in hydraulic rams and become a rover upon the seas.

The composer, it would seem, would then be in a particularly tight place; and if the commissioner of patents had any romance in his soul, he would permit me to cause that pirate to toss the musician overboard. Amelia would then tear herself from the pirate's loathsome embrace and plunge in after him. The two would float ashore on a life-raft, if any applications of that kind happened to be presented to the department. When they got to land, Amelia would shiver with cold until her jaws rattled, and the painful truth would be disclosed to her lover that she wore teeth which were attached to one of the gutta-percha plates about which there was a controversy in the courts.

Then, if we seemed to be approaching the end of the report, I think I would cause the composer to shriek "False! false!" or to use some exciting language of that kind, and to tear out his hair and wring his  nose and fly off with a broken heart and a blasted life to join the pirates and to play melancholy airs in a minor key, expressive of delusive dreams, for ever and for ever, upon some kind of a double-barreled flute with a copyright on it.

Thus even the prosaic material of which the patent-office reports are constructed could be made to yield entertainment and instruction, and afford a basis of succulent and suggestive fact for a superstructure of pathetic and blood-curdling fiction. The advantages of adopting such a method in constructing these documents would be especially marked in the case of Congressmen. The member who now sends a patent-office report to one of his constituents is regarded by that man as a kind of moral ruin who ought to be put in some place where it would be impossible for him to destroy the happiness and poison the peace of unoffending families. But when a competent novelist prepares those reports, when he throws over them the glamour of his fancy, when he adorns them with his graceful rhetoric, and gives a certain intense human interest to all the hay-rakes and gum rings and suction pumps which now fill the leaden pages, these reports will be sought after; their tone will be changed; children will cry for them; Sunday-schools will offer them as rewards, and the intelligent American voter whose mind craves healthy literature will elect to Congress the man who will promise to send him the greatest number of copies.

Here is the story of a tragical event of which I was a witness, and which has created a profound impression upon the people of this community.

An aunt of Bessie Magruder's lives at Salem; and as she had never seen Bob, she invited him and his betrothed to visit her one day last week, coupling the invitation with a request that we and the elder Magruders would come at the same time and take dinner with her. When the boat from up the river arrived at New Castle, the entire party of us went aboard. As the steamer shot across the water to Delaware City, Bob and Bessie wandered away by themselves,

while the rest of us passed the time pleasantly in conversation. At Delaware City we came out of the cabin to watch the people as they passed over the gangway. To our surprise and vexation, Lieutenant Smiley appeared among them. As he pressed forward in the throng some one jostled him roughly, when he uttered a fierce oath and aimed a blow at the offender. It missed the mark, and he plunged forward heavily. He would have fallen had not one of the boat's crew caught him in his arms. We saw then that he was intoxicated.

I watched Bob as he looked at the wretched man. His face flushed with indignation as he recalled the injury done to him by Smiley, and he looked as if he would have found intense satisfaction in an attempt to give the lieutenant a thrashing on the spot. But he did not contemplate such a performance, and Bessie clung tightly to his arm, half afraid that he might have a sudden and irresistible impulse to revenge, and half afraid lest Smiley might make some shocking demonstration against the party in that public place. As he staggered past us he recognized us; and, brutalized as he was with liquor, he seemed to feel the shame of his condition and the infamy of his past conduct. He went away to the other side of the boat and concealed himself from view.

When the vessel left the wharf and proceeded down the bay, past the fort, we walked about the lower deck, looking at the scenery and at the shipping which thronged the water. No one of us perceived Smiley or knew that he was near us. We had, indeed, suffered ourselves to forget the scene we had just witnessed, and we were speaking of other matters. As I stood by the railing with my wife and the Magruders, Bob and Bessie came out from the cabin, and Bob had just spoken one word, when a man came with a hurried and uneven step to the gangway. It was Smiley. He had been sitting in the corner behind one of the beams of the boat, with his hat pulled over his eyes. The rail at the gangway swings aside to admit of passage to and from the wharf. Now it opened out upon the water. Smiley paused for one moment, with his fingers clenched upon it; then he flung it wide open, and leaped forward into the sea.

A cry of horror came from the lips of those who saw him make the plunge, and instantly the steamer resounded with screams for help. Before any of us could recover from the paralysis of terror occasioned by the act, Smiley rose to the surface far away from the boat, and with a shriek so awful, so full of agony and despair, that it chilled the blood of those

who heard it, he threw up his arms and sank. In a second Bob tossed off his coat, and before I could restrain him he leaped into the water. He rose instantly, and struck out boldly in the direction in which Smiley had been seen.

Bessie almost fainted in her father's arms, and Mrs. Adeler was white with fear. The next moment the steamer stopped, and an attempt was made to lower the boat. The operation required time; and meanwhile, Bob, who is a good swimmer, gallantly cleft his way through the waves. I think Smiley never rose again. For as I entered the lifeboat I could see Bob turning about and endeavoring to swim toward the steamer. He was a long way from us, for the vessel had gone far before her headway could be over-come. Our boatmen pulled with desperate energy lest the brave fellow should be unable to sustain himself; and as I stood in the stern and watched him with eager eyes, I could see that he gave signs of being in distress. It was heavy work in the water, with his clothing on, and the sea was rough. We were within a hundred yards of him when he sank, and I felt my heart grow sick as I saw him dragged beneath the waves.

But as we reached the spot one of the men, who was lean-ing over the side, uttered an exclamation; and extending his arms, he pulled the lad's head and shoulders above the surface. A moment later he was in the boat, but insensible. As we turned about to seek the steamer, we rubbed his hands and his temples and strove to bring him back to life, and we seemed to have partial suc-cess.

But when we reached the vessel and placed him upon the cushions in the cabin, we committed him to better hands than ours. Mrs. Ma-gruder's medical skill then was of the highest service. She cared for the poor lad with a motherly tenderness which was as admirable as her art. In a brief while he revived; and though suffering greatly, he seemed sure of life. It would have made him blush, even in his weakness, to have heard the praises heaped upon him for his splendid courage; we rejoiced at them, but we rejoiced more to think how he had avenged himself upon his enemy by an act of sublime self-sacrifice.

And so, as he came back to consciousness, we neared our journey's end; and while we carried Bob from the boat to the carriage and placed him among his loving friends, we shuddered to think how the wretched man who had wrought so much evil was even now sweeping past us in the embrace of that swift current to burial beneath the rolling billows of the sea.

CHAPTER XXIII

PITMAN AS A POLITICIAN—HE IS NOMINATED FOR THE LEGIS-
LATURE—HOW HE WAS SERENADED, AND WHAT THE RE-
SULT WAS—I TAKE A HAND AT POLITICS—THE STORY OF
MY FIRST POLITICAL SPEECH—MY RECEPTION AT DOVER—
MISERY OF A MAN WITH ONLY ONE SPEECH—THE SCENE
AT THE MASS MEETING—A FRIGHTFUL DISCOMFITURE.

OME of the friends of Judge Pitman induced him, just before the last election, to permit himself to be nominated for the State Legislature, and accordingly he was presented to the people of this community as a candidate. Of course he was not selected because of his fitness for the position. The party managers knew him to be a very popular man; and as the success of the party is the only thing they care for, they chose Pitman as the person most likely to secure that result. I cannot say that I disapproved of the selection. For some reason, it appears to be entirely impossible for American citizens who live in any of the Middle States to find educated and intelligent men who are willing to represent them in the Legislatures. Those bodies are composed for the most part of men whose solitary purpose is plunder.

They are legislators simply because it pays better to blackmail railroad companies and to accept bribes from people who want votes for rascally measures than it does to pick pockets. They have the instincts and the principles of a pickpocket, but their ambition is greater. They do not steal handkerchiefs and watches, because they can filch fabulous sums of money from the public treasury and from villains who want to do dirty work under the color of the law. They know enough to enable them, with the assistance of party rings, to have themselves counted in at election-time, and to devise new and dexterous schemes of dishonesty; but in other and rather more desirable of the qualifications of law-makers they are deficient. They occupy the most important place in republican governments without knowing what republicanism means, and they create laws for the communities without having any knowledge of the science of law or the slightest acquaintance with the needs and requirements of the people for whom they act. The average American legislator is both ignorant and dishonest. Judge Pitman is ignorant, but he is honest; and as his election would secure at least a very important half of a fitting legislator, I supported him.

My other neighbor, Cooley, was the chairman of the committee to whose care was consigned the management of the campaign in which Judge Pitman played so prominent a part; and Cooley conducted the business with even an excess of enthusiasm. Just after the nomination of Pitman, Cooley called on him to say that a number of his friends had declared their intention to offer him a serenade. Cooley informed the judge that some refreshment must be given to the serenaders, but he, as the chairman of the committee, would attend to that; the judge need not make preparations of any kind. Accordingly, on the following evening a brass band, accompanied by a score or two politicians, entered Pitman's front yard, and for half an hour there was some very good music. Then the judge came out upon the porch and made a better speech than I had expected to hear from him. He concluded by asking the company to enter his house. Cooley was there with a wagon-load of meat and drink, including, of course, a large quantity of rum of the most impressive kinds. The judge, with the fear of the temperance society present in his mind, protested against the liquor; but Cooley demonstrated to him that he would be defeated and the party ruined if it was excluded, and so Pitman reluctantly permitted it to be placed upon his table. Besides, as Cooley had been so very liberal in undertaking to make this provision at his own cost, the judge disliked to hurt his feelings by refusing to permit the use of that which Cooley evidently considered the most important portion of it.

The guests remained at the banquet until four o'clock the next morning, the politicians meanwhile making speeches

and the band playing occasionally in the dining-room in a most uproarious manner. We could hear the noise at my house during the night, and sleep was possible only with the windows closed.

At four o'clock my door-bell rang violently; and upon descending to ascertain the cause of a visit at such an unseemly hour, I encountered Judge Pitman. He was nearly frantic with indignation.

"Adeler," he said, "them fellers is a-carryin' on scand'-lus over yer at my house. They're all drunk as owls; an' when I want 'em to go home, they laugh an' swear an' cheer

an' smash the furniture an' bu'st things generally. Mrs.
Pitman's 'bout skeered to death. Can't you come over an'
help me clear them out?"

"Why don't you call a couple of policemen? You hunt
up two or three officers while I dress myself, and we will see
if we can't adjourn the meeting."

By the time I was ready Pitman arrived with one policeman, and we proceeded to his house. As we entered, the
leader of the band was sitting upon the stairs, infamously
drunk, with the handle of his umbrella in his mouth, vainly
endeavoring to play a tune by fumbling his fingers among
the ribs. Mr. Cooley was in a corner of the parlor supporting himself by the wall while he endeavored to discuss the

question of the tariff with Pitman's plaster bust of Daniel
Webster, and to correct Daniel's view of the local option
law. Another politician was sitting upon the carpet crying
because, so he informed us, his wife's maiden name was Mc-

Carthy, and just as the policeman was removing him a combat occurred between the bass drummer and a man from Wilmington, during which the drummer was hurled against the pier glass and then dragged out to bleed upon the rug. The house was finally cleared of the company just as the church clock struck six, and then Pitman went to bed with sentiments of complete disgust for politics and politicians.

But he remained a candidate of the party. He had promised to run, and he determined to go through with the business.

"That serenade was rough enough without anythin' wuss," said the judge to me a day or two afterward; "but I did think Cooley was a-rubbin' it in 'most too hard when he come over yesterday with a bill for the refreshments which he wanted me to pay."

"Why, I thought he agreed to supply the supper?"

"So he did. But now he says that of course he was only actin' for me. 'The candidate,' he says, 'always foots all the bills.' I'll foot this one, an' then I'll foot Cooley if he ever brings them ruffians to my house agin. I expect nothin' else but the temperance society will shut down on me for that riot we had t'other night."

"I hope not; but I should think that affair would have made you sorry that you ever undertook this business."

"So it does," replied the judge, "but I never back down when I go into a thing. I 'm goin' to run for the Legislatur'; and if I'm elected, I'm goin' to serve my country honestly until my time's up. Then I'm comin' home, an' goin' to stay home. And what's more, I'll stir up that Legislatur' while I'm in it. You mind me!"

The result of the contest was that the judge was elected by a large majority, and he will sit in the next Assembly.

I played a peculiar part in the campaign; and although the narrative of my experience as an amateur politician is not a particularly grateful one to me, it might as well be given, if for no other reason, because it will serve to warn others against the fate that befel me.

I had for some time entertained a strong conviction that nature designed me for an orator. I was assured that I possessed the gift of eloquence which enables great speakers to sway the passions of the multitude, and I felt that I needed but the opportunity to reveal this fact to the world. Accordingly, at the beginning of the political campaign of which I speak I sent my name to one of the executive committees of the State, in Wilmington, with the request that it might be written down with the names of the speakers who could be called upon whenever important meetings were held. I waited impatiently all through the campaign for a summons to appear and electrify the people. It did not come, and I was almost in despair. But on the day before the election I received from the chairman a brief note, saying that I had been announced to speak at Dover that evening before a great mass meeting, and requesting me to take the early afternoon train, so that I might report to the local chairman in Dover before nightfall. The pleasure with which this summons was received was in some measure marred by the fact that I had not a speech ready, and the time was so short that elaborate preparation was impossible. But I determined to throw into some sort of shape the ideas and arguments which would readily occur to the mind of a man familiar with the ordinary political questions of the day and with the merits of the candidates, and to trust to the inspiration of the occasion for the power to present them forcibly and eloquently.

Of course it was plain that anything like an attempt at gorgeousness in such a speech would be foolish, so I concluded to speak plainly and directly to the point, and to enliven my argument with some amusing campaign stories. In order to fix my points firmly in my mind and to ensure their presentation in their proper order, they were numbered and committed to memory, each argument and its accompanying anecdote being associated with a particular arithmetical figure. The synopsis, if it may be called by that name, presented an appearance something like the following, excepting that it contained a specification of the points of the speech which need not be reproduced here.

The Speech.

1. Exordium, concluding with Scott's famous lines, "Breathes there a man with soul so dead," etc.

2. Arguments, introducing a narrative of the facts in the case of Hotchkiss, who was locked out upon the roof of his house all night. (See particulars farther on.) The design of the story is to give a striking picture of the manner in which the opposition party will be left out in the cold by the election. (Make this strong, and pause for cheers.)

3. Arguments, followed by the story of the Kickapoo Indian who saw a locomotive approaching upon the plains, and thinking it was a superior breed of buffalo, determined to capture it, so that he could take the first prize at the Kickapoo agricultural fair. He tied his lasso to his waist and threw the other end over

the smoke-stack. The locomotive did not stop; but when the engineer arrived at the next station, he went out and cut the string by which a small bit of copper-colored meat was tied to his smoke-stack. This is to illustrate the folly of the attempt of conservatism to check the onward career of pure and enlightened liberalism toward perfect civilization, etc., etc.

4. Arguments, and then the anecdote of that Dutchman in Berks county, Pa., who on the 10th of October, 1866, was observed to go out into his yard and raise the American flag; then he got his

gun and fired a salute seventeen or eighteen times, after which he consumed six packs of fire-crackers and gave three cheers for the Union. He enjoyed himself in this manner nearly all day, while his neighbors gathered around outside and placed their elbows upon the fence, watching him and wondering what on earth he meant. A peddler who came along stopped and had an interview with him. To his surprise, he found that the German agriculturist was celebrating the Fourth of July, 1859. He did not know that it was any later in the century, for he had been keeping his time on a notched stick; and having been sick a great deal, he had gotten the thing in a dreadful tangle. When he learned that he was seven Fourths in arrears, he was depressed; but he sent out and bought a box of fire-crackers and a barrel of gun-powder, and spent a week catching up.

(Tell this vivaciously, and make the point that none but a member of the other party could forget the glorious anniversary of our country's birth, and say that the whole party will have to do up a lot of back patriotism some day, if it desires to catch up with the people whose devotion to the country is encouraged and kept active by our side.)

5. Arguments, supplemented with the narrative of a confiding man who had such child-like faith in a patent fire-extinguisher which he had purchased that he set fire to his house merely to have the fun of putting it out. The

fire burned furiously, but the extinguisher gave only two or three imbecile squirts and then collapsed, and in two hours his residence was in ashes. Go on to say that our enemies have applied the torch of anarchy to the edifice of this government, but that there is an extinguisher which will not only *not* collapse, but will subdue the flames and quench the incendiary organization, and that extinguisher is our party. (Allow time for applause here.)

6. Arguments, introducing the story of the Sussex county farmer who was discouraged because his wife was perfidious. Before he was married she vowed over and over again that she could chop four cords of wood a day, but after the ceremony the

farmer found he was deceived. The treacherous woman could not chop more than two cords and a half, and so the dream of the husband was dissipated, and he demanded a divorce as the only balm for the wounds which lacerated his heart. Let this serve to illustrate the point that our political enemies have deceived us with promises to reduce the debt, to institute reforms, etc., etc., none of which they have kept, and now we must have the government separated from them by such a divorce as will be decreed to-morrow, etc., etc.

7. Peroration, working in if possible the story of Commodore Scudder's dog, which, while out with its master one day, pointed at some partridges. The commodore was about to fire, but he suddenly received orders to go off on a three years' cruise, so he dropped his gun, left the dog standing there and went right to sea. When he returned, three years later, he went back to the field, and there was his gun, there was the skeleton of the dog still standing and pointing just as he had left it, and a little farther on were the skeletons of the partridges. Show how our adversaries in their relations to the negro question resemble that dog. We came away years ago and left them pointing at the negro question, and we come back now to find that they are at it yet. Work this in carefully, and conclude in such a manner as to excite frantic applause.

It was not much of a speech, I know. Some of the arguments were weak, and several of the stories failed to fit into their places comfortably. But mass meetings do not criticise closely, and I was persuaded I should make a good impression, provoking laughter and perhaps exciting enthusiasm. The only time that could be procured for study of the speech was that consumed by the journey. So when the train started I took my notes from my pocket and learned them by heart. Then came the task of enlarging them, in my mind, into a speech. This was accomplished satisfactorily. I suppose that speech was repeated at least ten times between New Castle and Dover until at last I had it at my tongue's end. In the cars the seat next to mine was occupied by a colored gentleman, who seemed to be a little nervous when he perceived that I was muttering something continually; and he was actually alarmed once or twice when in exciting passages I would forget myself and gesticulate violently in his direction. Finally, when I came to the conclusion and was repeating to myself the exhortation, "Strike for your altars and your fires," etc., etc., I emphasized the language by striking fiercely at the floor with the ferule of my umbrella. It hit something soft. I think it was the corn of my colored friend, for he leaped up hurriedly, and ejaculating "Gosh!" went up and stood by the water-cooler during the rest of the journey, looking at me as if he thought it was dangerous for such a maniac to be at large.

When the train arrived at Dover, I was gratified to find the chairman of the local committee and eighteen of his fellow-citizens waiting for me with carriages and a brass band. As I stepped from the car the band played "See, the Conquering Hero comes!" I marched into the waiting-room of the dépôt, followed by the committee and the band. The chairman and his friends formed a semi-circle and stared at

me. I learned afterward that they had received information from Wilmington that I was one of the most remarkable orators in the State. It was impossible not to perceive that they regarded me already with enthusiastic admiration; and my heart sank a little as I reflected upon the possibility of failure.

Then the music ceased, and the chairman proposed "three cheers for our eloquent visitor." The devoted beings around him cheered lustily. The chairman thereupon came forward and welcomed me in the following terms:

"My dear sir, it is with unfeigned satisfaction that I have —may I say the exalted honor?—of welcoming you to the city of Dover. You come, sir, at a moment when the heart of every true patriot beats high with hope for a glorious triumph over the enemies of our cherished institutions; you come, sir, at a time when our great party, the true representative of American principles and the guardian of our liberties, bends to grapple with the deadly foe of our country; at a time, sir, when the American eagle—proud bird, which soars, as we would, to the sun—screams forth its defiance of treason, and when the banner of the free, the glorious emblem of our nationality, waves us onward to victory; you come, sir, to animate with your eloquence the hearts of our fellow-citizens; to inspire with your glowing language the souls of those who shrink from performing their duty in this contest; to depict in words of burning, scathing power the shame, the disgrace, the irretrievable ruin, which will befall our land if its enemies are victorious, and to hold up those enemies, as you well know how, to the scorn and contempt of all honest men. We give you a hearty welcome, then, and assure you that Dover will respond nobly to your appeal, giving to-morrow such a vote for justice, truth and the rights of man that the conservative wolf will shrink back in dismay to his lair. Welcome, sir, thrice welcome, to our city!"

I stood looking at this man throughout his speech with a conviction, constantly growing stronger, that I should be obliged to reply to him at some length. The contemplation of such a thing, I need hardly say, filled me with horror. I had never made a speech of the kind that would be required in my life, and I felt positively certain that I could not accomplish the task now. I had half a mind to hurl at the heads of this chairman and his attendant fiends the entire oration prepared for the evening; but that seemed so dreadfully inappropriate that the idea was abandoned. And besides, what would I say at the mass meeting? The comfort of the situation was not, by any means, improved by the fact that these persons entertained the belief that I was an experienced speaker who would probably throw off a dozen brilliant things in as many sentences. It was exceedingly embarrassing; and when the chairman concluded his remarks, the cold perspiration stood upon my forehead and my knees trembled.

Happily, the leader of the band desired to make himself conspicuous, so he embraced the opportunity afforded by the pause to give us some startling variations of "The Star-Spangled Banner."

As we stood there listening to the music, I observed that the energetic gentleman who played upon the drum and cymbals was looking at me with what seemed to be a scornful smile. He had a peculiarly cold eye, and 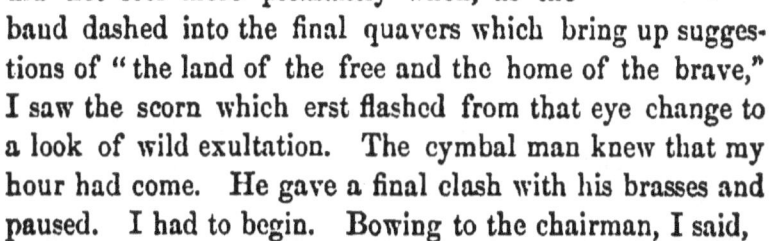 as he fixed it upon me I felt that the frigid optic pierced through and through my assumption of ease and perceived what a miserable sham it was for me to stand there pretending to be an orator. I quailed before that eye. Its glance humiliated me; and I did not feel more pleasantly when, as the band dashed into the final quavers which bring up suggestions of "the land of the free and the home of the brave," I saw the scorn which erst flashed from that eye change to a look of wild exultation. The cymbal man knew that my hour had come. He gave a final clash with his brasses and paused. I had to begin. Bowing to the chairman, I said,

"Mr. Chairman and fellow-citizens, there are times—times —there are times, fellow-citizens, when—times when—when the heart—there are times, I say, Mr. Chairman and fellow-citizens, when the heart—the heart of—of—" It wouldn't do. I stuck fast, and could not get out another word.

The cold-eyed man seemed ready to play triumphal strains upon his drum and to smash out a pæan upon his cymbals. In the frenzy and desperation of the moment, I determined to take the poetry from my exordium and to jam it into the

present speech, whether it was appropriate or not. I began
again :

"There are times, I say, fellow-citizens and Mr. Chairman, when the heart inquires if there breathes a man with
soul so dead, who never to himself hath said, 'This is my
own, my native land'—whose heart has ne'er within him

burned as home his footsteps he
hath turned from wanderings
on a foreign shore? If such
there breathe, go, mark him
well!" (Here I pointed to the
street, and one of the committee, who seemed not to
comprehend the thing exactly,
rushed to the window and
looked out, as if he intended
to call a policeman to arrest
the wretch referred to.) "For
him no minstrel raptures
swell." (Here the leader of the
band bowed, as if he had a vague idea that this was a com-
pliment ingeniously worked into the speech for his benefit;
but the cold-eyed man had a sneering smile which seemed to
say, "It won't do, my man, it won't do. I can't be bought
off in that manner.") "High though his titles, proud his
name, boundless his wealth as wish can claim ; despite these
titles, power and pelf, the wretch, concentred all in self,
living, shall forfeit fair renown, and doubly dying shall go
down to the vile dust from whence he sprung, unwept, un-
honored and unsung."

I stopped. There was embarrassing silence for a moment,
as if everybody thought I had something more to say. But
I put on my hat and shouldered my umbrella to assure them
that the affair was ended. Then it began to be apparent

that the company failed to grasp the purpose of my remarks. One man evidently thought I was complaining of something that happened to me while I was upon the train, for he took me aside and asked me in a confidential whisper if it wouldn't be better for him to see the conductor about it.

Another man inquired if the governor was the man referred to.

I said, "No; the remarks were of a poetical nature; they were quoted."

The man seemed surprised, and asked where I got them from.

"From *Marmion.*"

He considered a moment, and then said,

"Don't know him. Philadelphia man, I reckon?"

The occasion was too sad for words. I took the chairman's arm and we marched out to the carriages, the cold-eyed man thumping his drum as if his feeling of animosity for me would kill him if it did not find vigorous expression of that kind.

We entered the carriages and formed a procession, the band, on foot, leading the way and playing "Hail to the Chief." I rode with the chairman, who insisted that I should carry the American flag in my hand. As we passed up the street the crowd cheered us vehemently several times, and the chairman said he thought it would be better if I would rise occasionally and bow in response. I did so, remarking, at the last, that it was rather singular such a reception should be given to a complete stranger.

The chairman said he had been thinking of that, and it had occurred to him just at that moment that perhaps the populace had mistaken the character of the parade.

"You see," said he, "there is a circus in town, and I am a little bit afraid the people are impressed with the idea that this is the showman's procession, and that you are the

Aërial King. That monarch is a man of about your build, and he wears whiskers."

The Aërial King achieved distinction and a throne by leaping into the air and turning two backward somersaults before alighting, and also by standing poised upon one toe on a wire while he balanced a pole upon his nose. I had no desire to share the sceptre with that man, or to rob him of any of his renown, so I furled the flag of my beloved country, pulled my hat over my eyes and refused to bow again.

It was supper-time when we reached the hotel, and as soon as we entered, the chairman invited us into one of the parlors, where an elaborate repast had been prepared for the whole party. We went into the room, keeping step with a march played by the band, which was placed in the corner. When supper was over, it was with dismay that I saw the irrepressible chairman rise and propose a toast, to which he called upon one of the company to respond. I knew my turn would come presently, and there seemed to be no choice between the sacrifice of my great speech to this paltry occasion and utter ruin and disgrace. It appeared to me that the chairman must have guessed that I had but one speech, and that he had determined to force me to deliver it prematurely, so that I might be overwhelmed with mortification at the mass meeting. But I made up my mind to cling desperately to the solitary oration, no matter how much pressure was brought to bear to deprive me of it. So I resolved that if the chairman called upon me I would tell my number two story, giving the arguments, and omitting all of it from my speech in the evening.

He did call. When two or three men had spoken, the chairman offered the toast, "The orator of the evening," and it was received with applause. The chairman said: "It is with peculiar pleasure that I offer this sentiment. It gives to my eloquent young friend an opportunity which could not be obtained amid the embarrassments of the dépôt to offer, without restraint, such an exhibition of his powers as would prove to the company that the art which enabled Webster and Clay to win the admiration of an entranced world was not lost—that it found a master interpreter in the gentleman who sits before me."

This was severe. The cold-eyed child of the Muses sitting with the band looked as if he felt really and thoroughly glad in the inmost recesses of his soul for the first time in his life.

I rose, and said: "Mr. Chairman and gentlemen, I am too much fatigued to make a speech, and I wish to save my voice for to-night; so I will tell you a story of a man I used to know whose name was Hotchkiss. He lived up at New Castle, and one night he thought he would have a little innocent fun scaring his wife by dropping a loose brick or two down the chimney into the fireplace in her room. So he slipped softly out of bed; and dressed in his night-shirt, he stole up stairs and crept out upon the roof. Mr. Hotch-

kiss dropped nineteen bricks down that chimney, Mr. Chairman and gentlemen, each one with an emphatic slam, but his wife didn't scream once."

Everybody seemed to think this was the end of the story; so there was a roar of laughter, although I had not reached the humorous part or the real point of the anecdote, which

31 *

describes how Hotchkiss gave it up and tried to go down stairs, but was surprised to find that Mrs. Hotchkiss, who had been watching all the time, had retreated, fastening the trap-door, so that he spent the next four hours upon the comb of the roof with his trailing garments of the night fluttering in the evening breeze. But they all laughed and began to talk; and the leader of the band, considering that his turn must have come, struck out into "Hail Columbia," while the man with the cymbals seemed animated with fiendish glee.

I tried to explain to the chairman that it was all wrong, that the affair was terribly mixed.

He said he thought himself that it seemed so somehow, and he offered to explain the matter to the company and to give me a chance to tell the story over again properly.

I intimated, gloomily, that if he undertook such a thing I would blow out his brains with the very first horse-pistol I could lay my hands upon.

He said perhaps, then, it would be better not to do

The proceedings at the mass meeting were to begin at eight o'clock. At half-past seven I went to the telegraph office, and sent the following despatch to the Wilmington papers, fearing the office might be closed when the meeting adjourned :

"Dover, —— —, 18—: A tremendous mass meeting was held here to-night. The utmost enthusiasm was displayed by the crowd. Effective speeches were made by several prominent gentlemen, among them the eloquent young orator Mr. Max Adeler, whose spirited remarks, interspersed with sparkling anecdote, provoked uproarious applause. Dover is good for five hundred majority, and perhaps a thousand."

At eight o'clock a very large crowd really did assemble in front of the porch of one of the hotels. The speakers were placed upon the balcony, which was but a few feet above the pavement, and there was also a number of persons connected with the various political clubs of the town. I felt somewhat nervous; but I was tolerably certain I could speak my piece acceptably, even with the poetry torn out of the introduction and the number two story sacrificed. I took a seat upon the porch and waited while the band played a spirited air or two. It grieved me to perceive that the band stood directly in front of us upon the pavement, the cold-eyed drummer occupying a favorable position for staring at me.

The chairman began with a short speech in which he went over almost precisely the ground covered by my introduction; and as that portion of my oration was already reduced to a fragment by the use of the verses, I quietly resolved to begin, when my turn came, with point number two.

The chairman introduced to the crowd Mr. Keyser, who was received with cheers. He was a ready speaker, and he began, to my deep regret, by telling in capital style my story number three, after which he used up some of my number six arguments, and concluded with the remark that it was not his purpose to occupy the attention of the meeting for any length of time, because the executive committee in Wilmington had sent an eloquent orator who was now upon the platform and would present the cause of the party in a manner which he could not hope to approach.

Mr. Keyser then sat down, and Mr. Schwartz was introduced. Mr. Schwartz observed that it was hardly worth while for him to attempt to make anything like a speech, because the gentleman from New Castle had come down on purpose to discuss the issues of the campaign, and the audience, of course, was anxious to hear him. Mr. Schwartz would only tell a little story which seemed to illustrate a point he wished to make, and he thereupon related my anecdote number seven, making it appear that he was the bosom friend of Commodore Scudder and an acquaintance of the man who made the gun. The point illustrated I was shocked to find was almost precisely that which I had attached to my story number seven. The situation began to have a serious appearance. Here, at one fell swoop, two of my best stories and three of my sets of arguments were swept off into utter uselessness.

When Schwartz withdrew, a man named Krumbauer was brought forward. Krumbauer was a German, and the chairman announced that he would speak in that language for the benefit of those persons in the audience to whom the tongue was pleasantly familiar. Krumbauer went ahead, and the crowd received his remarks with roars of laughter. After one particularly exuberant outburst of merriment, I asked the man who sat next to me, and who seemed deeply interested in the story,

"What was that little joke of Krumbauer's? It must have been first rate."

"So it was," he said. "It was about a Dutchman up in Berks county, Penna., who got mixed up in his dates."

"What dates?" I gasped, in awful apprehension.

"Why, his Fourths of July, you know. Got seven or eight years in arrears and tried to make them all up at once. Good, wasn't it?"

"Good? I should think so; ha! ha! My very best story, as I'm a sinner!"

It was awfully bad. I could have strangled Krumbauer and then chopped him into bits. The ground seemed slipping away beneath me; there was the merest skeleton of a

speech left. But I determined to take that and do my best,
trusting to luck for a happy result.

But my turn had not yet come. Mr. Wilson was dragged
out next, and I thought I perceived a demoniac smile steal
over the countenance of the cymbal player as Wilson said
he was too hoarse to say much ; he would leave the heavy
work for the brilliant young orator who was here from New
Castle. He would skim rapidly over the ground and then
retire. He did. Wilson rapidly skimmed all the cream off
of my arguments numbers two, five and six, and wound up
by offering the whole of my number four argument. My
hair fairly stood on end when Wilson bowed and left the
stand. What on earth was I to do now? Not an argument
left to stand upon ; all my anecdotes gone but two, and my
mind in such a condition of frenzied bewilderment that it
seemed as if there was not another available argument or
suggestion or hint or anecdote remaining in the entire universe. In an agony of despair, I turned to the man next to
me and asked him if I would have to follow Wilson.

He said it was his turn now.

"And what are you going to say?" I demanded, suspiciously.

"Oh, nothing," he replied—"nothing at all. I want to
leave room for you. I'll just tell a little story or so, to
amuse them, and then sit down."

"What story, for instance?" I asked.

"Oh, nothing, nothing; only a little yarn I happen to remember about a farmer who married a woman who said she
could cut four cords of wood, when she couldn't."

My worst fears were realized. I turned to the man next
to me, and said, with suppressed emotion,

"May I ask your name, my friend?"

He said his name was Gumbs.

"May I inquire what your Christian name is?"

He said it was William Henry.

"Well, William Henry Gumbs," I exclaimed, "gaze at me! Do I look like a man who would slay a human being in cold blood?"

"Hm-m-m, n-no; you don't," he replied, with an air of critical consideration.

"But I AM!" said I, fiercely—"I AM; and I tell you now that if you undertake to relate that anecdote about the farmer's wife I will blow you into eternity without a moment's warning; I will, by George!"

Mr. Gumbs instantly jumped up, placed his hand on the railing of the porch, and got over suddenly into the crowd. He stood there pointing me out to the bystanders, and doubtless advancing the theory that I was an original kind of a lunatic, who might be expected to have at any moment a fit which would be interesting when studied from a distance.

The chairman looked around, intending to call upon my friend Mr. Gumbs; but not perceiving him, he came to me and said:

"Now is your chance, sir; splendid opportunity; crowd worked up to just the proper pitch. We have paved the way for you; go in and do your best."

"Oh yes; but hold on for a few moments, will you? I can't speak now; the fact is I am not quite ready. Run out some other man."

"Haven't got another man. Kept you for the last purposely, and the crowd is waiting. Come ahead and pitch in, and give it to 'em hot and heavy."

It was very easy for him to say "give it to them," but I had nothing to give. Beautifully they paved the way for me! Nicely they had worked up the crowd to the proper pitch! Here I was in a condition of frantic despair, with a crowd of one thousand people expecting a brilliant oration from me who had not a thing in my mind but a beggarly story about a fire-extinguisher and a worse one about a farmer's wife. I groaned in spirit and wished I had been born far away in some distant clime among savages who knew not of mass meetings, and whose language contained such a small number of words that speech-making was impossible.

But the chairman was determined. He seized me by the arm and fairly dragged me to the front. He introduced me to the crowd in flattering, and I may say outrageously ridiculous, terms, and then whispering in my ear, " Hit 'em hard, old fellow, hit 'em hard," he sat down.

The crowd received me with three hearty cheers. As I heard them I began to feel dizzy. The audience seemed to swim around and to increase tenfold in size. By a resolute effort I recovered my self-possession partially, and determined to begin. I could not think of anything but the two stories, and I resolved to tell them as well as I could. I said,

" Fellow-citizens : It is so late now that I will not attempt to make a speech to you." (Cries of " Yes !" " Go ahead !" " Never mind the time !" etc., etc.) Elevating my voice, I repeated : " I say it is so late now that I can't make a speech as I intended on account of its being so late that the speech which I intended to make would keep you here too late if I made it as I intended to. So I will tell you a story about a man who bought a patent fire-extinguisher which was warranted to split four cords of wood a day ; so he set fire to his house to try her, and— No, it was his wife who was warranted to split four cords of wood—I got it wrong; and when the flames obtained full headway, he found she could only split two cords and a half, and it made him— What I mean is that the farmer, when he bought the exting— courted her, that is, she said she could set fire to the house, and when he tried her, she collapsed the first time—the extinguisher did, and·he wanted a divorce because his house— Oh, hang it, fellow-citizens, you understand that this man, or . farmer, rather, bought a—I should say courted a—that is, a fire-ex—" (Desperately.) "Fellow-citizens! IF ANY MAN SHOOTS THE AMERICAN FLAG, PULL HIM DOWN UPON THE SPOT; BUT AS FOR ME, GIVE ME LIBERTY OR GIVE ME DEATH!"

As I shouted this out at the top of my voice, in an ecstasy

of confusion, a wild, tumultuous yell of laughter came up from the crowd. I paused for a second beneath the spell of that cold eye in the band, and then, dashing through the throng at the back of the porch, I rushed down the street to the dépôt, with the shouts of the crowd and the uproarious music of the band ringing in my ears. I got upon a freight train, gave the engineer five dollars to take me along on the locomotive, and spent the night riding to New Castle.

CHAPTER XXIV.

ESTERDAY was the day of the wedding.

I suppose no one can hope to describe accurately the sensation that is created by such an event in a little community like ours. It has supplied the ladies of the village with material for discussion for several weeks past, and the extraordinary interest manifested in it has constantly grown stronger until it culminated in a blaze of excitement which made calmness upon the part of any New Castilian upon the great day a wholly impossible condition. My own wife has introduced the subject in her conversation with me at every available opportunity; and when I have grown weary of hearing about the preparations for the wedding, about the purchases made by the Magruders for Bessie, about the presents given to the bride by her friends, about the future prospects of the pair, and about other matrimonial

things innumerable, the excellent partner of my joys, still
with unabated enthusiasm, has turned from so dull a listener,
and seizing her bonnet and shawl, has darted off to visit Mrs.
Jones or Mrs. Hopkins, and has found them eager to participate in conversation upon these subjects.   During the past
month this sympathetic woman has called at Magruder's at
least three times a day to ascertain the latest facts respecting
the situation, and to give advice and assistance to the busy
workers who have been preparing the multitude of articles
which a girl must have before she is married.   Every woman in the village was familiar, long ago, with the minutest
details of the arrangements, and all of them were so deeply
absorbed in the preparations and in contemplation of the
approaching catastrophe that they cared for nothing else.
If there had been revolutions, if thrones had tottered to their
fall, if hurricanes had swept over the land and the nations
had been stricken by the scourge, I verily believe that these
devoted women of New Castle would have regarded these
calamities with steadfast composure, and would have excluded
them from a place in the social debates wherein the wedding
of Bessie Magruder was the one great subject of discussion.

There is nothing more intense in nature than the interest
felt by a woman in the marriage of another woman.   The
fanatic fury of a Hindoo devotee is mere icy indifference in
comparison to it.

It was entertaining to watch Bob Parker upon the evening before the wedding and upon the morning of the great
day itself.   He had everything ready a week before the
time, and upon the last night of his bachelor life he had
nothing to do but to sit at home with us and think.   And
so, while I read my book and while Mrs. Adeler finished the
bonnet that she had made for the occasion from old material
(the dexterous economy of that woman, by the way, is simply
phenomenal), Bob fidgeted about.   He pretended to read the

paper; he threw himself upon the lounge and counterfeited
sleep; he darted suddenly up stairs to see if he had put a
sufficient number of collars in his trunk; he darted down

again and tried on his new hat for the fiftieth time; he stood
by the fire and expressed his fear, often repeated during the
day, that there would be rain on the morrow; he tried to
wind up his watch four times, and he examined his pocketbook over and over again to ascertain if the ring was safe.
At a ridiculously early hour he said he was tired and must
go to bed; but when I ascended the stairs about midnight,
I could hear him still moving about. He was nervous, excited and anxious.

Before daylight dawned Bob was out of bed and down
stairs smoking and guessing at the weather. When we descended, he was in extreme agitation lest the man should not
come with the bouquets. When the flowers did arrive, they
looked so much like business that he immediately flew up to
his room and put on his wedding suit.

Then we had to wait nearly two hours for the carriages,
and Bob was harassed by doubts as to the correctness of the
appearance of his neck-tie. Three times Mrs. Adeler applied thread and needle to that article of adornment, and at

last Bob threw it away and assumed another. He seemed
to have a strong conviction that the eyes of the entire assembly would be concentrated upon that white tie. Then he
put on his gloves and sat, flushed and uncomfortable in his
new clothing, waiting for the moment of his departure. Pres-

ently he discovered that he had lost one of his
gold shirt buttons; and after a very long and
very warm search for it, he thought he felt it in
his boot. I procured a boot-jack for him; and
when the button was found, he had to remove
his gloves again in order to pull his boot on.
He was beginning to be acutely miserable when,
at last, the carriages arrived. Then Mrs. Adeler came down; and when I had buttoned her
gloves with a hair-pin and criticised the appearance of her dress, we went out to the street and drove away.

When we reached Magruder's, the doorway was surrounded
by quite a throng of persons. The excitement had reached
even the lower classes, and a crowd composed of slatternly
women with babies in their arms, of truant servant-girls, of

unclean children, of idle men and noisy boys, stood upon the
pavement waiting for the bride to come out. As we descended from the carriages, Bob was the chief object of
interest, and while the women eyed him with admiration the
boys made very unpleasant remarks concerning his clothing,
particularly his "claw-hammer coat."   When we entered
the house, Bob ascended to some mysterious region above to
wait for Bessie, while we examined the bridal gifts and con-

versed with the paternal Magruder, who was plainly uncomfortable in his wedding garments.

Then the bride descended amid exclamations of admiration from the servants and their friends, who were collected in a knot at the rear of the hall. She did look very sweet and pretty, that little maiden, in her lovely white dress, with orange blossoms in her dark hair, with a radiant light in her brown eyes and with a faint glow warming her cheek. Bob Parker had good reason to feel proud as he led the fair girl to the altar; and he was proud, despite his trepidation.

And when our salutations were over, when the satins and silks were all arranged and the bridesmaids and groomsmen were ready, we marched through the critical assembly outside the door and drove swiftly to the church. At the gate we found, awaiting the wedding party, another throng of spectators, among them that gloomy undertaker, with his chin hooked upon the wall, and his mind still brooding over his wrongs.

Then we heard the organ playing the Coronation March, and as the bridal party entered the church and swept up the aisle the Wedding March burst forth. There was a fluttering and a turning of heads in the pews; then silence, and then the ceremony began. Bob was pale as a ghost, and his replies could hardly be heard, but Bessie spoke with perfect distinctness. It is strange that women on these occasions should always be more composed than men.

And when the solemn words were said, Bob kissed his wife gallantly, and then, as the organ uttered Mendelssohn's lovely melody "I waited for the Lord," the two turned about and in the aisle met hosts of friends eager to congratulate them. At any other time Bob might have been mortified that he was a person of secondary importance. It was the bride that the people looked at, and not the groom. But now he was too happy and too ready to forget himself

32 *

He was too glad to have his wife greeted warmly to think
of any other thing. By the time the church porch was
reached every woman present had the details of Bessie's
costume fixed indelibly in her mind, ready for description
and explanation to her friends; and while the bell in the
steeple rang out a merry peal, we returned to the Magruder
mansion, where, in the company of friends, we passed the
few hours before the departure of Mr. and Mrs. Parker.

Rev. Dr. Hopkins was there, beaming at the guests through
his gold spectacles, and making himself very comfortable
with the oysters and terrapin and chicken salad. He even
had a smile for Colonel Bangs, who was discussing with Mr.
Magruder the probable effect upon the railway interests of
the country of an article in the *Argus* of that morning upon

"Our Grinding Monopolies."   It was interesting to listen to
the colonel.

"I tell you," said he, with vehemence, "the time has come

for the overthrow of these gigantic railroad corporations;
the time has come for a free press to open its batteries upon
the monopolies which are trampling the rights of the people
beneath their feet. There will be a bitter fight, sir, mark
me; it will be a battle to the death. But the *Argus* enters
the lists boldly and without fear. The article of to-day un-
sheaths the sword; it warns the railway tyrants that the
battle has begun."

"I am sure it will alarm them," said Mr. Magruder.
"And you, I suppose, are willing to give up everything
for the cause? How about your annual free pass to Philadelphia?"

"Oh, ah! as for that," exclaimed the colonel, "you perhaps observed that I expressly excepted our own road and
complimented its officers. A man must not go to extremes
in these matters, Magruder. And then there's the advertising, you know! No, sir; we must proceed, as it were,
cautiously at first. Precipitate action might ruin everything."

Dr. Tobias Jones also had overcome his professional animosity to Mrs. Magruder, and he was not only present, but
he was conversing pleasantly with that lady, probably upon
the subjects of bilious fever and aneurisms. Benjamin P.
Gunn was there, bustling around among the guests and paying especial attention to Bob. When I saw Gunn in earnest
conversation with the groom and caught the words, "in favor
of your wife, you know," I became aware of the fact that
Benjamin was improving the festive hour with an attempt
to do a bit of business. Even Judge Pitman was present,
for Mr. Magruder liked the old man and was in a gracious
mood upon that day. I welcomed the judge heartily when,
dressed in a swallow-tail coat of a surprising pattern, he
came up to me and said,

"Splendid send-off for them young folks, ain't it? I tell

you, they didn't do things this way when me an' Harriet consolidated! We lived down yer in Kent; an' when we were married by the squire, I give him fifty cents an' then

went out an' borrowed a waggin so's me an' Harriet could take a little drive. We come up yer to New Cassel an' stayed two days at the tavern, an' then drove back an' begun work agin, jes' 's if nothin' oncommon had happened."

"It was not the custom then, I suppose, to make a display on such occasions?"

"No, *sir!* People hadn't no money to git up sich fodderin' as this yer. They had to go slower. Still," mused the judge, "it's all right—it's all right. Gittin' married 's a big event; an' if you kin make a fuss over it, you ought to. If my daughter ever tries it, I'll give her the best I kin buy. A weddin' like this is nice all 'round, but the wimmen in partickler is amazin' fond of sich things. If you'll excuse me, I believe I'll try another fried oyster."

There was another exciting time when Bessie, at last, came down in her traveling dress and stood with Bob ready to depart. While the cabman carried the trunks to the carriage, Bessie said her farewells. There was a good-bye for mother, uttered with tears in the eyes of both of them, a tender adieu to father, kisses for the women and a shake of the hand for the men, and then they entered the carriage. We flung an old shoe or two after them and waved our hands; and

Cooley's boy gave them a parting salute with a stone that shivered the carriage window. We watched them as they went down the street, and saw, now and then, a handkerchief fluttered toward us; then they turned a corner and disappeared.

It was a little lonely in the cottage upon that evening with Bob no longer a member of the family. We shall miss him, with his sprightliness and fun; and we shall half incline to regret that the little drama we have watched so long with eager interest is ended, even though the prince, after all his suffering, has found the princess and wedded her, and though at last they have gone "across the hills and far away" beyond "the utmost purple rim of that new world, which is the old."

We sat in the old room in silence for a while, both looking at the fire and both thinking, not so much of the events of the day as of the promise of the future for those two voyagers into the golden regions of delight. Then Mrs. Adeler said, with half a sigh:

"I do hope they will be happy!"

"And so do I; and I really believe they will be, for both of them have sweet tempers and good common sense; those are the qualities that are likely to ensure the felicity of married folks."

"But it is a great risk for Bob to run; and for Bessie too, for that matter."

"So it is; but it is a risk that may fairly be taken when the judgment gives approval to the choice of the heart. Lovers do not bother themselves, however, a great deal with the possibilities of the future. They have only sunshine now, and it seems as if so clear a sky could never breed cloud and storm. It is a happy thing for them, as well as for the rest of us, that no human ingenuity can lift the veil that shuts from our eyes the mysteries of the years to come. Think what a journey it is that began to-day! Separate and apart they have come thus far; but now they are to travel during all their lives together, over rough places as well as where the way is smooth. The power of each over the happiness of the other is infinite. He can make her wholly miserable, and she can utterly destroy his peace. A violent demonstration is not required. A little indifference at first, a harsh word, then a growing coldness, then neglect, and for ever afterward complete separation of heart and soul and feeling, though outwardly they seem united.

"And even if they should be as happy as the most blessed of us, it is well that their imaginations should throw about the future a glamour which will hide the reality. A tried and well-proved love will hardly bear the shock when misfortune and poverty come; it sometimes permits an almost fatal display of ill-temper when there are sleepless nights with sick and peevish children, when the soul is vexed with the cares of business, with the smaller trials of life, and with the myriad petty annoyances that are encountered in the path of every man. There are few of us who are heroes among the troubles of common life. Perhaps we bear the heavy blows courageously enough; but we cry out when we are stung by the pigmy arrows that are shot at us every day, at home and in the world. The truly great man is he who is patient and forbearing beneath small vexations. The real hero is he who bears the burden of his life, with its swarm of minor troubles, with calm, sweet evenness of temper and with steadfast courage. The peevish and the irritable are the enemies of peace in this world. Our lad and lass, we may hope, will find a place for themselves among those who wisely choose the better part.

"And now, Mrs. Adeler, would it not be well to close our record, as the hero and the heroine depart? It is the custom.

in the novel and upon the stage, to end the story when the knight and the lady who have loved and suffered through all the pages and all the acts are made man and wife. We have not done much with our pair; but it is enough that we have told a simple story of an old passion in still another form, and that we have given the chronicles of the village with what quality of humor we could infuse into them, but without malice or vulgarity and without irreverence. I have no patience with those who seek to find amusement by committing these faults. There is matter enough in harmless things for sportiveness; and rather than try to excite mirth by hurting the feelings of my neighbors, by stooping to coarseness, or by speaking with levity of things that are sacred, I would consent to write only books that should be as solemn as tragedy itself. We have had some strange experiences since the record began, and we should be very dull indeed if we had not learned something from them. Of one thing we are completely convinced: it is that a man who is made miserable because his neighbors will not do as he wishes them to do had better not come to this or any other village with the intent to be made happy. The man who voluntarily becomes a hermit is a fool. A man of sense must necessarily desire to live with his fellows and to enjoy their society, their sympathy and the comforts that can be obtained with their assistance. He can have these only by making sacrifices for them. He must not only give up some of his natural rights as an individual, but he must make up his mind to endure patiently disagreeable things that are done by his neighbors. He may flee from the city to escape the professor of music who hammers a piano ceaselessly, but in his new home he will certainly find a compensating nuisance of some kind. Until all men learn to think and act alike, he will find everywhere in the world those who are fond of the things that he hates, and who will do things that he thinks should be left undone. The man, therefore, who comes to the village in pursuit of perfect peace and quiet of course will not find them. He will encounter the disagreeable practices and peculiarities of other people precisely as he did in the city; he will be called upon to endure annoyances as aggravating as any of those from which he has flown. He can have comparativo contentment and repose in either place only by determining to have them despite his neighbors. It is probable that men will always have in this world sharp corners and rough surfaces with which they will jag and tear each other as they roll onward in the swift current of life. Perhaps we shall have smoothness and evenness when we enter Paradise. I hope so, at any rate. And meantime let us all stop growling about evils which cannot be cured.

"And now I will conclude our meek little story. Perhaps regretfully I will close the door through which the public has been suffered to peep in upon the movements of our quiet life at home and in the village, and thus will end the spectacle. That life will continue, but it shall be sacred to ourselves, and the events that give it interest shall go unrecorded."